On the Wings of Condor

by John M. Cortes

The contents of this work, including, but not limited to, the accuracy of events, people, and places depicted; opinions expressed; permission to use previously published materials included; and any advice given or actions advocated are solely the responsibility of the author, who assumes all liability for said work and indemnifies the publisher against any claims stemming from publication of the work.

All Rights Reserved
Copyright © 2014 by John M. Cortes

No part of this book may be reproduced or transmitted, downloaded, distributed, reverse engineered, or stored in or introduced into any information storage and retrieval system, in any form or by any means, including photocopying and recording, whether electronic or mechanical, now known or hereinafter invented without permission in writing from the publisher.

Dorrance Publishing Co
701 Smithfield Street
Pittsburgh, PA 15222
Visit our website at *www.dorrancebookstore.com*

ISBN: 978-1-4809-1062-1
eISBN 978-1-4809-1384-4

To my beloved wife Maver Anne

"And in the days of those kings
the God of Heaven will set up a kingdom
that will never be brought to ruin.
And the kingdom itself will not
be passed on to any other people.
It will crush and put an end to all these kingdoms,
and it itself will stand to times indefinite."
Daniel 2:44

PROLOGUE

During the aftermath of the Al-Qaeda attack on the World Trade Center in New York, John Curtis, a former Central Intelligence Agency operative and now a retired agent for the Federal Bureau of Investigation, solemnly contemplated the ruins of what had once been the pride of New York City.

He reasoned that in certain parts of the world some would say that the attack on the Towers was retribution — just retribution for the crimes perpetrated against humanity by the United States' foreign policy in its use of its armed forces and the relentless presence of the CIA in the affairs of foreign governments.

There was a time that he had been part of the CIA. He knew the agency's role in American foreign policy well. The sole role of the CIA since its conception was the destabilization and elimination, by any means necessary, of governments that were unfriendly to the United States. The CIA would use that sort of policy as a deterrent to keep other friendly governments in constant awareness that Uncle Sam was watching their affairs.

The attack on New York was not the only time that a foreign terrorist group had attacked the continental United States. In the American minds, the attack by Japan on Pearl Harbor in 1941 and the assassination of Orlando Letelier, a former Chilean ambassador in Washington D.C., in 1976 still lingered. Some would have considered the attack on Pearl Harbor by the Japanese a terrorist attack, but in reality it was an act of war. Pearl Harbor was actually a direct attack by Japan's military establishment, a sort of formal declaration of war by a foreign nation. The answer to the attack was an immediate declaration of war by the United State against Japan; it was a just act against a known debtor because it represented a recognized legitimate government.

However, the assassination of Letelier in Washington D.C. was an act of terrorism that the Chilean government seemingly had not officially promoted or approved. The Chilean aggression of 1976 had defied the sovereignty of the United States and fulfilled the criteria of terrorism. Based on these criteria, the United States pursued the perpetrators and brought some of them to justice without declaring a state of war against Chile.

The terrorist attack on New York was to a greater degree similar to the Chilean attack on Washington D.C. years earlier, and it had crossed international boundaries. However, it had not necessarily represented the policy or attitudes of the countries where they had originated, and the attack on New York would not generate a Pearl Harbor retaliation.

The only alternative left for the United States to retaliate was to seek the perpetrators on a clandestine pursuit that definitely would not recognize the sovereignty of the countries harboring the terrorists that had brought death and suffering to thousands of U.S. citizens. The attack in New York had ramifications that were already signaling scattered terrorist cells throughout the Middle East involving different countries. Current information was leading to Osama bin Laden, the leader of Al-Qaeda, a recognized Arab terrorist group operating in several Arab countries.

What was most unsavory and unwelcoming to the American mind was the fact that most of the known enemies of the United States had at one time or another been created by CIA and American funds, and one of these enemies was Osama bin Laden.

There were no doubts in the intelligent services at home and abroad that Al-Qaeda had planned and executed the attack on the World Trade Center. It was now imperative to bring its leader to justice — dead or alive.

John already knew that Osama would not be an easy prey; Osama had the support of most of the Arab people, and he had enough wealth to provide himself a comfortable zone to survive. Some even suspected Osama to have at one time been a CIA operative, and it was probable that he still had friends inside the agency.

John knew that his friend Spencer, a CIA operative, had befriended Arabs who once had fought the Soviets in Afghanistan. He knew that Spencer at a very young age had lived in Jordan, where his parents had served for several years in the American Foreign Service. John knew that Spencer, while serving in Chile, had flown several times to Jordan and Saudi Arabia on some sort of CIA business, and Spencer could have befriended Osama at that time. In his mind, agents like Spencer who were unhappy with U.S. foreign policy would not hesitate to throw a protective umbrella over him, at least for a while.

John would not question that reasoning. From his CIA experience, he knew it was possible. How long would Osama survive the American wrath? It did not really matter. In the end, Osama would be killed. It was only a matter of time. Osama would not survive the American resolve to avenge this attack, which had struck not only the image of the American government abroad but had struck the heart of the American people. There was no room for forgiveness.

He now wondered if Spencer was also one of the many figures lurking in the shadows of Al-Qaeda's planning. Most Americans would find it unconceivable that an American like Spencer, who had fought at Vietnam and later had become one of the CIA's most able operatives during the 1970's in the countries of the Southern Cone in South America, would turn against his country. But he knew Spencer well, and he just could not help thinking about it. As a CIA operative, Spencer had been instrumental in the Chilean terrorist attack.

John was now in his early sixties and had recently retired from the FBI. He regretted the fact that in 1976 he had not been able to stop Spencer from intruding in the sovereignty of the United States to commit a terrorist attack. He himself had also been guilty, for he had been part of Operation Condor, a terrorist organization that had once swept the countries of the Southern Cone in South America, and Condor was responsible for the attack on D.C.

Operation Condor was the offspring of DINA, the Chilean military secret police, one of the most repressive police agencies that had ever existed in the countries of the Southern Cone. Operation Condor at its beginning had the financial support of the American government and had benefited from the expertise given by the CIA and DINA.

John knew that in the early 1980's, when Condor had already spread its wings beyond the borders of the countries of the Southern Cone, the CIA and the Chilean government found it necessary to stop Condor. Operation Condor's repressive policy of torture and murder against all known Marxists and Communists within and beyond the boundaries of the countries of the Southern Cone had become detrimental to the United States' foreign policy and to Chile's appeasement of world opinion. In a combined effort, the CIA and DINA brought Operation Condor seemingly to an end by delivering to the civilian authorities the same people to whom they had entrusted the operation. But Spencer, who had taken over Operation Condor, managed to escape, and for several years to come, Condor kept flying the skies of the countries of the

Southern Cone, bringing death wherever it chose to land. Finally in the late 1980's, Operation Condor seemed to cease, but now with the attack in New York, John could not help from wondering if Spencer, who seemingly was now in the Middle East, had also taken Operation Condor with him in support of his friends.

The idea of Spencer helping the terrorist groups did not truly represent the Spencer that John once knew. True, Spencer had masterminded the attack on Washington D.C., but on that attack he had singled out a foreigner known to be a Marxist and friend of Castro, not the American people. Feeling tired John sought the comfort of a nearby bench and sat down. Burying his head in his hands, he sought for an answer. Spencer's face now became more visible in his mind, and he still could feel his scrutinizing eyes on him.

After a while, he gained some composure and just sat looking at the desolated landscape in front of him, ruins of steel and concrete of what only recently had been magnificent buildings. Everything was depressing. Just the thought of the thousands who had died here was too overwhelming to behold. He recalled a Biblical passage found in Daniel that read, "…that in the days of those kings the God of Heaven will set up a kingdom that will never be brought to ruin….that it will crush and put an end to all these kingdoms." It was a sobering thought that had kept him alive all these years, years that he had never wanted since his wife and child had passed away. Mankind would never be able to rule itself without terror and death — the only hope was God's Kingdom.

Again he thought of Spencer and wondered where he really was. He had never met or known anyone as intelligent and intriguing as Spencer. When Operation Condor ceased operation, most of the top men seemingly running Condor were prosecuted, and several of them received life prison terms, including an American assassin. Spencer just vanished. What was most intriguing to John was that Spencer faded away as if he had never existed. He assumed that Spencer had travelled the same road he had once followed by assuming a new identity.

Damn! He told himself that Spencer was too good. When he had tried to find Spencer's mother, she had also disappeared and had left no traces that she had ever lived in Boston. He had thought of visiting Spencer's grandfather at Puerto William but changed his mind. It was better to let it go, to put it to rest. He never doubted that Spencer was somewhere still in the world of espionage, the only world Spencer ever knew.

At one point, he had wondered if Spencer had been a double agent and was part of the British MI6. He regretted that he had not asked Spencer's grandfather if Spencer was also working for the British in Chile.

In December of 1991, John found himself to be right — Spencer was still a factor in the world of espionage. Suddenly Spencer broke the silence of the years by sending him a brief note which read, "The swallow is flying east." The cable had been sent from Buenos Aires, Argentina. He knew then that Spencer was going to the Middle East, where he had friends. He speculated that Spencer was probably in Cairo, Jordan, or Saudi Arabia.

Spencer had many friends among the Jordanians, Saudis and Egyptians who disliked their own government and were sworn enemies of the United States. At the time that Spencer had gone to the Middle East, the Arabs were trying to help the Afghan mujahedeen on their effort to oust the Soviets from Afghanistan. Osama bin Laden, then a young Arab idealist, was becoming an influential, effective leader in the Arab efforts to repel the intruders.

John again speculated that Spencer had probably met the young Osama at that time. It was known that the CIA had armed and funded the Afghan mujahedeen who were fighting the Soviets in Afghanistan. Spencer had been instrumental in the deliverance of money to the opposition in Chile when the United States sought the ousting of President Allende, and in all probabilities, the CIA had used him again to transfer funds to the Afghan Arabs being trained by Osama in Saudi Arabia and other Arab countries.

It would not surprise him at all if Spencer was active in the Middle East and perhaps a part of Al-Qaeda. What had occurred in Chile was similar to what was happening in the Middle East. In 1970 when it had become obvious that the Chilean government was being friendly with the Soviets, the United States promoted the assassination of the Chilean president in order to install a friendly regime to the United States. The CIA then took total control of the destabilization of the Chilean civilian government by all means necessary. That resulted in giving the Chilean military total control of the government. The installing of a new government friendly to the United States in time created a suppressive government that became defiant of its benefactor, consequently giving birth to Operation Condor.

John wished he knew Spencer's real name, but while in Chile, even he himself had an assumed name. Back in the States, he could not revert back to his real name for it meant death, and he had acquired an entirely different identity. The only thing that he truly knew was that Operation Condor had existed. He himself had flown on the wings of Condor....

It began in September 11, 1973.
Santiago, Chile.

Part I

On the morning of the tenth day in September, I was able to put my wife on one of the last flights to the United States. The bloody military coup about to occur had already been anticipated by our people days earlier. Although I was attached to the State Department, I was one of those whom they preferred to ignore. The less the Embassy personnel knew about it, the better.

It was only because of my friend Spencer Truman, an operative of the CIA, and his close ties with some of my superiors at the American Embassy that he was able to learn of the incoming coup. Spencer immediately contacted me, and we were able to arrange my wife's departure to the States.

It seemed like a stroke of luck because the nightmare was just about to begin. The State Department and the CIA had been working toward the elimination of the Marxist government by a military coup for several years. Its sudden occurrence surprised all of us, perhaps due to the fact that the Chilean military had moved against the civilian government of President Salvador Allende without waiting for the final approval of its northern benefactor, the United States.

The military coup started at 7:00 A.M. on the eleventh of September in 1973. It began at the city port of Valparaiso by the Chilean Navy, to be followed by the Army, the National Police, and the Air Force. By the end of the day, Salvador Allende, the Chilean president, and his cabinet had been eliminated and replaced by a military junta.

The junta was an alliance of the three branches of the Armed Forces and the National Police: General Augusto Pinochet represented the Army; Admiral Jose Toribio Merino represented the Navy; General Gustavo Leigh represented the Air Force; and General Cesar Mendoza represented the Carabineros or National Police.

The junta immediately took over the legislative and executive branches of the government and brought all functions of the Congress to a halt. General Pinochet seemed to be the junta's strong man because the Army was dictating the pace of events. Afterward, the persecution, arrest, and elimination of the opposition began. It was brutal and merciless; hundreds of detainees were now being tortured and killed by summary execution or at random by the security forces roaming the streets of Santiago, the Chilean capital. At this time, another fearful figure began to project a large deadly shadow. This was Colonel Manuel Contreras, head of the military security forces and a protégé of General Pinochet.

Realizing the seriousness of the situation, I rushed to locate young Frank, a journalist and a student at the University of Chile. Frank, a liberal and strong supporter of the Allende government, was now in danger and could be considered by the military a Marxist and be executed.

On several occasions, Frank had stopped at my office at the embassy to chat about current events affecting Chile, and though I disliked his negative views on American foreign policy, I could not help from admiring his sense of value of the American Constitution. However, being aware of his liberal views on the Chilean situation, at times I had jokingly introduced him to some of my associates as my Marxist friend, a statement I was to regret the rest of my life. Being a Marxist, being thought of as one, or even associating with one was now having deadly repercussions. Marxists and Communists were being killed by the military security forces wherever they were found. It was of the utmost urgency to find Frank, as soon as possible. And the only person who could help me in locating Frank and get him out of Chile was Spencer.

The problem I was now facing on getting Spencer's help was the fact that he was deeply involved with the military on hunting leftists, and Frank was a leftist. The only difference was that Frank was an American leftist, and Spencer and I at times had discussed this difference. Both of us thought that American leftists, at least Frank and Charles whom we both knew, were not truly representatives of the Communists we knew. We thought of them as misguided American liberals. Charles was another American journalist who like Frank was also well known for his leftist view on the politics of Chile; Charles in a strange way had sort of cemented a friendship with Spencer — perhaps it was as a result of their love for soccer. They both had attended many soccer games.

Charles was a fan of the University of Chile soccer team and Spencer was a fan of Colo-Colo, a popular local team which identified itself with the common people. Would this friendship alter slightly the course that Spencer had taken lately? Only time had the answer, and that time was still ahead.

Spencer seemed to relish in what was occurring: Getting rid of the Communists was top priority in his agenda. I knew Spencer had a great deal of hate toward the Communists, a hate that was rooted deep inside him beginning in Vietnam, where he had served as a first lieutenant with the marines. Now the very thought of being part of the Chilean military push to get rid of all Marxists and Communists had given him a reason and an incentive to continue a fight for what had been lost in Vietnam. Would he spare Frank and Charles? I was not sure, but I needed his help.

Being aware of Spencer's hatred toward the Communists and Marxists, I was apprehensive about approaching him to help me get Frank out of Chile; I had no choice but to seek his help. There was no doubt in my mind that Charles was also in danger of being detained and killed, and knowing Spencer and his sense of Americanism, I did not think that he would knowingly allow an American to be killed by foreigners, regardless of his ideology.

I called him at Valparaiso, where he was stationed. Spencer's response was very receptive on helping our friends, and though he had agreed to help me, I could not totally dissipate a feeling of apprehension. That very morning before talking to him, we had been briefed at the embassy on what was occurring at Valparaiso, Vina del Mar and San Antonio. Many had been detained, tortured and killed, among them women and children. James, my superior, informed me that Spencer had been helping the military by rounding up the opposition at Valparaiso and Vina del Mar, and now he was on his way to Santiago to support the military security forces. At this time, I had no choice but to rely on Spencer and on our friendship that had started nearly ten years earlier in Vietnam, where both of us had served in the same unit.

Thinking about the Americans we were about to help, I was filled with a sense of urgency and anxiety because it seemed that time was running too fast for them. I kept telling myself that their escapes had to be now, not later. And I could not help from thinking of them. Charles did most of his journalism in Valparaiso, while Frank worked in Santiago and in some of the Northern provinces. I did not think of them as being Marxists or Communists, but their closeness to the people, their keen awareness of the Chilean social and economic structure which negatively affected the working class, and the deplorable condition of the poor had played a part in their being sympathetic to the Marxist cause.

Once someone on the embassy staff had suggested to Frank to join some of the American university students who had recently arrived from the States to help the Peace Corps with a special project among the Mapuche Indians south of the city of Temuco. Frank had rejected the offer by saying that he was not going to be part of another CIA scheme; he considered the Peace Corps another American plot to further American interest among the peasants. His response was not taken lightly by the staff, and he severed his friendly ties with some of them.

Frank was right. At that time, the Peace Corps was a CIA front. A CIA operative known as Michael was running some of the Peace Corps in the vicinity of Temuco and Concepcion, and I assumed the same was true for other sections of the country where the Peace Corps operated.

Frank was an idealist, a writer. By reading some of his pieces of work that he had brought to me, I felt that in time he was to achieve some degree of success. Now I needed to find him and bring him into the sanctuary of our embassy and provide him with American protection and a flight out of the country. In the meantime, Spencer was to locate Charles and bring him to Santiago. We would then place both of them on the very laps of the ambassador and let the events take their course.

A few days into these tragic moments of Chilean history, Spencer contacted me. He still had not located Charles. He told me I was to let him know as soon as I found Frank so that he could come and help me get him to the embassy. Then he informed me that the Chilean military intelligence had relayed to the CIA that they definitely wanted Frank and Charles for questioning. It was imperative to find them before they could get a hold of our friends.

Aware of the gravity of the times and anticipating the usual denial by the embassy that these two Americans were in Chile, I addressed the issue with James and with the ambassador's secretary. Though they seemed sympathetic and took the matter into consideration, I sensed I was getting nowhere. Hours later, I was informed by the office of the secretary that the names of these two Americans were not on the official embassy log register. I was not surprised. The embassy was to follow the usual State Department policy of denying Americans who could become potential liabilities and an embarrassment to our government.

Americans coming into Chile were not required to report to the embassy, and it was true that some chose not to report themselves. In the case of Frank and Charles however, the ambassador and most of us knew they were in Chile. They had visited the compound many times and had talked to the staff of several departments. They were journalists, and it was not only their job to ask questions, but it was part of their personas.

There was Anderson from the public affairs section who had taken a liking to Frank. Frank was from Chicago, Anderson's hometown. This same individual chose to remain indifferent when I asked for his help. I quickly received orders from James to stop inquiring about Frank or Charles. I was not to help either of them. James' orders ignited a fire of defiance in me and cemented my resolve to help them.

Several days passed and I was not able to locate Frank. Spencer had still not found Charles either. It seemed as if the ground had swallowed them up, and I deeply worried that perhaps the Chilean military had captured them. To my relief, I received a note from Spencer through one of the CIA officers attached to the embassy that the Chileans were still looking for them. It was good news; it meant they were still alive.

A week into the military takeover, Spencer came to see me. He filled me in on what was occurring throughout the country. Still there was no news about our friends. He told me his efforts to find Charles had been delayed due to other assignments. Usually he would not tell me the nature of these assignments. This was a mutual understanding between us. There were things in my work that I would not disclose to him either. He would have assignments that were "strictly company," as he sometimes referred to the CIA, and he would not discuss it with me. Sometimes he would ask for my opinion on a particular subject that we both knew was part of his work, and we would sort of tackle the issue in an indirect way, and I would reciprocate by doing the same when I needed advice on a matter of importance. It was our way to strengthen our friendship without breaking the rules on confidentiality.

My efforts to find Frank had also been slowed down due to the overwhelming amount of work engulfing all of us at the embassy. In a few days, the whole country had become a chaotic situation, and it had turned the international community into a diplomatic nightmare as each foreign mission scrambled to find a favorable niche of its own.

Spencer was now on his way to San Antonio for a meeting with Colonel Contreras and told me that he would see me in a few days. I assumed that he was heading there as an adviser to Contreras units now combing the countryside for dissidents.

I knew that the CIA and the Chilean military intelligence headed by Colonel Contreras were jointly trying to locate and liquidate the framework of MIR, the Revolutionary Left Movement. MIR was the most militant political unit of the UP, the Popular Union. The other lesser units, such as the Lautaro and the Manuel Rodriguez Patriotic Front, had already been put out of action. Through James and leaks at the CIA army station at the embassy, I knew that Spencer and others CIA operatives were part of this suppression that had already claimed hundreds of lives and tortured hundreds of detainees.

The day after Spencer left, reports came to the embassy that several hundreds of elements of MIR were cornered at some passes in the Andean Mountains and would surely be destroyed by army units on the Chilean side of the mountains or by the Argentinean army on the other side. There was no way out. It was just a matter of time. I assumed that Spencer was in the midst of it. It was at this time that I also ran into information coming from some mining towns in the north of the country that was channeled directly to us by the Peace Corps. It should not have surprised me. After all, the Peace Corps had been created by the Alliance for Progress, an American project created to disengage any of Fidel Castro's influence among the poor, the peasants, and the lower working class. The Peace Corps was fulfilling its obligation to the Alliance for Progress.

The situation in northern Chile was to become worse as we received news that Generals Stark and Espinoza, two of Pinochet's most feared generals, were on their way to Copiapo, a town in northern Chile, to bring order to the region. The Peace Corps was providing information on the military of that region. Seemingly some of the generals in charge of the northern provinces had taken a low approach in dealing with subversives. James confided to me that according to Colonel Manuel Contreras, General Stark would definitely bring order to the region. Stark was as ruthless as Contreras.

I was very familiar with the Alliance for Progress projects. Since the early sixties, the United States had provided nearly 300 million dollars to different segments of the Chilean society. The concept of the Peace Corps — to educate and help ones in need — had appealed to the American public and hundreds of well-intentioned young university students had responded to the call.

I was not totally ignorant of the role of the CIA in the Peace Corps, but I had never been confronted directly by its presence. The Peace Corps role was now evident in the form of information that kept coming from the different Peace Corps camps scattered throughout the northern region.

The Peace Corps was a paradox in itself. Here we had an unselfish, idealist, dedicated army of American youngsters who were trying in a sublime gesture of generosity to do their best to educate and help ones in need. On the other hand, our government was using them to further American interest, which in my field was copper, a metallic item that was far from being sublime. This knowledge about the Peace Corps bothered me, but I managed to dissuade myself from my own discontent because I was part of the same package of American deception. I was an American sworn to defend the interests of the American government, and deception was a needed commodity to secure those interests.

Meanwhile the persecution of dissidents was gaining momentum as the killing continued unopposed. In just a few days following the coup, hundreds had already been killed; it was a blood bath. The awareness of being part of this madness was eroding the clarity of my thinking, and at times I felt like throwing in the towel and walking away from this madness, which definitely was not part of my persona. "You must meet challenges as they come and don't focus on the outcome for the outcome is not necessarily what you see first," my father would tell me when I was very young. When I joined the marines, this concept was accentuated by the many challenges that we met on the battlefield. It did not matter the terrain or the size of the enemy, we were there to stay. I was here in Chile, and I was determined to stay until my assignment was over.

On this particular night, I was extremely tired and mentally exhausted, and I was anticipating a good night's sleep. It was going on midnight, and no sooner had I closed my eyes when the loud noise in the street brought me out of the bed. I looked outside the window. It was the same regular parade of earlier nights of those who welcomed the new government. In the dark, I sat in the recliner and listened.

The noise increased, and soon I heard the sounds of gunfire and the triumphal shouts of approval of those who had welcomed the takeover: the rich, the well-to-do, the political right, the fascists, the so-called Christian Democrats, the people in our pockets bought by the Yanqui dollar, and by those who, like in most societies, wait for the window of opportunity to be open.

All of these people — under the watchful eye and blessing of the Vatican and the religious protestant right — were now adding more wood to the blazing flame of the military that had already consumed hundreds of their own people. At the other end of this madness were the Soviets, the European

Eastern Block, and the Cubans. They kept fueling a hopeless case with shouts of empty dreams and promises that had never materialized. "Where was Fidel Castro?" I asked myself several times. It reminded me of President Johnson calling for young American blood to be spilled on foreign soil in a senseless war that the U.S. Congress would not allow us to win. Chile was no different; Chile was just another move in a game of chess played by the superpowers, and the people...the Chilean people were ordinary pawns moved at will by whoever was making the move.

As the sounds outside subsided and the night unfolded, my mind kept tune with this unfolding madness. I just could not understand these countries — Argentina and Chile were supposed to be Roman Catholic and what was occurring here was abhorrent to Christianity. The Catholic Church, since their independence from Spain, had a firm grip not only upon their civilians but also on their governments and military as well.

All of us in the diplomatic circle were very much aware of the strong influence that the Vatican had in the politics of Chile and Argentina, but it never occurred to us the extent of that hold. Several days after the military coup had brought President Allende down, James had walked into the office shaking his head and telling me that Cardinal Angelo Sodano, the Vatican's ambassador in Chile, had that very morning recognized the junta as the legitimate government of Chile. Then a few days later Spencer told me that the Archbishop of Valparaiso had given the military his blessing. It just did not make any sense. Here we had a Catholic military regime bringing suffering and death to thousands of devoted Catholics.

At this time in Argentina, Brigadier General Jorge Videla, a devout Catholic just like Pinochet, had given indication to move against Peron's government. Accordingly, Videla had already been giving the blessing from all of the Argentinian Catholic bishops and of the Vatican to take over the Argentinian government. The irony in these human dramas was that all of them were Roman Catholics and all of them worship the pope with the same ardor. But this unfolding madness was not a religious one, it was a political one, and devoted Catholics could blow each other's brains out with no remorse as long as they had their priest's blessings, and both sides had plenty of blessing.

I grew restless and resentful of the human race. We were creatures supposedly created in the image of God! What an insult to the Creator...if there was one. Then as sudden as these thoughts appeared, I rejected them. I felt very deeply that far away my Anne was praying for me to her God whom I was now denying. This sense of knowing that her prayers had some sort of trueness was becoming an undeniable part of my thinking, and it was there so close to me that at times I could feel its effect. "Was there a God?" I asked myself. Was there a supreme being who was watching all our moves, a God like Anne's God, a God who really cared? But where was He now if he really cared? If there was a God, then...why all this suffering? Feeling the need to rest, I stopped wondering because I knew it would take me nowhere. It always did, and each time it filled me with a form of anxiety because I really wanted an answer which kept eluding me. The only thing I was sure of was that my Anne was there praying for me.

It was in this state of mind that Spencer found me on this September's morning. We were both glad to see each other, and immediately I could tell that he had been thru some fighting. He looked exhausted. He told me he had returned with some units returning to Santiago and that MIR's combatants in the interior east of the capital had been eliminated He then told me that he had already seen James earlier that morning and that he was now on his way to Valparaiso for a debriefing on the fighting in which he had participated.

He confirmed what we had heard about the situation in northern Chile. It seemed that in the northern provinces where the military had adopted a lesser, nonbelligerent policy toward the populace, now they themselves had felt the iron hand of General Stark. Many civilians and also some of the military personnel who had been lenient to the dissidents had been executed.

He also told me that Orlando Letelier, the defense minister under the Allende regime and probably the only survivor of Allende's cabinet, had been taken to a prison camp in southern Chile. Letelier was a well-liked Chilean international political figure who had been a former ambassador in Washington D.C. He was an economist like me, with a great deal of expertise in a field that I was just exploring. Like any other politician associated with Allende's regime, however, he had not escaped the military momentum sweeping the country. It was a miracle that he was still alive.

Perhaps Letelier's survival was due to being an internationally well-known figure in Washington. The military did not want to upset Washington and had not killed him yet. Sparing Letelier's life at this time was a political necessity; it was a way to appease those who were now criticizing the brutality of the junta. In doing so, the military was showing the world that it respected the process of law.

However, the military security forces roaming the country contradicted appeasement in all fronts, and at this time it dictated the military and civilian affairs of Chile by suppression and fear. In time Chile's military security forces would turn into a military secret intelligence agency that would become the dominant factor on deciding who was going to live or die.

The appointment of Contreras to command the military security forces had left me wondering why Pinochet had not chosen Stark or Espinoza as the head of the security forces, both of them being the closest generals to Pinochet.

"Spencer, tell me, I am just curious," I asked. "Why didn't Pinochet appoint General Stark or Espinoza as head of the military security forces, which now seem to be controlling all aspect of the armed forces. I know that Contreras has the power to arrest or execute within the armed forces anyone considered an enemy of the state regardless of rank. It is a powerful post. General Stark and Espinoza seem closer to Pinochet than Contreras, who is only a colonel."

"Don't let appearances fool you, my friend," he responded, on the verge of a smile at the corner of his mouth. "Pinochet is a fox. He knows well that those two have his position in mind while Colonel Contreras doesn't. Pinochet knows that the colonel is a man he can trust. Those generals wouldn't waste a minute if the opportunity to get rid of him came their way." He paused briefly and added, "People can say anything about the colonel, that he is a man without a conscience, ruthless, merciless, a cold killer, but no one can question his sense of loyalty to Pinochet."

"Really! Why is that? The colonel is just like any other colonel. They all want to come up through the ranks to become top dog. What makes Contreras any different?"

"Loyalty, my friend. I know the colonel. You see, Pinochet and Contreras are old friends, and both have a deep respect for each other. At one point in their military career, General Pinochet was Contreras' teacher at the War Academy where Pinochet was teaching strategy," Spencer said. He grinned upon seeing an inquisitive expression on my face. "Sometimes we Americans tend to look at them as just military people coming up through the ranks without a formal education. Did you know that Contreras spent two years at Fort Benning studying intelligence, and some of us in the CIA do not even have that sort of training? Yeah... he is a well-educated, trained soldier. There is no doubt in my mind that Pinochet has a great deal of trust and confidence in him."

"To tell you the truth, I did not have the vaguest idea. I just thought that he was a common soldier coming up through the ranks. One thing I do know

— he does speak English well," I replied. In my brief conversations with him, Contreras always spoke to me in English, something that was of no surprise to me for most of the Chilean military officers I had met spoke English.

Spencer continued, "Also Pinochet has nothing but admiration for the way Contreras handled the first phase of the coup and how he coordinated the roundups of the Communists and Socialists at San Antonio, and not only that, he was a key person for our own people at Valparaiso and Vina del Mar."

"That is what James told me," I responded. "But I also know that he doesn't play second to Stark or Espinoza in the way he handles the opposition. From what I know, he is as ruthless as they are in the way he treats his prisoners. He is known to be a cold killer, showing mercy to no one."

"Yeah, he has a reputation for having no mercy on his opponents, but who among us in times like these are not forgivers or killers?" he responded and looked at me expecting a reply.

Sensing where he was leading, I chose not to answer because he was right. The current madness was a direct result of our own effort to destabilize the country and bring Chile to our own mode of democracy, and the price was now being paid in Chilean blood. Contreras, like Pinochet and many other killers, including myself, were part of that great American effort to re- establish democracy in Chile.

We ourselves were definite parts now of this military killing machine rolling on the paved and unpaved roads of the Chilean landscape. Spencer and I looked at each other and moved our heads slightly in acceptance and grinned realizing that we had agreed on something. I changed the direction of the conversation to what was our own immediate concern at the moment, the safety of our American friends.

Spencer proceeded to tell me he was now on his way to find Charles for he had received information that he was hiding in a location near Vina del Mar. He had to find Charles soon. He had the same urgency as I had in locating Frank. If the Chileans got to them first, they would be killed. The Chilean military was not a forgiving lot. We already knew what was happening at that very moment at the National Stadium soccer field where the military was torturing and killing presumable enemies of the state by the hundreds.

He also related to me that General Pinochet, commander of the army, was now taking over all the functions of the junta. In Spencer's mind, Pinochet was the undisputable leader of the junta, something that we at the embassy had anticipated. I confided to him that the State Department had already given indication that Pinochet's intention was to declare himself president of the junta with the intention of becoming president of Chile sometime in the next year. General Augusto Pinochet had the full support and loyalty of the army, and the army was the dominant force within the armed forces. More so, he had the approval of President Richard Nixon and Secretary of State Henry Kissinger.

"Yeah, Don Augusto is the strong man. There is no doubt about it. He is calling the shots," Spencer commented and then he changed the conversation toward Frank and Charles.

Spencer admitted that locating Charles and Frank had proved difficult because they had gone into hiding, and he could not blame either of them, for they in all probabilities knew that they were marked for death. In the case of Frank, both of us agreed that definitely his college friends were hiding him. Charles' emergence in the resort city of Vina del Mar indicated to us that some of the well-to-do and local celebrities that had befriended Charles had given him protection.

Frank's friends were university students and intellectuals. Some of them were dissidents and probable supporters of MIR but also sons and daughters of prominent families that were actually on the side of the military. This paradox made my search more difficult, more so when one must dig in one's own backyard. I had contacted several friends of Frank, but knowing that I was an American, they were reluctant to offer any information. They did not trust the Americans. Most of them felt that we had helped the military bring down the presidency of Salvador Allende. They were absolutely right. There was no sense in denying it. It was a constant truth in my mind that was haunting me. The White House had given the order and we had abided by their decision by pressing upon the military that the only solution to Chile's problem was a military coup.

Then Spencer told me about an execution that he had witnessed on his way to my place. He told me that by the side of the Mapocho River he had seen the execution of some young people. I knew that it had bothered him, and a light of hope shone at that moment. My friend had a conscience after all.

"There were at least two dozen kids, just kids, maybe high school kids. They shot them all and then the soldiers threw them into the river," he said in a voice that sounded strange and lowly tragic. His eyes seemed to be looking back at time, but I sensed much farther back, perhaps it had to do with another place besides Vietnam. It was something that at times I had wondered about and I had not asked, for in some way Spencer was sort of a private person.

I remembered that there had been many occasions in which we had witnessed the killing of many young people. There was one however that typified the cruelty of war and still echoed in our minds. The elders at a village friendly to us had refused to let their young people join the Viet Cong, and in retaliation the Viet Cong executed more than two dozen young boys and girls, the youngest being nine years old. I could still see Spencer falling on his knees, cursing God and the Viet Cong. On that day a young girl whom he had befriended had also been raped, tortured, and killed. After that he never showed any emotion when faced with killings, and there were many to occur, and some were worse.

I looked at him. He was perturbed. Had he reached the point of limitation? There is always a certain place in the lives of people where most come to question their limitation. Had my friend reached this point?

"At the embassy, we are divided," I said. "Most of us are against the torture and killing of the detainees, and we have presented a letter of protest to the ambassador. There is no due process of law in Chile." I sought an answer, but he remained silent.

"It does not matter if they are dissidents or not," I continued. "They are human beings, and we know that the American people do not like it. Even our friends at The Times ran an article against this inhumanity." Still, there was no immediate response from Spencer.

He looked at me and grinned. In silence he approached the window, and for several minutes, he just looked out. I joined him and looked outside; the street was deserted. It seemed strange. In past weeks, there was always movement of people, vehicles and sometimes wandering dogs. Across the street lived an old man who owned a Great Dane, a huge dog, but I had not seen either of them. The truth is that it was not strange at all. The people knew that the military was there, and everybody knew their places. This time it was inside their homes.

Spencer reached for the couch and sat while I stayed by the window, keeping my eyes on the deserted street which at that moment seemed so pitifully lonely. After a while, I turned my attention to him and found him looking at me. He grinned as if he had been trying to probe into my mind, which now was impenetrable for it was flooded with disquieting thoughts coming ceaselessly from the inners chambers of a mind dressed in distressful attires. I looked at him wondering, just wondering, waiting for him to say something.

"Of all the people in the world and considering the type of work we do," he finally said, "we are the most sanitary of them all." He stopped briefly and laughed seeing my questioning look.

"I smoke some, you don't," he continued. "I drink some, you don't. I fool around some, you are married. Seldom do we go to the movies, yet we can talk a lot. And some time we do enjoy a soccer game and comment about it, during and after the game. In a sense, as friends, we do share something that escapes most friends. We can talk to each other. There is something that we do not do… drugs! Believe me, in the CIA we do have a high percent of drug addicts and drunkards, not to mention broken marriages, homosexuals, and so on."

I did not respond and waited for him to continue. I sensed that he was going to say something that could shine more light on his profound hatred toward the opposition. Again he kept silent. He continued this silence for some seemingly long moments. I moved toward the recliner and sat, waiting for him to continue. In the past, there had been moments like these between us, where silence had engulfed as a blanket of soothing protection and yet, I still could not get used to its awkwardness; silence can be so awkward.

"You see John," he said, "sometimes we are aware of things that happen around us, and because it does not affect us personally, we just keep on living as if these things never happened. But then….you are there, and it does touch you, whether indirectly or directly. We do feel that touch, and then before we know it, we become part of it. We feel it, we taste it, but then we have to keep on living. We are part of this madness, as you call it. It has swallowed us, and it won't spit us out until it is over, and believe me it is not over, and it won't be over for a while…a long while."

"I know what you mean," I answered, "but being here does not mean that we have to be part of it."

And as I responded I became aware of my own contradiction. I questioned myself. Who was I fooling? Was I that stupid? We were part of it.

"Really, my naive friend," Spencer replied, "the fact that we are here is enough proof that we are part of it. Including you! The White House sends the orders, the diplomats like you write the documents and deliver them, and we enforce it to make sure that it is accepted, at any cost, including murder."

I did not reply because I knew that he was right, absolutely right. The success of our mission depended so much on agents like Spencer who would go beyond reasoning to make sure that we achieve our goals whether they agreed or not with those goals. Their jobs were to secure the State Department's objectives.

"I guess I give you the impression that I like what I do, all these killings in the name of freedom. You should know better," he said with his eyes nailed to the wall.

"Don't you? I saw the excitement in your face when this killing started, when the military took over. I was there when General Espinoza gave the orders to round up the opposition, and you wasted no time in joining them. Hundreds upon hundreds are now at the stadium being tortured and killed in part thanks to the generosity of the CIA," I said, and immediately I apologized to him for I was part of the slaughter.

I realized then that in trying to justify myself I was pacing frantically the hallway of denial, my own denial. The United States had sought the ouster of President Allende by any means, and we the diplomats had given the orders to the CIA to execute the orders given to us by the State Department. And I was there when the orders were given to the CIA station in Santiago to support the coup by any means necessary. And now all of these were lingering in my conscience.

"I am not going to deny the fact that I was glad when it happened," Spencer said, cutting short my thoughts. "All of us were glad that the military had taken over, including you, not to mention Old Nathan's unwavering support for Don Augusto Pinochet and his idiotic ideas on how to set up concentration camps for the prisoners."

I laughed because I remembered when James had told me about the ambassador's ideas on setting up camps throughout the country. German concentration camps for the Jews were still fresh in the American mind; the State Department shut down Nathan Davis' solution to the prisoner's containment. There were enough buildings to keep the prisoners in, rather than place them in camps surrounded by barbed wire. The exception was in southern Chile, where prisoners in rural areas had been delegated to camps due to the lack of building shelter, but they were now being transferred to the cities for proper sheltering.

Spencer, still with a grin on his face, looked straight at my eyes and said, " John, you must admit that the coup, though unpleasant as it is, it assured you that you were not going to lose that precious copper. After all, our interest in Chile is not only its strategic location in the Pacific but its raw material as well, and in Chile, copper is our most coveted metal. However, to tell you the truth, I was not ready for the magnitude of the military response. But here I am, and I will continue my work. This is also an opportunity for us to get rid of the Communist menace in this part of the world."

"I do agree with you in principles, but what we are talking now is about the ordinary people, the common people. They do not deserve to be treated as animals. These people here are not the Communists we know them to be.

We must have room for others who do not think like we do. There are others, whom because of their economic situations, have no other recourse but to embrace Communism as a way out. It is our obligation to show them that there is another way, but we cannot do it if we choose to kill them rather than show them the way," I replied.

"My friend, there are only two things in the world: the Soviets and us. If ever there was to be an encounter with the Soviets, I am sure that the Communists won't be with us," he responded, raising his voice slightly. He was visibly annoyed.

"Spencer, what I am trying to tell you as a friend is that it is time for us to find a better way to deal with situations like this in Chile. You are behaving as if you were in Vietnam. Vietnam is long gone. Vietnam is only a memory, and we are here in the present."

He looked at me in a disapproving way, and I knew why. Most of us still had fresh memories of fallen friends. Vietnam was still a very vivid memory for me as well. Five years of continuous fighting was engraved in my memory for years to come, and sometimes it was not easy to put away the fallen ones.

"I'm sorry. I did not mean it that way," I said.. "What I mean is that we should leave those memories just as they are…dear memories, to both of us. What I am trying to say as a friend is that whatever bad happened then, it shouldn't have a hold in our present. I know that is hard not to remember, but sometimes it is good to put it away momentarily. These people here have done nothing to us. True, we still have a pocket of insurgents here and there, but they are just insignificant pockets, and most of them have already been taken out. What we have now are unarmed civilians, and they present no threat to us."

"As long as there are Marxists or Communists, whether armed or unarmed, they will always be a threat to us. Have you ever read the Bible?" he asked. His questioning surprised me for I always thought that he had no religion at all. And immediately I asked myself: What did the Bible have to do with what we were talking about? Maybe he had just asked for the sake of asking.

"My mother had one, and when I was a kid, she told me some Bible stories, and my teacher at Sunday School told me some, but to tell you the truth, I did not pay too much attention," I responded. "Anne has a Bible that she reads daily, but it does not mean too much to me. Sometimes she does get upset when I do not pay attention to it. After going through the hell of Nam, I do not think much about the Christian or Moslem god or any other god, and you well know that."

As I said those words, I could not repress a feeling of regret knowing that at this very moment my wife perhaps was reading her Bible, which gave her the needed strength in this time of separation, and she was probably at this very moment praying for me.

"Did your Mom or Anne ever read to you about Joshua?" he asked.

"Yeah, about the walls of Jericho falling due to the shouting…Pretty far-fetched, don't you think so? Still I just remember some of the account. Why?" I responded.

"Not if you believe in the Bible. The Bible is for men of faith, and most of us have no faith at all, except in ourselves. But tell me, what do you remember of Joshua?" he asked.

"All I know is that he was the military leader of the Israelites." I responded. "He became the commander of the Israelite's army after Moses' death."

"Yes, you are correct, but did you know that in some courses in military maneuvers, he is considered next to Napoleon, Wellington, General Lee and MacArthur, as one of the great military commanders? He is perhaps the first one to have used commandos. When Joshua entered the Promised Land, he sent commandos ahead of his army." He stopped upon seeing my expression that he took as disbelief.

Looking at him, I could not help from wondering how a man like him could be referring to the Bible, a holy book. Sacredness should not be coming from the lips of a professional killer.

"I am sorry. It never crossed my mind that you may know anything about the Bible. I never took you as a religious man," I said.

"I am not, but Joshua is a subject that is taught in military schools, and you will find it in texts on tactical maneuvers."

"But what does Joshua have to do with what we are talking about?" I questioned.

"You see," he said with excitement in his voice, "when the Israelis came to the Promised Land after leaving Egypt, Jehovah their God told them that in order to have the Promised Land they would not only have to fight the people of the land, but they also had to destroy them completely. Therefore, when Joshua went into battle, he ordered the destruction of everyone in the conquered territory. He left nothing alive, human or beast. Hard to understand how a loving God could give such an order, especially one God that seems so holy, so good to some of us. However in retrospect, one can understand why Jehovah gave that command. Jehovah did not want his people contaminated with the pagan nations. Jehovah told the Israelites not to have mercy upon their enemies if they were going to be a great people."

Spencer paused briefly and continued. "You see John, Jehovah knew if they were to take prisoners, sooner or later these same people would be part of the nation, and their ways would eventually influence the very fiber of the nation. After Joshua died, the Israelis did come to terms with some of the people that were still in the land and assimilated them into their culture. Idolatry and pagan customs plagued the chosen people, and finally their ways destroyed Israel. So there is a lesson to be learned. In war there can be no compromise. We cannot compromise with the Communists and Marxists; they have to be destroyed."

Though as hard as it seemed to be, it did make sense. We both looked at each other as we were in some way trying to understand each other. In silence we shook hands, and unexpectedly he embraced me. It meant a lot to me because Spencer was not the emotional type.

Then he left, leaving me with mixed feelings. Suddenly after so many years, he had dug into a religious source that I had not ever considered being part of his persona. His understanding of the Bible was surprising for never once in our conversations had he referred to the Bible. His genuine show of emotion had also in some way overwhelmed me for I had no recollection of having ever been embraced by him. And yet this sudden show of genuine love did not speak about the degree of tolerance he had shown toward those he considered his enemies. Maybe Charles could escape his definition of Communists...but what about Frank? And yet Spencer was my friend, and I trusted him even against the shadow of apprehension. Perhaps this trust was also due to my desires to bring Frank out of danger. That young man's life was very dear. I did not want him or any American to fall into the hands of the Chilean military security forces.

Finding myself alone with these thoughts, I could not help from grinning for, in a sense, I was another Spencer. In Vietnam we did not leave Americans behind, dead or alive, and in Chile we were not about to leave two Americans behind. But these two Americans were leftists, and Spencer would not tolerate them. It was a dilemma that only time would answer. It was like holding onto the edge of a precipice and looking at my rescuer. Would Spencer step on my hand or would he offer me a rescuing hand? Time had the answer, and time was walking a fast pace.

Our plan was to bring them into the embassy at all costs, where I myself would register their name in the official log and leave no room for the embassy or the State Department to deny their presence in the country. Spencer and I knew of the fallout that was to occur afterward. At this point, it did not matter. All that they could do was fire us or send us to other assignments.

Since the State Department policy code name 'Track I" had failed, 'Track II" was now in effect, and the CIA was in total control of the State Department's affairs in Chile. The U.S. Army station at the embassy was now under the direct order of Kissinger, the American secretary of state. The embassy was now a mere token of American political presence, but in that sense, to some of us it would make no difference at all. Ambassador Nathaniel Davis had always been sort of a White House puppet, with no politics of his own, a man whom I thought to have no principles at all; it seemed to some of us that he only cared about just having a good time. More than once I heard James saying that "Old Nathan knows his brandy and can throw good parties, but he doesn't know a damn about the politics of this country."

Nearly three years had passed since I had joined the staff of the American Embassy at Santiago, the capital of Chile. My role was to enhance the American perspective on international trade between the United States and Chile. Copper was the main commodity on our agenda. Copper was, to us, as important as oil in the Persian Gulf and at that time was in the balance of a negotiating scale dangerously tilting in favor of the Marxist government.

The State Department prior to 1970 had recognized that a Marxist regime in Chile was not in the interest of the United States. Salvador Allende, a Marxist backed by the Socialists and the Communist Party in a common front known as the "UP" or "Popular Union," was the candidate most likely to be elected president in the election of September 3, 1970.

As a deterrent to this Communist effort to elect Allende, the United States embarked on a policy that entrenched all internal affairs in Chile. Cuba was now a recognizable Communist entity in Latin America, and the Soviet Union had already projected a fearsome presence in South America. Nixon, the American president, would not allow Chile to become a Communist state and directed two initiatives to that effect, Track I and Track II.

Track I, ran directly by the State Department with some cooperation from the CIA, was an intensified political effort to discredit Allende and the Left. It involved making Alessandri, one of the other presidential runners and a conservative, most appealing to the voters and definitely to the United States. It was a combination of propaganda and political operations aimed at bringing public distrust of the Left.

Track II was a more aggressive initiative that required a military coup in case the Marxist candidate was elected, and Track II was to be solely run by the CIA. If Allende was to be elected, immediately afterward the Allende's regime was to be eliminated by all means necessary, including the assassination of Allende.

Despite these two American initiatives at the cost of millions of dollars, Salvador Allende won 36.8 percent of the votes. That was slightly higher than Alessandri, who came in second. Allende definitely had not won an absolute majority, and the Chilean Constitution called for an absolute majority. Now it was up to the Congress to decide who would be elected president.

Seeing the gravity of the moment and anticipating the possible election of Allende, the State Department did not want to wait for a Congressional decision and immediately released to the CIA Track II, which unleashed all clandestine efforts to abort the election of Allende.

The CIA now dictated the course of action, assigning lesser roles to the embassy. The aim was clear: to influence the Chilean Congress by any means and gain the necessary votes to declare Alessandri the winner. Also as a backup plan in case our efforts were to fail, a military coup had been prepared. This plan already had the approval of some of the most influential generals in the armed forces, except for General Schneider, the commander of the army and a Constitution Loyalist who had expressed his disapproval of a possible coup.

Schneider's rejection of the plan made it imperative for us that he had to be removed. He was to be replaced with General Carlos Prats, who seemed to be friendly to American interests. A plan was conceived by the CIA to kidnap Schneider and blame the kidnapping on forces loyal to Allende. The plan had the approval of the State Department and the White House. It could have worked, but it became another major blunder for the CIA. It resulted in the death of Schneider.

It was also a blunder to all of us. Some of us still had fresh memories of the CIA's blunder at Bay of Pigs in 1961 and also of their inability to reach President Johnson with vital information on the Tet Offensive in Vietnam in 1968, which could have saved many American lives .

At the embassy, we felt that the removal of Schneider and placing General Prats as commander-in-chief of the army was essential for a military coup to take effect as to prevent Congress from electing Allende. We had all the means necessary to execute the kidnapping of Schneider and blame it on the left, thus gaining the Congressional votes in favor of Alessandri, but somehow it had not worked as planned.

The CIA had engaged two groups of Chilean army officers, headed by retired General Robert Viaux and General Camilo Valenzuela, to plot the abduction of Schneider. At the CIA station, those of us who knew of the plan favored the group headed by Valenzuela. We felt that he had the capability to carry out the kidnapping because Valenzuela was still active in the army. Viaux, aware that the CIA was inclined toward the Valenzuela group to execute the mission, went ahead and carried out the attempt that resulted in Schneider's death. The death of the general was shocking to the armed forces and other influential political leaders who had favored the removal of General Schneider. His death became the bonding of a divided Congress. Though Schneider's death had been blamed on the left, most Chileans felt that the Americans were behind the death of Schneider.

Even Eduardo Frei, the then-current president and staunch ally of the United States who had welcomed a United States sponsored military coup, denounced the assassination of Schneider. General Carlos Prats, who replaced Schneider as commander of the army, backed the Congress, thus giving a death blow to our expectations.

Eventually Salvador Allende became the first Marxist president in the Western Hemisphere elected in a democratic election on October 24, 1970. He was inaugurated as president of Chile on November 3, 1970.

Although Allende had been elected as president, he was still not liked by a large segment of Chileans — mostly the rich and upper and middle classes, plus the armed forces, which still favored the American presence. Though the army had backed the Congress as an expression of disgust in the assassination of one of its own most respected citizens, it was still against a Marxist government and still considered the United States its friend. We were aware of what was truly breathing behind the political scene and moved promptly to gain the momentum.

In the aftermath of the election of Salvador Allende, the United States engaged in an all-out effort to bring down the presidency of Allende. Yanqui dollars flowed in all directions buying politicians, leaders of most segments of the Chilean society, and military officers by the hundreds, plus we started exerting economic pressure in the national industry as well at the exterior by cutting foreign loans to a regime already in default. Also the role of the Vatican in the effort to bring down Allende's government was crucial. Cardinal Angelo Sodano

Papal Nuncio in Chile and Archbishop Jorge Medina were supportive of the American initiative.

It was in this time of political upheaval that Anne and I had arrived in January of 1971 to Santiago after being nearly two years in Argentina serving at the American Embassy in Buenos Aires. It was a sudden departure due to the seriousness of what was occurring in Chile. The State Department felt that my success as a negotiator with the meat industry in Argentina would strengthen the American position in the anticipated Chilean nationalization of the American companies and the call for the total expropriation of all American property. Expropriation was not acceptable to President Richard Nixon, and he sought the forcible removal of President Salvador Allende by any means necessary.

I was to be part of the negotiating team headed by James Farewell, the American representative to the Marxist government of President Allende. The main issue was the nationalization of the copper mines owned by the Anaconda Copper Company and Kennecott Copper Corporation. The nationalization was not a new issue for it had already started during the presidency of Carlos Ibanez in the 1950s and a second stage of nationalization called the Negotiated Nationalization was established in 1960 during the presidency of Eduardo Frei. That called for a fair compensation to the American companies and had been accepted by us in principle. However in 1971, the Marxist government would not abide by the principles established in the Negotiated Nationalization Agreement and called for its rejection, thus antagonizing the president of the United States.

Eventually the trends of events culminated with the military coup that ended the Marxist government of President Allende. The military coup eased the position of American interest, but it also brought darkness to a large segment of the Chilean population. Chilean dissidents were now being hunted inexorably and mercilessly by the military secret service, among them Charles and Frank, who were merely spectators in this human drama.

Spencer, who had talked about not compromising at all with the Marxists, had now compromised himself by agreeing to help our American friends. It seemed a paradoxical situation, but it had to do mostly with our friendship. Most of us human beings at one time or another contradict ourselves by word and action. It all depends on one's viewpoint of the situation and the time when it occurs.

After Spencer left for Vina del Mar, I spent the following morning calling some of my contacts, trying to find the whereabouts of Frank. All I could gather was that he was being protected by some university students. This group was hard to crack; it was known to us that most students due to their youth and sense of idealism had many times chosen to die rather than to give up their friends. .

On the evening of the same day, I waited at my office at the embassy for a call from Spencer, still hoping that Spencer was on my side. At the same time, I kept calling on some of my associates at the State Department for any information that they might have received about Frank. I was very cautious on whom to trust as to avoid any confrontation with James, who had already told me to leave this matter of the journalists alone.

Then to my surprise after leaving my office for a short time, on my return I found a note on my desk. It was an address at Hernan Cortes Street and the name of Frank. I immediately assumed that it had come from James though I knew that he did not want me to be involved. Was it James pretending not to care when in reality he did care about these two Americans in harm's way? Why not? After all James was an American. I went to his office, but he was not there.

I pulled my gun from the drawer of my desk and put it inside my coat's pocket. Then I placed my wallet containing my ID and credentials as a diplomat in the desk's drawer and locked it. I was determined to do whatever was necessary to save Frank. I called Mario Arriaga, a taxi driver and a close friend whom I trusted completely. Anne and I had cemented a genuine friendship with Mario's family. My wife was very close with Julia, and their two small children, Mario and Carmen, called us Aunt Anne and Uncle John.

At the gate, I went to one of the marines on duty, and I told him that I was leaving and that a friend of mine was to pick me up. A short time later, Mario picked me up by the curb. It was a while later that Mario told me that we were being followed, and we kept the same pace waiting for the opportune time to make a break. Mario's familiarity with the city made it possible for us to lose them when the opportunity came.

We drove through the back streets to our destination, trying to avoid any checkpoints set by the military. As we drove, I became aware that Mario was unusually quiet, and he was quite a talker. He was no stranger to danger for we had in the last year faced some unforeseen predicaments that could have easily taken our lives. A year earlier, Mario had helped me to abort an attempt to abduct me and Anne. Mario, who was driving us, took us out of the spot by running over one of them. In another occasion, he had gunned down a robber. Therefore, I had total trust in him. What was unique about him was his sense of humor that he kept during both ordeals. We both knew that the danger ahead in our efforts in finding Frank and bringing him to the embassy could end our lives. Perhaps he was thinking of his family, and I respected his silence.

After nearly an hour driving and avoiding patrols and checkpoints, I noticed we were going in the opposite direction of our destination. The many unknown streets that we had taken had probably changed the course of our destination, but Mario was familiar with the city. It just did not make any sense.

I turned to Mario to express my concern, but he did not reply. Instead he abruptly turned a corner, and we came into what seemed to be an army post with several army trucks lined up neatly against the curb. He came to a stop between several patrols units parked near the entrance to a military compound. Fully surprised I tried to make sense at what was occurring. It made no sense at all. I looked at Mario, then at the soldiers approaching our car. It never occurred to me that Mario would betray me. I realized at this moment the gravity of my situation. Here I was at an army post without my credentials or identity and carrying a weapon. I was a sure candidate for the slaughter.

"Why? Why, Mario?" I asked in disbelief.

He buried his head on the steering wheel and wept. I put my hand on his shoulder at the same time that an officer opened the door and asked me to get out of the car. As I was stepping out, Mario grabbed my arm and in tears told me that the military had Julia and the children. My heart sunk as my eyes found the hard concrete staring at me. Of all the crazy unexpected thoughts that might come to someone's mind at the worst moment in his life, I thought of the first fish that I had caught when I was a small boy and how reluctant I was to throw it back in the water because the fish was too small to keep. Then as quick as I had been thrown back into memory, I emerged into reality and found myself flanked by soldiers following the officer. Resigned to whatever life had in store for me, I pictured myself facing a firing squad. Life seemed at that moment a fleeting thought, just a thought.

Part II

Following an officer and escorted by several soldiers, I walked the narrow corridor along the exterior of the building wondering about my destination. So far it did not look good at all. Not far from us in the spacious yard were several tanks and armored cars. I remembered that I had been here in the month of June after the failed coup of General Souper. This was the headquarters of the Second Armored Battalion.

Back in June, General Souper had taken more than a dozen armored cars and several tanks and laid siege to The Moneda, the presidential palace where President Allende was staying. The ill-conceived coup had not succeeded because the army commander-in-chief, General Carlos Prats, had intervened in bringing down the rebellious group. After the failed coup, the embassy had sent me here to deliver some documents to the new commander.

Now I had been arrested, and I could sense some distasteful moments ahead. I had no identification with me, and they had my gun. I had to rely on the fact that they already knew who I was. It was obvious to me that my arrest had been planned. While we were walking, I voiced my protest several times to the officer, telling him that I was an American diplomat, but he ignored me.

The room where I was taken was rather small. The only furniture in it was two chairs and a calendar hanging on a naked wall. Alone and facing some sort of interrogation, I grew uneasy to the awareness that they could easily deny that I had ever been detained and I could just follow the same fate as so many other detainees. It was a sobering thought, which made me consider the alternatives available, which in no time came to none, except overpowering my captors. Now it was only a matter of waiting. I looked at the calendar hanging on the wall. It was odd; today was September the 18th, Chile's Independence Day, and it seemed as the day was passing unnoticed.

In past years, parades and celebrations were everywhere. Only a year ago at this time, Chile was celebrating Independence Day at the tune of friendly military parades where the military shone in its past glories. Their well-pressed, immaculate uniforms showing medals by the dozens spoke of splendor as they passed along thousands of spectators with their flawless marching of impressive goose steps. The sound of thousands of boots hitting the paved street and the sound of trumpets and drums stirring the air brought nothing but praise from the crowd. The crowd then became frantic in approval of their defenders; their applauses and shouts were expressions of their appreciation for their service to the Fatherland.

And now…in September of 1973…on their Independence Day, their soldiers…their children…their offspring…their army…were killing them. Now there was terror and death lurking at every corner, of every street, in every city, town, and village in this day of independence.

Santiago on this day was a grotesque graveyard dressed in military attire as thousands of their citizens sought the restful refuge of unmarked graves. And as I reflected on what Chile was just a year ago, I could not refrain from painful emotions reaching my heart for then I was not alone — Anne was at my side. And at these moments, her presence became stronger in my thoughts. She was there telling me not to worry, that everything would be alright, that I had nothing to fear for her prayers were with me, that God would look after me. Thinking of God, this time I chose not to question, not to even wonder if He existed or not.

Several hours later I heard movement at the door, and two officers came in. Both were in their early thirties, tall, and probably of German stock. With the exception of large pockets of Chinese and Arabs, Chile was a European niche in South America with a large influx of German immigration after the Second World War. There was also a large British ethnic presence in the southern part of the country — descendants of English blood since the days of Francis Drake and of the past glory of the British Empire, very noticeable in the current make up of the Chilean Navy. All of these ethnicities added to the Spanish flavor a definite European accent to Chile's populace and culture. However, the German presence was most obvious in the makeup of the army, which dated to the nineteenth century when Chile asked for Prussian military officers to train their officers at the Chilean Military Academy. Also their constant reliance on Germany assistance since then had definitely given the Chilean Army its German appearance.

"I am Lieutenant Warner, and this is my assistant," the taller one said as he circled me. "You claim to be an American diplomat, but you have no sort of identification, and you were carrying a weapon. How do we know that you are what you claim to be?" he asked.

"I am attached to the American Embassy. All you have to do is to contact them. Also I have an American friend who is an adviser to Contreras security forces. His name is Spencer," I responded, this time in English.

He did not respond. Instead he leaned toward me as I sat in the chair. His penetrating eyes were on mine, searching for any sort of clues that could convince him.

"You have an Argentinian accent. You may speak to me in English, but as I am not fluent in the language, I cannot distinguish if you are speaking like an American or not. I can tell, however, from your Spanish that you are Argentinian. Right now Monteneros are coming across the border to help MIR," he said, referring to the Monteneros, an Argentinian Leftist group, and to MIR, the Revolutionary Left Movement.

At that moment, I could recall the many times that Spencer had tried to help me try to remove the accent in my Spanish. Back then it had been comical. Now it was a matter of life or death.

"I spent several years at the American Embassy in Buenos Aires, and I picked up the accent there. It can happen to anyone," I replied.

He gave me an inquisitive look. Then glancing at his assistant, he reached for the door without saying a word and left. Alone and probably facing a death sentence, I considered the only alternative left was for me to escape. Being inside a military compound, escape was next to impossible. It had to happen on the way to the stadium where all the killings were being done. Then it occurred to me. They could kill me in this very room. Nothing was stopping them from coming inside at any time and shooting me. This was the Chilean Army tailored to the German Army of the Second War. Its military secret intelligence was now being recognized as the most feared military secret agency not only in Chile but in all the countries of the Southern Cone.

Only a few days earlier information came to us at the embassy that Chilean military agents were already in Argentina interrogating prisoners. Falling in the hands of them was a frightening prospect to consider, but at the same time it could be my way out. All I had to do is to tell them to take me to Spencer.

Spencer was now an adviser to Contreras. But what if for some reason they would decide to ignore my plea or Spencer was working with them under a code name that he did not provide to me? As my mind frantically considered my precarious situation, the door opened, and the same lieutenant ordered me out.

In the corridor, I was met by three civilians who I immediately recognized as military personnel by their neat, short haircut and shiny shoes. All this time there was no interchange of words. Not one word was spoken. My fears increased for I realized now that I had been handed over to the military security personnel, and as far as I knew, I was already a dead man.

At the patio, a car was waiting, and one of the three civilians, a short stocky man in his forties, signaled me to get in. "Where were they taking me?" I asked myself several times, once even asking aloud. There was no answer. Aware that they were wearing civilian clothing, I had a sliver of hope; maybe they were taking me to the embassy. Then I told them that there was an American adviser called Spencer who would vouch for me, but again as at the military compound, my plea fell into deaf ears.

In total silence, we drove many streets. Each time the car slowed down at the intersections or corners, the thought of escaping was nailed to my mind. I could have just opened the door and rolled onto the pavement. The hope or expectancy of being taken to the embassy held me back.

Then unexpectedly, the man sitting next to me produced handcuffs. His gun pointing at my chest did the talking as he handcuffed me to his left wrist. It did surprise me for he acted as if he had been reading my mind. The whole scenario had drastically changed, narrowing my chances for escape. Soon the car took the familiar turn onto Grecia Avenue. I often went this way to watch a soccer game at the National Stadium. My hope for freedom was now shattered, and this time I was not going into the stadium to watch a soccer game.

The car came to a stop close to the entrance of the stadium, and strangely there was a noticeable absence of the usual heavy guarding of the area although there was a heavy military presence. We stood at the entrance as a large group of prisoners started to come in. They were led by two young soldiers. It seemed strange that the group was not guarded appropriately, especially for a large group. If they made a break now, some would get killed but others could get away. But there was no fighting spirit left in any of them.

Some of the prisoners glanced at me briefly because I was still handcuffed to the security man. They all seemed to have the same lost expression. Their eyes, in their brief encounter with mine, seemed to be alive still in the quest for answers that no one could answer except God, if there was a god.

As they moved along, it seemed as if time had slowed down considerably. It was as if we were spectators in a slow-motion picture that had no ending on a background of total silence. A silence that now spoke. It was a silence that was becoming a deafening loud scream, a scream of the spirit that broke the soul. I fought the tears as they moved along to an uncertain destination of which I was to follow.

The burst of machine-gun fire abruptly brought me back to reality. The firing was coming from inside the stadium. All of these sounds, and yet it was just background noise in this dreadful silence.

As we walked into the stadium following a military officer, the soccer field came into view, and the scene of the thousands of detainees occupying the green field and galleries was to become an unforgettable part of my memory. At this precise moment, soldiers were dragging bodies everywhere in the field.

My captors then stopped. The officer in charge, a very young lieutenant, took a waiting position as if he was waiting for someone. From time to time, he would glance at me and then return his attention to somewhere else. I figured that probably he was waiting for someone to take me to the tribune where condemned men were to receive the death penalty. "Who else would he be waiting for?" I asked myself. The dreaded thought that he may have called a priest was obscene. At this moment when my life was at its very end, a priest was the last thing I wanted to see. If there was a hell, now more than ever I would go to that hell. A profound hateful feeling was overpowering me at the thought of a Catholic priest coming to me.

The scene rapidly unfolding not too far from me stopped my thoughts. From the doorway where the teams would come out to the soccer field, the figures of two men appeared. They walked a few steps toward the field and fell. An officer and two soldiers came to the fallen men, and the officer calmly aimed his pistol upon each one of them and shot them point blank in the head. The scene seemed unreal, but the breath of reality was too strong to ignore. It was as if I was watching a World War II film reel of German soldiers shooting down civilians. It was the nightmare of Nazism recurring all over again.

At the nearby corridor, the crying and painful screams of women pierced my ears. As I turned toward the noise, I saw soldiers beating several women with their rifle butts. Some women remained motionless on the hard concrete floor while others tried to stand and continue marching toward their destination. An older woman in her late sixties fell against the wall and remained there, in a sitting position, blood pouring from her mouth, her face shattered by the butt of a rifle.

Not far from this madness, a strange scene unfolded. Several rows of soldiers were on their knees participating in some sort of Catholic ritual as a priest placed something in their mouth; all this sacredness with so much evil, I thought. These same soldiers were to torture and kill with no guilt attached to their actions. They thought they had already been forgiven. At that moment, I became as angry as I was a few minutes earlier. Deep inside of me a hate came rushing through, and I damned the whole Catholic Church, the pope, and the priesthood.

But then I looked up, and I saw an intense blue sky. It was a clean sky, and this sky spoke of something greater that could not be defined in terms of humanity. It filled me with a sense of acceptance in a mantle of awesome silence. But this acceptance lasted for a few, so brief moments, as the sounds returned to me engulfed in veils of madness. And it seemed awkward to me that the sky would still remain silent while I was here on the ground beaten by the vicious sounds of the dying.

These were the sounds of soldiers shouting orders and obscenities; the sounds of the sporadic bursts of cursing from defying prisoners who were about to die and had nothing to lose; and the cries of intense pain coming from human beings under torture and from the wounded who were also about to die. It was odd; something was definitely wrong. There was sound and silence, and the silence at times seemed to dull the sound. The stadium was in agony, in a graveyard of silence. A silence that ever so often was also broken by the unmistakable sound of bullets tearing the flesh and bones of some poor soul somewhere in this soccer field that once had been filled with laughter and shouts of excitement and happy voices of people enjoying a soccer game.

In these moments of unbelievable inhumanity when things are deplorably wrong, I find myself reaching for my wife. Desperately, I brought her close to me. Madness sometimes brings out the best in a man's life, and the best of my entire life was Anne. And now my life was coming to an end. I had to do something soon; Anne was waiting and I would not disappoint her. The moment that I could get close enough to one of the guards, I would make my move. I had to grab a rifle or a pistol, leaving them no alternative but to shoot both of us — myself and the man to whom I was handcuffed. Would I survive? Hardly, but it would be for a worthy cause. I would not leave my Anne alone. I had to live. It was now or never.

I glanced at my captors; there was no fear in me as I felt my whole body relax. It relaxed with that kind of relaxed mode that comes before an extraneous, desperate action. But then precisely at that instant when I was about to make my move, the sound of shots brought my entire being to a halt — body and thoughts.

Nearby a young man succumbed to a hail of bullets from his pursuers. His lifeless body was quickly retrieved by his executioners. Then at a glance, I thought I saw James, and I became anxious and surprised. James was not just a thought. He was real, and he was coming toward us accompanied by an officer whom I recognized as Colonel Manuel Contreras, the feared head of the military security forces.

As they came toward us, both men were looking toward where the young man was being dragged. The colonel was moving his head like he did not agree with what had occurred. Seeing them I became overwhelmed with emotions. Anne's prayer had done it, and I fought the tears from appearing. I was not going to share tears, not with them.

As they reached us, the colonel immediately told my captors to remove the handcuffs and told them to leave. He then apologized for what I had just experienced. "Mister Curtis, I am very sorry for what could have happened to you," he said, reaching for my hand. "I do wish that I had known earlier, but I only learned of your misfortune this afternoon when you had already been taken to this dreadful place."

"The Colonel is right," James said, "but it turned out all right for the call came to the colonel here, the very place where you had been taken."

Feeling the colonel's firm grip, I felt a sudden strength. It was the realization and assurance that I was to live — life was here staring at me in the face of a man who was lenient to no one.

"When Lieutenant Warner told me that the prisoner claimed to be a friend of Mr. Spencer Truman and a diplomat, I immediately knew that it was you and told him to release you, but you were already on the way here," the colonel said. "Lucky for both of us, for it would have been dreadful and embarrassing for us if something would have happened to you."

"An unfortunate happening, but an understandable one considering that you forgot to carry with you your identification," James said, and I noticed a slight sort of reproach in his voice.

"It could have happened to anyone," the colonel said in my defense, "Mistakes in times like these are bound to happen. I was just telling James about that poor misguided young man whom you witnessed being shot. It should have not happened if he had made the right choice, the correct choice, instead of running around with the wrong crowd." There was regret in his words as he looked toward the place where moments earlier the young man had been killed.

James drew a smile, seemingly agreeing with him, but I sensed a sort of disbelief in his expression. Everyone in Chile knew who Colonel Manuel Contreras was. Contreras did not know the meaning of regret, and James knew it.

"I better take you back. I think that you have had enough," James said.

He was absolutely right. I had more than enough for one day. Surprisingly James grabbed my arm in a show of affection, which was rare in his persona. "I am glad that we reached you in time. I am so sorry, my friend, that you went through this dreadful ordeal," he said, raising to a higher degree my expectation of the human race. James proved to me at that moment that there was still some good left in all of us.

Then he thanked Contreras and apologized for the inconvenience. I also thanked the colonel, and we left.

As we drove to the embassy, James' demeanor changed. His replies to my questions were short and rather cutting. Then later at the embassy, unable to control himself, he launched a tirade of accusations and observations that I found improper and totally unacceptable. He accused me of discrediting the Office of Foreign Affairs by getting myself involved in private matters and interfering in the internal politics of Chile, which could damage the relationship between the State Department and the junta. I broke into laugher, aware of his cynical and hypocritical accusation, and reminded him that our government, the State Department as well as the embassy, not to mention the CIA, had already interfered in the internal politics of Chile.

Then I reminded him about the note he had left at my desk. He grew angry. He told me that he had not left such a note, that someone else had done it. At this point in our arguing, he pointed out that he had only known about my detention through the Chilean military intelligence.

Aware that we were going nowhere in this interchange of words and reminding myself that I was still a diplomat, I abruptly changed the course of the conversation and asked him if he still needed my help on a project called the White Book. Project White Book was some sort of reconciliation between the military and the world press that was now at odds with the junta and its oppressive policies toward the Chilean populace.

He did not reply immediately, but his expression changed. Then he looked at me and apologized. He blamed the whole mess on the now overwhelming pressure we were under.

"I must tell you now that there is nothing we can do about Frank and Charles. Whoever placed that note on your desk had no idea that the information on it was already a day old. Chilean intelligence got hold of Frank yesterday morning," he said, lowering his eyes to the floor. He had been annoyed at me earlier; now his whole demeanor was sort of stressful and laboriously apologetic. The seconds became unending moments of unbearable waiting, and I sensed that it had to do with Frank.

"You know," he said as he looked at me seeking some understanding, "in our business some things remain unanswerable. We as people would like to have answers. However, sometimes there are tasks that we would like to question, but we cannot." He paused and lowered his eyes to floor.

He remained silent for several moments. He was silent, but in this instance his silence spoke before the sound of words ever came out of his mouth, and my eyes were instantly filled with tears that I did not want.

Suddenly I had become vulnerable. I could not understand it. Most of my life I had been exposed to the hard facts of life. Vietnam had been an experience that had considerably hardened my views about life, but then Anne had come into my life. She brought softness to my spirit that I did not really want, but it was there to stay, and it was becoming more transparent in my demeanor more often.

"This morning when I was contacted by Colonel Contreras and told that you had been detained, he also informed me that they had apprehended Frank yesterday morning and that last night he had been released. Early this morning however, he was found dead on a deserted street. According to Contreras, Frank was killed by Communists who blamed the Americans for the coup. Of course, you well know that is not true. Frank was arrested at his place by military intelligence agents. One thing I do know, Spencer was not involved," he said.

I fought the tears and cleared my throat. "I guess the only thing left for us to do is to notify his parents. Then we can send the body home," I said, pacing the room.

"That's out of the question. The State Department has no knowledge of Frank ever having been in Chile. Officially he never came to register here."

"Yes I know, but you and I know that he was here," I said. "How can you say that you had no knowledge that Frank was not in Chile? You have spoken to him several times, and you once even told me that you liked the kid!"

"I speak for the State Department, and the ambassador agrees. That is the official word."

I knew he was right. Our government was of the position that there would be no interference. At least, that was the "official position." However, on the practical side, we had already interfered. We had already been given the green light from Kissinger to support the junta. The CIA had been given absolute independence from us and was acting on its own.

"I guess you are aware that Spencer is trying to find Charles. Is there any news about Charles?" I asked.

"Yes, Spencer was contacted this morning, and he should be here tomorrow morning. As for Charles, we just don't know. I just hope he is heading north and can get to Peru. Argentina is out of the question. There are only a few passes in the Andes. and the military on both sides control them."

"I would like to see Frank," I said impulsively, and I saw a questioning look in James's face. "Yes, I know. It sounds out of our characters being diplomats, but it is personal, and I will keep it that way," I added to reassure him of my heartfelt feelings for the young man.

"Alright, I can understand that. I think that it can be arranged. I will make some calls and find out where he was taken. I think I would like to know too. Don't think of me as being too callous. I have a son about his age in the States."

I did not respond although my expression spoke of understanding. Who wouldn't try to understand the feelings of a father? Perhaps the most callous, and I was not that callous. James drew the faintest hint of a smile, seemingly grateful to me for expressing a voiceless understanding. He then picked up a note off his desk and said, "Anne called this morning. Why don't you call her now? You can use my phone to call her." He pointed at the phone at his desk and left the room.

I picked up the phone. As I was dialing her number, my hand started trembling, and I became overwhelmed by the unexpected mixture of feelings — sadness and joy — coming over me at the sound of her voice. I had no choice but to remain silent for some moments, desperately trying to calm myself. Finally I spoke, but this time it was her who had succumbed to her feelings.

After gaining her composure, she managed to tell me how much she missed me and that during the night she could not sleep, worrying to death about me. Earlier in the day she had not been able to shake a fearsome feeling that something had happened to me. I eased her feelings by telling her that I was all right. I assured her that I was not taking any risks that could place me in danger. I told her that I loved her deeply and that I was thinking of my future with her in the States this December. After a while she seemed to gain a great deal of peace of mind and told me that she prayed constantly for my sake. It was hard to say goodbye to her. I wanted to keep hearing her voice. When I finally placed the phone down, I was not able to ease my feelings. Pressing my head upon the desk, I wept.

Later that day as I watched television on the only channel controlled by the junta, I tried to make sense of what was now occurring. It was not easy to focus on it because Anne's voice was still fresh in my mind. But the need to know what was going on was imperative. There were too many unanswered questions in my mind. The most pressing now was Mario. I wondered about him. Was the military really holding his family hostage or…was he working for the Chilean military secret service or for the CIA?

I was sure that all of these recent events had to be staged. From the note that had been left at my desk, to Mario turning me in to the military, to the agents taking me to the stadium, and to the timely arrival of Contreras and James to save me from being tortured and killed.

I wondered about what role James played in all of these occurrences. Was he *that* innocent about Frank's death? What about Spencer? Taking his position within the CIA into consideration and being an adviser to Colonel Contreras, Spencer should have known about Frank. Was Spencer taking me for a ride on a path that had already been determined? There were too many questions and doubts. I had to find the answer, and the answer would not come easy, not now as I had to face the reality of Frank's death.

The night was harsh as the face of Frank obscured most of my thoughts. There were intervals of Anne's face appearing and the sound of her voice that kept breaking the silence in my mind. Finally I fell asleep on a night that went too fast.

In the early hours of the morning, I was already awake and waiting for the arrival of James and Spencer, who were going to take me to the place where Frank's body was supposed to have been taken.

Around eleven in the morning, they picked me up. Spencer seemed glad to see me and expressed what I thought was a heartfelt emotion for what had happened to Frank. I asked him about Charles, and he told me that he had probably gone into hiding with his friends and left it at that, something unusual for him because he always liked to express different possibilities. At one point he told me that soon communications would be faster. Someone at the States had come out with a portable cell phone. The agency was doing everything possible to make it available to all the operatives. Soon they would be able to communicate with each other instantaneously. "Soon we will all be just like agent 007. My friend we are James Bonds in the making," he said jokingly.

About half an hour later, at the outskirts of the District of Nunoa, we stopped in front of what seemed to be a large warehouse. Outside there were several military units, and several soldiers were guarding the main entrance.

As we left the car, I sensed that James was familiar with the building. He approached one of the guards and then he signaled to us, waiting by the curb. Once inside we went to a large office, and James was greeted by a colonel who knew him for he addressed James by his name. James then introduced Spencer and I to the colonel; his name was Jose Urriaga.

Colonel Urriaga then told us that one of his units had found Frank's body on a street. According to him, Frank had probably been killed by leftist insurgents. He assured us that Frank, after being detained by the military, had been set free.

"You know how much these Communist hate the Americans," he said in an apologetic tone.

James thanked him. I looked at Spencer for a reaction, but his expression remained calm. We both knew that Frank had been arrested by DINA and had later been executed. We then followed the colonel, who guided us into a large hall that contained several hundred bodies lying on a concrete floor covered with white linen.

I had seen dead bodies by the hundreds in Vietnam, and at the time it seemed normal. It was an expected occurrence of war. But now it was a strange happening that did not fit with the civilized world we were in. These killings should not be happening, and the scene confronting me was revolting and tragic.

Part III

In the war, I had seen many mutilated, burned, torn bodies. And sometimes I had found young Americans, their bodies showing visible signs of having been tortured. There have been several occasions that left deep impressions on me on how I perceived war. These impressions had affected me and lasted for the rest of my service in Vietnam, and now years later, the recollection still bothered me.

Spencer went thru the same thing, but at that particular time Spencer was already a seasoned warrior; he had already been there since 1961. Killing for him had become sort of normal. I say sort of because killing a human being is never normal. But for Spencer this normality was to change into an unchecked hate that with time also would become normal.

In my case, I justified it to myself as occurrences of war. Yes I did come to hate the Communists, but that was war. Casualties of war have no face to reckon with, just war. But here in Chile, there was no war as I knew it. The enemy was only a remnant of a few hundred Communist militants who had presented a token resistance. Now most of those who were falling to the military were defenseless civilians. Here inhumanity to mankind had a face — Pinochet and his henchmen...and to a lesser degree us, the Americans.

I slowly moved along the corridor separating the dead, fearful to find my friend. I stopped. My curiosity took me to a body to my left. I lowered myself down to the figure wrapped in white. I raised the sheet and found a young man probably in his early teens. What captured my attention were the exposed feet that had a bluish coloring and large toes that were unusually black in color. Perhaps he had been subjected to electric charges. His face was all bruised up and still showed expression of intense pain, and at both sides of his temple two neat holes that had been washed clean still had signs of dry blood in them.

There was no doubt that this poor soul had been tortured — the only mercy he had received was the bullet in his brain that had stopped all pain. I imagined the horrible pain that his parents would go through once they found his lifeless body, unless they as well had fallen victim to the military.

Absorbed in my thoughts, I did not hear the voice of Spencer calling me, and it took several seconds before I heard him. I stood still frozen to my feet, which seemed to ignore my brain's calling for movement. At that moment I did not want to move — afraid, afraid that they had found Frank.

Moments later I found myself staring at the nearly unrecognizable face of my young friend. He had been severely beaten. Someone had viciously tortured him, his face the face of unbearable suffering. For some reason, I felt detached from what I was seeing. The surroundings became somber and dreadful, the walls too tall, the large windows too opaque and denying entrance to any daylight, and the ceiling was an uninviting height.

Then I became aware of the silence. It was the same type of silence I had experienced at the stadium. This was a silence that penetrated all of my surroundings and scrutinized my whole being. I heard its sound — an overwhelming sound that came like a gentle breeze and inversely roared like the fiercest wind — and I listened…I listened to what it was saying, and I felt the pain of humanity, the suffering, the frailty, the motionless coldness of the dead who now had a voice. I felt this numbness; it seemed that there were no feelings in me.

After a while things took form and shape, and the snap of heels as a soldier saluted an officer brought me to my reality. I looked at Spencer, who kept his eyes on the floor. Nearby James was hitting the wall, seemingly profoundly disturbed. The thought that James had succumbed to some unexpected feeling of remorse rushed through my mind, but it was quickly replaced by a feeling of distrust toward him, and I told myself that he was just pretending.

Spencer methodically showed me and explained the many wounds and bruises on Frank's body. I listened and listened well, as if my mind wanted to record every word that my friend was saying. He pointed at the many bruises all over his body and told me that Frank had probably been kicked viciously and beaten when he had been first brought to the National Stadium where he had been shot. The deep abrasion around his neck showed that his torturers had used a wire, probably a clothes hanger, as a choker. However, the many bullets did not speak of a summary execution. More than a dozen bullets of a high-caliber rifle indicated something else, a purposefully sinister intention. The killers were making a statement, not just to nationals but to foreigners, especially Americans.

"What was so important for them to know? This kid didn't know more than what the public already knows. My God...Why?" I asked.

"You are right. They are making a statement. By killing an American, they are telling the opposition that they will stop at nothing," Spencer answered.

I lowered myself to the floor and sat on the cold concrete. I pulled the sheet back over Frank's body. At a glance, I saw Spencer pulling James away, and moments later I saw them leaving this place of death. Nearby a guard, a very young soldier, stood at attention. His uniform and helmet reminded me of the German soldiers of the Second War.

Looking at the figure of Frank brought brief memories. The few instances that I had exchanges with him became as vivid as if I had just seen him. I wished I had known him more. I wished I could go back in time so I could ask him personal questions. What kind of family did he have? Did he have any brothers or sisters? What about his parents? Thoughts upon thoughts came and went; there were no answers. There was so much I could have asked him, so much I wanted to know. Really I knew little about him. He had come to mean so much to me at this time. This was the reality of the living — the reality that most of us become important to others after we die.

All I knew about Frank was that he came from Chicago and was enrolled at the University of Chile. He was well-educated and did not hide from us. He sympathized with the philosophy of Carl Marx and Lenin but refrained from the rawness of Mao's teaching. It seemed to me that he lacked perception and was sort of naive. But all of this made him a sensitive human being — an imperfect human, but after all, we were all imperfect.

Once I had reminded him that we were following the policy of the Monroe Doctrine, which made the United States the protectors of the Latin American countries. But according to him, the Monroe Doctrine was a perverse policy, and it denied the Latin American countries self-determination. It was an American policy aimed solely at protecting American interests. He had been absolutely right, and I had to agree with him, but that was the nature of American foreign policy, and I was a representative of that policy.

Absorbed in thoughts, I did not hear the guard calling out to me until he touched my shoulder.

"Sir," he said. "You should leave. It is getting late."

I stood up, my eyes glued to the inert figure of my young friend. After a few moments, I found myself looking at the forms of so many dead. They looked insolent, clean, and grotesque. There was always something grotesque about death. I had felt it in Vietnam, so many young lives just wasted away and for no purpose at all.

Here in Chile, death seemed more grotesque. Here was a purpose — an evil, diabolical purpose — and what was more revolting was the undeniable factor that I was part of this evil. "Did I still have that hate that had rooted so deep inside of me while I was in Vietnam?" I asked myself. If Frank had truly been a Communist, would I have just accepted it and walked away? I grew confused. All I could see, and I was very much aware of this, was the fact that this young man had never been a threat to us.

I glanced at the face of the young soldier who stood stoic, as rigid as the dead. I was about to move when I heard him saying something. I looked at him. His eyes were focused, buried in the wall across from us.

"I am sorry, Sir," he said without looking at me.

I looked down as if I had not heard him. I knew that he wanted to say something, but his being associated with this demanded an explanation. Across the hall, an officer focused his eyes on us. I knew then that this young soldier was on duty, and he did not have permission to address me.

"I understand," I replied. "And I am grateful."

"Was he your brother?" he asked in a low voice.

"No, but he could have been," I responded as I walked away.

Outside the morgue, life was everywhere. A mockingbird was whistling a happy tune as a gentle breeze rocked him back and forth on the exposed limb of a tree. It was a sunny day, a beautiful day. As I walked toward the curb where the car was waiting, I resented that good smell of life. It did not seem right after seeing so much death.

On the way to the embassy, we hardly spoke — only once when Spencer made a comment that neither James nor I bothered to answer. As we approached the British Embassy, I told James to let me out. I wanted to see an old friend.

"If any correspondence has arrived there for me, pick it up," Spencer said as I was leaving the car.

At that moment, I turned toward Spencer without looking at James and asked him, "What about Charles, Spencer? Tell me, what about him?"

"I'll do all I can. So far, he is nowhere to be found," he answered, avoiding my eyes and showing some distress in his voice.

"Why don't you ask your friend here? Maybe he will take you to the right morgue," I said, trying to perceive some sort of honesty somewhere in his eyes, hoping I could see something that could tell me that I was totally wrong. Spencer looked at me and hardened his expression. His eyes were impenetrable, and I was beaten. He knew me too well.

As I came closer to the gates of the British Embassy, the guards stood at attention. I had known both of them for quite some time, and they let me in without requesting my identification. At the entrance, I tried to gain my composure. I was not so naive as to deny completely that maybe Spencer had deceived me. After all, deception was an essential part of the makeup of any operative. This was a sobering thought. I analyzed myself in different times and circumstances with different degrees of necessity and if they could have placed me in a double play with a friendship that wouldn't matter. The results are always what really matter on any play. And yet somewhere inside of me a disquieting thought considered him a trustworthy friend. Was I wrong? Perhaps.

The sight of Sir Percil by the waiting room had a soothing effect on me. Whenever I gave him the time, he wasted no time occupying it. His main and favorite theme was his recollections of his staying in Burma during the Second World War.

For me at least, it was fascinating the way he presented his adventures. Perhaps it was that particular British sound and wording — elegant and respectful, an assuming sense of moral cleanliness even at its worse. It seemed that the British, even when being engaged in their own bloody mess, always came out pure and clean.

I greeted him and sat down. He gave me a friendly welcome as he always did. Then as we spoke, I suddenly felt impelled to tell him what had been occurring. I was careful to not divulge sensitive matter. He was a man of insight however, and I sensed he knew that something was bothering me, but he did no inquiring. This time he refrained from saying anything that could lead into one of his stories; he just sat and waited.

"What a bloody mess, my friend," he said, breaking the awkwardness of the moment. "Early this morning, more than a dozen bodies were found floating on the San Carlos Channel. Most of them were students."

"Courtesy of the beloved Pinochet," I replied with sarcasm. "Soon we'll start calling him The George Washington of Chile."

"Be careful, John. Most of your people are very sympathetic to the junta. Also Contreras' ears are everywhere."

"I know, Sir Percil."

"Too bad about your friend, but staying alive is extremely important to us. Never forget that those who are alive are doing the changes — the dead are dead. As for your friend, those who murdered him will face justice. Just let time take its course."

I looked at him, realizing that he already knew about Frank.

"Colonel Contreras is unreachable, one of those untouchable people. He is Pinochet's right hand man. I do not see justice at all," I said.

He grinned and replied, "My young friend, nothing remains untouchable. Ten or twenty years from now a new generation will be coming for them. Pinochet, Contreras, Larios, Starks, and so many others will pay as Hitler or Mussolini did."

"Perhaps. Only time can tell. But now I can only hope that Spencer can find Charles," I said. "He may be luckier than I."

He stretched his legs and turned slightly toward me, glaring at me. I sensed something was coming. After a long awkward moment of silence, he said, "Charles is dead. He was shot this morning." His eyes were on mine, eager to read my reaction.

My reaction was anger as I suddenly burst out cursing the whole Chilean military establishment and its damned class of well-to-do citizens and socialist idealists who had brought this seemingly unending nightmare. Then I stopped cursing, realizing that there was something odd about the whole thing. James and Spencer had just told me that they did not know about Charles, and here at the British Embassy, they already knew that Charles had been shot. James had been at the embassy earlier in the morning. He should have known. Sir Percil, anticipating my thought, said, "They already know. Spencer got to Charles, but he had to hand him over to the military security after some sort of scuffle with them. My guess is that Spencer had no choice. You must take into consideration that Spencer is attached to them only as an adviser."

I was bewildered. "Spencer?" I questioned him in silence, but Sir Percil lowered his eyes for he himself had no answer. How could he? But in my emotional state, I needed an answer. It had to be an answer. It could not be possible, not Spencer. I had asked him about Charles this morning, and he had told me that he thought Charles had probably gone into hiding with some of his friends. There was no way Spencer could have lied to me so brazenly. Someone was lying, and it was not Spencer. It just did not make any sense. What about James? Did he know about Charles? I had seen him.

He was deeply moved when he saw Frank's body. He could not be that deceiving...could he have been?

"I just left James and Spencer. They did not mention anything. On the contrary, they led me to believe that he was still alive," I said. "I don't think that Spencer could do that. Maybe James, but not Spencer."

He did not reply. Silence was the spokesman. Everything was being told, a whole picture in front of me. Yet even still, I could not tell its meaning. The ending was too vague, but the lantern had been placed in my hands. All I had to do was to focus the light on the path ahead. On the other hand, I was too afraid to light the way, afraid to know the truth. I could not accept that Spencer had betrayed me. Not Spencer.

"John!" Sir Percil said after a few long awkward moments. "Sometimes I wonder what made you join the Foreign Service. You know well that we are players in a chess game of nations. We use people, and they use us. Spencer plays his part, as both of us do. We diplomats like to think of ourselves as honorable men serving our country, as if it was a matter of gallant duty, which it is not. Most of us play dirty to achieve the interest of our countries although we do try our best to project an honorable distinguished presence in the midst of deception."

"You are right, Sir Percil. Sometimes I wonder myself," I said. "However, the interest of my country does benefit my people, and that gives me a good feeling."

"And yet in the process, sometimes we hurt others, and our victims have no country. The cemeteries of the world hold only flesh and bones. Death holds no flags," he responded in a tone of voice that was reassuring and soothing. "True, it does benefit your people, but...what about these people?"

"They are well rewarded. We have brought progress," I said.

"For a short period of time, I suppose. What will happen to them when they run out of copper? The United States still has untapped copper resources for centuries to come."

He was right; I had no rebuttal. We had followed the Monroe Doctrine for two centuries. It had nothing to do with the protection of the Americas from European imperialism. On the contrary, once England had ruled the oceans of the world. Now it was a formidable ally of the United States. The Monroe Doctrine was here to stay solely for the interest of the United States, nothing else. I was here to make sure that the trade between the United States and Chile would remain unchanged for the benefit of the United States. As I became engulfed in this thinking, I became aware then that I had detached myself momentarily from what had just transpired. Frank, Charles, Spencer, James, they all seemed like characters of a passing transcript. All I wanted now was to see Anne. God...how much I was missing her.

I left the chair, and I thanked him for his time. He gave some correspondence for Spencer, a letter from Spencer's mother to him.

"I notice that Stella always sends her correspondence to Spencer through you. It seems to me she does not trust our embassy," I said.

"To some degree, my boy; she is British all the way. She won't have it any other way," he responded. After a brief pause he said, "Try to understand your friend. I know Spencer well; he is after all half British. I assume that after seeing what you went through with Frank, he did not have the presence of mind to add more pain to a cup that was already full. Perhaps tomorrow or later he will tell you about it. Sometimes our agencies do not allow us to be informative, at least for the moment. There are matters that are only the CIA's concern and others only ours. They do what they must do, and we do the same. Think about it. What we as diplomats want to accomplish sometimes can only be done by unpleasant means. We get the glory and they... they remain unnoticed."

"I don't know. Time will tell. I just don't know," I said, and as I started to leave I recalled what I had seen at the stadium. "I guess it is the fact that I know that there are things occurring around me, and there is nothing I can do about it. It is like what I saw yesterday at the stadium. It reminded me of those documentaries of the Second War where you see thousands of prisoners being taken away to labor camps or to be killed, being led by a few dozen soldiers. I always wondered why they did not overpower their guards if they outnumbered them by so many."

"After a long period of suffering all sorts of deprivations, soldiers and civilians lose their will to resist or fight." he responded.

"Yeah, I suppose we all have a breaking point," I replied and looked at him for a response, but he did not respond. I continued, "There was a group of about thirty prisoners guarded by two young guards. A thought crossed my mind — they were seemingly willing to accept their imprisonment though they knew that they were going to be tortured and most likely killed. But what made the biggest impression on me was their silence, an intense silence that engulfed everything. At least that is how I felt. Maybe it was just me."

I paused for several moments as my voice momentarily lost strength to continue. "You see..there was this silence, the same silence I felt this morning when I came upon young Frank. You know that in Vietnam I saw all kinds of atrocities, but I had never heard true silence, the silence that penetrates the deepest part of one's being. The people kept looking at me as they passed by. I felt their eyes on me and thought they were oddly expressionless. I felt their intensity. They were silent, and yet I heard their cry. It was like a deafening scream, a scream of the spirit coming from their broken souls. It wasn't a scream for mercy or pity…just despair…deep despair. Sir Percil, have you ever heard the sound of that sort of silence?"

Sir Percil slowly turned his chair slightly toward the wall, giving his back to me.

"Yes my boy, many times in my life," he replied and became silent.

I left without saying goodbye. I knew he understood my departure. Words at that moment were better heard in the silence of our hearts. Outside the building, September met me with all the beauty of life. September in Chile had always been refreshing, but this year it had been somber and bloody. And yet the surroundings were awesomely beautiful against that deep blue sky above the white snow crowning the Andes mountains. It was as if the surroundings were telling me that there was a God after all. Could it be that my Anne was right and there was a God? Perhaps…but regardless, it felt good to be alive.

Part IV

Shortly after Charles' and Frank's deaths, I became involved in the gathering of material favorable to the junta. It was an effort by the State Department to soften world criticism of Chile's current government. By now Augusto Pinochet was the recognized undisputed leader of the junta, and rumors at the embassy were that he was planning to assume the presidency of Chile by December.

On November 12, three months after the military coup, the formation of the agency Dirección de Inteligencia Nacional, which came to be known as DINA, was established. DINA was to control all Chilean internal and external affairs and all branches of the armed forces. DINA was the Gestapo of the army, the overseer of civilians and military alike. Under Decree 521, DINA had the power in a declared state of emergency to detain any individual. Shortly after its inception, DINA extended its iron grip to all the countries of the Southern Cone, squeezing the lives out of thousands of leftist subversives and sympathizers.

The notion that Spencer had turned Charles over to the military drove a wedge between Spencer and me. Now Spencer was an adviser to DINA. Our friendship in these days had become only formalities and casual exchanges of concern toward our loved ones. Sometimes on his way to the ambassador's office, he would ask about Anne, and I would inquire about his mother. Even though James had told me about the circumstances in which Spencer had turned Charles over to the military, which from the practical intelligence point of view had been the sensible thing to do, I still felt Spencer had not done enough to save him. Somehow I had grown reluctant to accept that Spencer was attached to DINA and in all probability had no choice but to deliver him to the Chileans.

Also since I had found that the executions of Frank and Charles had been approved by an American, probably a CIA officer, my disdain toward the agency and its operatives became known in the embassy's circle to the point that the assistant to the ambassador found it appropriate to express his concern by calling me to his office to express his displeasure.

At this time, I was also having a hard time coping with the disappearance of Mario and his family. The last time I had seen him was when I had been arrested by the military. All that I had were his last words that the military had taken his family. Later I went looking for him, but there was no sign of them or neighbors. The whole complex where they were living was emptied.

There were no civil authorities that could give me any information on Mario and his family. Fernando Ruiz, a friend of Mario and owner of a small coffee shop which I used to frequent in better days, told me that entire families were disappearing. He as well had relatives who had just vanished.

I wrote to Anne about Mario, Julia, and the children. I also told her that I had been informed by some of their friends that they had left the city to avoid the dangers of living in Santiago, that they had probably moved to northern Chile with their relatives. Fully aware that Anne cared for the family, I could not tell her my fears. More than once I became very depressed, sensing the worse. On my desk, dozens of reports about entire families that had been executed or disappeared were piling up.

At one point, moved by fears that Mario and his family would follow the same fate of Frank and Charles, I left my pride aside, and I asked for Spencer's help in locating Mario and his family. I knew Spencer had never met Mario, but he was the only hope I had to find Mario. Spencer had connections inside DINA. Spencer did his best to try and locate them but to no avail. Mario and his family had disappeared.

As I had not seen or witnessed what had happened to them, it was easier to push them into the back of my mind. I was to remember them as I had seen them the last time. It was easier to pretend than to try to know the truth. I convinced myself that they had moved north.

In the case of Frank and Charles, I could not avoid reality. I had been there, and I had seen what had happened to them. The possible role of Spencer in their deaths was important to me, important in the sense that I considered him a man of integrity and principles although the essence of his work denied both virtues. But some of us like to see virtues in a friend whom we respect and love. It is a paradox for some, but some do care when friendship is involved. Also by this time, I felt that I myself had wronged him for I knew the kind of work that he did. After all he was an operative, a CIA man.

At one time, Spencer and I were soldiers — American soldiers. We both believed that American soldiers do not kill Americans. This sort of misguided thinking was important to both of us though deep inside we knew that were totally wrong. Our history books were filled with Americans betraying and killing Americans. The American Civil War was an example where Americans fought and killed Americans on both sides of that conflict.

Spencer was my friend. In true friendship, sometimes we tend to look for the less obvious, a sanitizing of the spirit, and be less apologetic about facts. I could not accept the thought of him participating in the death of both Americans, and if he had, I wanted in some way to find a reason for justification. Maybe his handing over Charles to the military could be justified due to the gravity of the situation. His seemingly willing spirit to accept their deaths as part of the time in which we were living had some justification. But somehow I just needed to know, and it was an awkward confusing feeling, sort of needing to know though by this time it did not really matter. But it was there, and I had to know.

When I finally did question him to see if he had anything to do with the deaths of Frank or Charles, he became angry and told me that by accusing Americans for their deaths, I was helping the opposition, and that even if he knew it, he was not about to tell me. He said Charles and Frank had stumbled in the crossfire of events, and there was nothing that he or I could have done to avoid their deaths. Then he told me that I was siding too much with the Communists and that I should remember Vietnam.

"If we do not stop the Communists now, sooner or later we would have another Nam," he said. "The US is not going to allow a Communist state in the Americas. Especially with the natural resources that Chile has. Of all people, you should know that. Copper is an essential and precious commodity to us. Otherwise you or I wouldn't be here. If we had allowed a Marxist regime, sooner or later, we would have to intervene. Thousands of American boys would die, just like in Vietnam."

He was right. When I had considered the alternatives, there were none left. If Allende had been allowed to continue, the Soviets gradually would have tilted the balance of power in their favor. I was sort of divided — on one hand what was occurring was not acceptable, yet the occurrence itself was acceptable.

Spencer asked me to accept what had happened to our friends as an unpleasant episode and to let it go. He reminded me of what had been told to him about Vietnam, about letting go of some unsavory things that had occurred to him. I told him that I would, but he knew that my search for the identity of the American who had approved of our friend's death would not end.

In time I realized that I was going nowhere with my search, and I found it wise to channel my attention to the demands of my work, which was to provide data favorable to the junta. Although I tried to find something positive concerning human rights, all things pointed in a different direction.

The State Department, realizing that most of the world press that once had welcomed the fall of Marxism in Chile was now critical of the junta, sought to improve the image of Chile's government by establishing a policy of appeasement that would present to the world a peaceful nation. It was ironic that the Times and other American and European newspapers, newspapers that a year earlier had sent reporters to discredit the Allende regime, were now at odds with Chile's military regime. It was ironic in the sense that some of the reporters who had actually been paid by the CIA to discredit President Allende were now discrediting the government that they had helped to establish. But I also realized that sometimes a continuous wrong cannot continue when that wrong is recognized. Perhaps the world press had a conscience.

There was no denial from the State Department that mass executions, torture and imprisonment of alleged enemies of the state had alienated even those who had favored the military coup. Even Kissinger had expressed his disapproval — a mere token of conscience, but at least a token. Accepting in part the blame, the American government brought to the world's attention some justifiable actions that took place solely for the interest of the Chilean people.

However, some events were not justifiable. Just recently, and still very fresh in my mind, was the decision by the Chilean government to bring back the dissidents in exile. The State Department approved the plan, and even I myself felt that there was still hope — finally the Chilean government was on its course toward redemption.

Assured that the opposition had been neutralized, the Chilean government, headed by Pinochet, announced that because the political upheaval had been stabilized, all Chilean citizens and their families that had traveled abroad during the first weeks of the military takeover could now return to their home. It was a tragic event. Those who had in good faith returned were put in prison, and hundreds just disappeared. DINA swallowed them by the hundreds. For the State Department, it was a hard pill to swallow that they were the ones who had backed the plan. It was Pinochet's finest master piece of deception, framed by Contreras on a cold, solid frame of blood and death.

And yet there was also no denial that the military had brought stability to Chile; its economy was on the rise. Prior to the military coup, the Chilean economy had been in total disarray. Allende had suffered a setback from his own follower, the Popular Unity. It had embarked in the takeover of private firms by trade unions, which gave the workers the full ownership over these companies without any compensation to the legal owners. This alarmed foreign investors and halted investments in Chile.

The nationalization of the American copper mines had also frozen foreign investment in Chile. There were strikes made at the copper mines of El Teniente, El Salvador and Chuquicamata. The trucker strike had been a major blow to the economy; it paralyzed the entire country for several months and had seriously damaged the economy. Also the harsh economic sanctions imposed by the Nixon administration to an economy in decline had been a major factor in the destabilization of Chile's economy.

Now with Marxism gone, it was an opportunity for financial conglomerates to invest in Chile. I was already visualizing an influx of foreign bank loans. These banks were already reinstating the credit to revitalize the Chilean economy.

As I paged the many drafts that I was to submit for release of the sanctions on Chile, James told me that Nixon had approved an accelerated loan of forty million dollars. Within two weeks, another forty million dollars would be added. He had, earlier in the day, received assurance of loans from the World Bank, the International Monetary Fund, and the Inter-American Development Bank. Also all the nationalized foreign corporations, such as Dow Chemical, Firestone and International Telephone and Telegraph, were returning to the country and the Alliance for Progress had added more funds to the infrastructure of the country in general.

All of this was good news that favored the Chilean economy. However, in the aspect of human rights, the news was detrimental to the image of Chile. In my desk, in separate files, were dozens of documents on the summary executions that were now taking place. CIA reports on tortures, on detainees, and on killing of innocent civilians were damaging to Chile. I did not think that the State Department could do anything to lessen the truth behind these occurrences.

And yet the CIA station chief who had taken over the U.S. Army attaché at the embassy thought that we still could change the face of the Chilean military in the West by minimizing some of the reports that had already reached us.

Walter, one of the assistants for the CIA station, was not pleased with my report. Although it was favorable to the government on the economic aspect, it offered no encouragement on the hostile nature of the government toward the populace. He was annoyed at me and expressed his thought on the matter to James, who shrugged his shoulders and just walked away.

Walter told me that the Chilean admiral who was in charge of the publication of the findings, or so called White Book, needed a favorable input. The White Book was an attempt by the military to justify the coup on the ground that the coup had been necessary to prevent a Marxist takeover of the country by force, a plan known as Plan Z. This Plan Z was known to us as political propaganda used by the military to discredit President Allende and his followers.

I told Walter that the number of executions given to us by the military did not coincide with the actual figures given to us by other reliable sources and that the number of detainees who were friends or relatives of suspected Communists or Socialists was on an increase. Not to mention the torture of countless prisoners that was still happening.

Also extremely concerning was the information that we had gathered on a detainee center called Colonia Dignidad where prisoners were tortured and used as guinea pigs in experiments by elements of the biochemical warfare branch of the army. The imprisonment of Orlando Letelier, former ambassador to the United States and former minister of defense under the Allende government, was a matter of deep concern to the United States, which now had called for his release.

I also told Walter that the objective of the White Book was to justify the military coup, and this Plan Z alleged by the military was nonfactual. Most of us knew that the coup had not been necessary to prevent an armed takeover by the paramilitary units of the Popular Unity. They supposedly had the backing of Castro and the Soviets. The Soviets, since the coup had remained unusually quiet, and the Cubans were offering verbal support to a Left that had been liquidated, except for a few pockets of resistance of no great concern. This White Book was only an attempt by the military junta to soften the world criticism by presenting Chile as a calm, peaceful nation going through a transitional period that needed the support and understanding of the world community.

Walter became upset. According to him, Chile's enemies had been suppressed and normality was returning to the country, and now was time for the world community to give Chile a hand on its way to full recovery.

However, Chile's situation at the start of 1974 was far from being normal. DINA was now a recognizable entity of its own, an administrative state force that relentlessly continued the executions of suspected political dissidents and torture of thousands of detainees. Among the detainees were hundreds of innocent prisoners who were only guilty of being relatives, friends or sympathizers of the opposition. It had also extended abroad its distorted sense of justice by going after the exiles in different countries and murdering them. The State Department was now receiving information that Chilean exiles had been murdered in Mexico, Argentina, Uruguay, and in some European countries.

Former Ambassador Nathaniel Davis had been instrumental to the fall of Allende by fully supporting the military coup and recognizing the military junta as Chile's legitimate government. In turn, Ambassador David Popper, who had become the new ambassador to Chile in February 1974, accentuated the American support. He established a policy of cynicism, of appeasement to supporters and critics of Pinochet's government. Perhaps being closer to the players in this big chess game of nations made me apprehensive and distrustful of those I came into contact with at the embassy.

The conviction of President Nixon's former aids on March 1 regarding the Watergate scandal had all of us uncertain as to what definite role we would play in Chile. If things were to continue on as they were, there was no doubt that Nixon would be impeached. Afterward, in all probabilities, he could be indicted by the Senate and forced out of office. Then what? The USA could change its current policy in Chile, and most of us would have to return home, including Ambassador Popper.

At this time, I was eagerly looking forward to getting back to the States and to start a new life with Anne. My assignment in Chile would end on December 31, 1974. It was time to start a family, and the thought of it was pleasant and soothing. Now more than ever I needed to visualize my life with Anne. My present nightmare would cease to exist in less than a year.

The month of March became too long, and time seemed to drag as I focused on December, when Chile was to be a thing of the past. At this time, I could not help from missing Spencer, who for several months had just disappeared. I realized then that he was perhaps the only friend I had in Chile besides old man Percy and the only friend I had ever had besides my Anne.

Then in April, a visit by Spencer to my office at the embassy took me by surprise. This time I received him in a different light. I viewed him as a true friend whom I had not seen for quite a while. Also at this time, I already knew that the killing of Frank and Charles had been ordered by General Manuel Contreras and Brigadier Espinoza and another general called Gonzales. I also knew that it had been approved by an American who still remained unidentified. Somehow the identity of the American had lost its importance; it did not matter. After all, we were all guilty in regards to what had happened to Charles and Frank. I had also accepted the circumstances in which Spencer had handed over Charles to the military. I learned through James that the vehicle bringing Charles had been intercepted by a military unit, and Spencer had no choice but to surrender Charles to them.

In the past, I had been aware that Spencer had been reporting to the CIA station at Valparaiso, and I assumed he had been sent from Valparaiso to Santiago on some assignment. But I was wrong. He and a Chilean agent codenamed Claver were on their way to Argentina to attend a CIA meeting with SIDE, the Argentinian military intelligence.

He told me that the meeting objective was to find a way to neutralize MIR cells that had escaped to Argentina and to eliminate the Monteneros, an extreme leftist organization operating in Argentina, and also the Uruguayan Resistance OPR-33, which was assisting MIR. He was also to meet with General Prats to try to find an acceptable political solution or compromise for the current political status of Chile where General Augusto Pinochet was the president of the junta.

The CIA was trying to get the support of the retired General Prats, a former commander-in-chief of the Chilean Army who had been a supporter of the Allende government not because he was a Marxist but due to the legal position of the army, which was to preserve the constitution regardless of who was the president.

General Prats was definitely not a leftist, but he was a "military loyal" to the constitution who had legitimized the Allende regime as a government chosen by the votes of a people in a democratic state. Shortly after the coup, he and his family had moved to Buenos Aires in Argentina to distance himself from the junta.

Pinochet was now the president of junta, and there was a strong rumor that he planned to become president of Chile in the nearby future, perhaps in November or December. Pinochet considered Prats a threat to him because he had the potential to become the leader of a government in exile. The CIA understood Prats' potential and Pinochet's concern. The CIA had to prevent any moves from the exiles to form a government headed by Prats in Argentina.

I personally felt that the CIA station in Santiago and DINA had chosen Spencer for the assignment to persuade the general. Spencer had come to know the general closer than any other American and seemingly knew the general's family well.

At this time, Spencer told me the news about the possible, very unwelcoming release of Orlando Letelier. Spencer thought that Allende's former minister should have been shot. I chose to keep my own feelings about Letelier to myself. I considered him a diplomat first, then a politician — more of a Socialist than a Marxist.

Letelier was still a prisoner at Dawson Island at Magallanes Strait. Dozens of detainees were still held in concentration camps where shelters offered very little protection to the cold, merciless weathers of the Antarctic front. According to Spencer, an unexpected dispatch from Washington had reached the junta; it came from Henry Kissinger. Kissinger had asked the junta to release Letelier. The junta recognized that it was an American diplomatic move to appease world criticism and had agreed to release Letelier. Soon Letelier was to be flown to Caracas, Venezuela.

For a while, we also discussed what was happening in the States. The Watergate issue was gaining momentum by the hours. Two years earlier, no one would think that a botched break-in to the Democratic National Committee at the Watergate complex in Washington, D.C., in June of 1972 by elements of the Republican Committee to Re-elect President Nixon could have developed into the possible impeachment and conviction of Nixon. Knowing that the CIA was deeply involved in the Watergate scandal, it was obvious to us that some of the top brass would end up in prison. The CIA had no business getting involved in the internal affairs of the United States government. Spencer's only comment was that those involved were "office boys" and deserved what was coming to them.

Prior to his flying to Buenos Aires, Spencer and I spent a few hours at one of the balconies of the Carrera Hotel talking about times we had shared in the past. We sat across from one another at a small table. His expression became distant and thoughtful as he reminisced about the past.

"A dollar for your thought," I said jokingly.

The mood became serious, however, when he brought up the memory of our two friends that we had lost at Hue City.

"Strange. Just last night I was thinking of them." I said.

"No kidding! On the way here, I saw two young soldiers walking down the street. They seemed to have a hell of a time. They were talking loud and laughing, like they were the only ones in the world. It reminded me of Ricky and Lancy," he said.

"Yeah, last night before I went to sleep, their faces kept popping up in my mind. It kept me awake for a long time. Those two kids saw the best in everything. They always seemed to have a good time. Ricky's laughter was contagious, and Lancy had a way with telling a story. He could have been another Mark Twain."

"Both were smart kids. Sometime I wonder…why them? There were thousands just like them who were killed in their youth. Ricky was nineteen, and Lancy was twenty as I recall."

"You are probably right. Ricky enjoyed calling me Old Man, though at that time, I was only twenty-six years old. But to him, I was an old man," I said.

"Yeah, they were two happy young men," he said as he put out the cigarette's butt with his fingers. He leaned heavily on the chair. "I hated that war…but what I really hated was the way our country treated our fighting men after the war. It seemed that the whole country blamed us for the war and put less blame on the politicians who sent us there in the first place. Damn politicians! Twenty years from now, the Viets are going to be on Wall Street, and rich Americans are going to be down the Delta looking for opportunities to make a buck."

"That's where you are wrong. Let's say ten years from now," I added with sarcasm.

Spencer smirked and kept silent. His eyes were focused on a time not too long ago, a painful moment that had driven both of us against a vicious enemy. I could see the pictures in his mind. They were the same in my mind. I recalled the time I saw the mutilated body of Frank. The faces of Ricky and Lancy were also there staring at me asking the same question. Why? What the Viet Cong had done to them had cut deep inside of us. There was no mercy shown to them whenever we met them. We were as vicious and inhumane as they were. Until then we had seen hundreds of thousands of atrocities from both sides, but what they did to these young soldiers was beyond comprehension. For any soldier in war who has lost a friend, the desire for revenge comes quickly. In the frenzy of getting even, atrocities are perpetrated. I can still hear the screaming and the shouting when the Viet Cong threw their bodies into our camp.

At that time, we were surrounded by a large number of Viet Cong, and the thought had crossed our minds that they could overrun us. The sight of the mutilated bodies of these two marines filled us with such hatred that we did not only repulse the onslaught but went on killing each one of them. We took no prisoners and killed all their wounded.

Shortly thereafter we came to that friendly village where all the young people had been killed and mutilated. All of this left a sense of aberration toward the Communists —more so for Spencer. Years later he still could not shake this hatred. I felt deeply for him. This was the village where his girlfriend had been murdered.

Five years later, the hatred I had felt against the Vietnamese had diminished. Being married to Anne had changed some aspects of my life, and I was able to see the goodness of most people. In Spencer's life, there was no one who could have softened him. From that view point, I could understand and accept some of his hatred toward the Communists.

However, I still had a problem accepting his hatred toward the Chilean leftists who at this time had already been neutralized. At this time, there was only scattered fighting from the opposition. I knew that some leaders of the Union Popular and MIR had been killed in a gun battle. The military and most of the armed groups had already been eliminated. In general the country was not in a state of war, except some units of MIR were cornered at the Andes Mountains.

Now Spencer was leaving on a mission to Argentina. Spencer was at odds with himself. He did not like the assignment. He had come to know General Prats well, and he was considered a friend of the family. In several conversations, Spencer had referred to Don Carlos as a good man. Now he was on a mission that could place the general in harm's way.

"If something happens to me there, just make sure you send my ashes to Mom. Let her scatter them over American soil," he said. "You being a marine, I hope you understand that."

I laughed and promised him that I would, feeling the invincibility that Spencer projected. Many times we had joked at the idea of getting killed, and we both felt in some way that if we had survived Nam, nothing would prevent us from surviving the worst.

After he left, I could not suppress my feeling of guilt toward accusing him of being the American who had given our friends to the Chileans. After all, he worked for the CIA, and the CIA was one of the tools that the United

States government had at its disposal to further secure American interests around the world.

I knew already that some assignments were distasteful to the American public, but at the time, I felt that these breaches of moral values were for its own security. Copper was a needed commodity in the industrialized world. Chile, being the largest provider of copper, had fallen into a place of extreme importance to the realities of American external policy that would ultimately benefit the American public. How long would the United States economy last if it was to be deprived of raw material such as oil, copper, and other substances essential to the survival of the country and its people? Even the staunchest of liberals needed oil for his vehicle, and his vehicle needed copper as its components. Without copper, his vehicle would not run. Neither would his computer and other essentials. Copper was the main means to bring electricity to cities. The whole of the country was entangled in billions upon billions of miles of copper cables and wiring. This realization would have a sobering effect on the average citizen if he really wanted to place things in perspective.

A week after Spencer had left for Argentina, Anne unexpectedly came to stay with me for two weeks during July, during the seemingly coldest weeks of the Chilean winter. She came at a time when I was feeling pretty down. Taking advantage of summer school vacation in the States, she thought of it as a nice surprise. Earlier in the year, we had already made plans for her to come back in December and travel to Osorno — one of the most beautiful places in southern Chile. But in July, Osorno was a very cold place.

During these two weeks, we stayed in Santiago at a housing complex close to the embassy where other State Department families lived. It gave us a degree of security. I appreciated these two weeks tremendously. Most of the time we just stayed home making plans for the future. Anne did her best to convince me to let her stay until the end of the year when my assignment would be over in Chile. I felt that by staying she wanted to make sure that I would end my assignment for good, which prompted me to reassure her that this was my last year in the diplomatic field.

Sometimes we could not help from wondering what had happened to Mario, Julia, and the children. I never mentioned my experience with the military arresting me and the role that Mario had played in my arrest. I had no idea what happened to Mario except on the occasion of my arrest when he told me that the military had taken them. I told her that they did have relatives in the north of the country and that they were just weathering the political storm, being that the north was the more peaceful section of the country. It was a total lie for I knew well that General Stark had already brought death and suffering to that region.

Anne agreed that most likely they had escaped to northern Chile to avoid the chaotic situation in Santiago. She wished that we could see them again, and thinking that I was getting too worried about them, she gave me assurance that they were out of harm's way. I appreciated her support for it also alleviated her fears. She felt that I had done everything possible to find them and that God would bless me and that I should try not to think too negatively about their situation. It was too painful to even guess their whereabouts. Most likely they had been shot and buried in mass graves like thousands who followed the same fate.

Anne kept expressing her feelings of gratefulness that I had not applied for any other assignment at the Foreign Service. My assignment was to end by the end of the year, just before Christmas. My application at a junior college close to where Anne was teaching had been accepted. She seemed happier than ever and was looking forward to those peaceful days.

She had bought a two-bedroom house at Idyllwild, a resort town in the San Jacinto Mountains in California, close to her parents who lived in the small town of Hemet. Whether in summer or winter, weather in that part of California was milder than in Santiago, where winter was always cold. Idyllwild was not too far from the ocean, and it was close to the most beautiful places on earth — the Sequoias and Yosemite, the United States' top national parks.

One afternoon prior to her departure to the States, we went to San Cristobal Hill and spent time enjoying the beauty offered by the city against the majestic Cordillera de los Andes. Her light brown hair slightly blown by the early evening breeze revealed her entire face and sent a guilty feeling over me. She seemed too young and too clean to be in Chile, where a human tragedy was still in the making. The city spoke of beauty, a false beauty. In its core, human beings had and continued to be tortured and killed.

"This is a beautiful country," she said while we sat on a bench. She leaned against me, and I embraced her. "And at the same time, it is such an ugly country," she added.

"I agree with you. Chile is one of the most beautiful countries in the world. Southern Chile always reminds me of some places in the Sequoias and Yosemite. Remember Osorno and Villarrica and how beautiful it was to just look across the lake and see those volcanoes covered with snow reflecting their might, beauty and awesomeness against the blue of the sky and lake? You even told me that you wanted to stay there forever."

"Yeah, I remember."

"You see, the country and the people are a beautiful people, but it is their government that brings the ugliness to them. And really…it happens all around the world."

"So you think that humans will never be able to govern themselves?"

"I am afraid so, and I am afraid that we will perish if we continue setting up governments that will finally destroy us."

She drew one of her smiles that could melt an iceberg and looked at me with that clear honest intensity that she always projected. "Then you do agree with me on what I was telling you the other night?"

I could not help from laughing for I remembered that she had told me about God's kingdom several nights earlier and how emphatic I was in rejecting that notion for I could not see that God being a spiritual being could deal with the likes of us, a sinful materialistic species. Now I had let my guard down and finally she had cornered me, and really at this moment, I had no way out, and I had to listen to what she felt was God's kingdom.

"Don't you think that it will be a marvelous life in that kingdom, to live forever under a paradise condition?" she asked.

I assented in silence. Silence spoke louder and voiced no opinion. She reached for me and gently caressed my face. I had always felt a sense of security when she was close to me. It was the feeling of being needed; it was what had attracted me to her when I started dating her shortly after returning from Nam. She looked at me and smiled.

"I remember the first time I saw you at the campus. You stood at the line to enroll in the same class I was taking. You were there, but the look in your eyes was distant. Yes…you were there, but a part of you was somewhere else."

I did not respond. I just kept the touch of a smile on my lips. Anne's nearness had always soothed me.

"It was that look of yours, that expression of detachment from your surroundings that attracted me to you. It kept me closer and closer to you," she said. "Each time I found your eyes looking somewhere else, I was filled with a desire to go wherever you were. I wanted to be there…did not matter where… as long as I was there with you. That is when you told me you wanted to be a diplomat. I had no objections to you serving the country in different parts of the world. To tell you the truth, I enjoyed Argentina. The people there always seemed happy — sort of loud, but it was all right."

"Yeah, I agree with you. Remember the two weeks we spent at the Pampas — the late evenings when we went to sleep in our sleeping bags by the warmth of the dying fire? When the night came in its fullness, we saw stars as we had never seen before," I said in a nostalgic tone.
Anne squeezed my hand hard. She did not speak. Her silence was saying everything I needed to know.

It was sort of funny; here we were away from the security that the nearness of the American Embassy or some of the American recreational circles could offer, and we had not even given it a thought. As we descended down the slopes of the hill toward our place, the world surrounding us did not matter. We were in a world of our own.

On the following day, James drove us to Pudahuel Airport where Anne was to take a flight to the States. Sensing our state of mind, James found it proper to say goodbye to Anne when he dropped us at the entrance to the building. After we checked in and her luggage was taken away, we moved toward where the passengers sat waiting for their flights, but we decided instead to stand by holding hands. Departing from each other as in others occasions would surely leave us broken hearted. I did not want her to go, and I did my utmost not to reveal my inner feelings. I felt her sadness when we embraced each other; her body trembled as she sobbed against my chest. I felt overwhelmed by her open intense love pouring all over me. At that moment, she felt so light, so fragile.

In the midst of people in a hurry, we locked in an embrace of sharing, giving to each other the love that came from the inner recesses of our aching hearts. At those moments, we were detached from the world surrounding us, together in a speck of time that seemingly was timeless though time was racing, moments escaping in an unforgiving reality. And then it was time for her to leave. Her flight had come, and I gently pushed her away still holding her hands. I looked at her face, and my eyes frantically tore the hard granite of my mind to engrave on it each detail, each feature of her face, kindly and lovingly giving me an everlasting memory. Then we heard the loud voice in the speaker reminding everyone that it was time to take the flight. I grabbed the small briefcase that she had left on the floor and placed it in her hand. We kissed and said goodbye. Tears ran down her face. She drew a smile when I playfully pushed her away as the last seconds came for her to walk away. At the last instant, nearly submerged by other passengers, she lifted her hand in a loving and sad goodbye. At that moment, I wished it was December and that I could have gone with her.

For several moments I stood motionless, staring at the doorway where she had vanished and that now was filled by numbers of strange faces. Suddenly I felt tired and reached for the nearby empty bench where I sat. Now I could not refrain from the tears appearing and flooding my eyes for I felt deeply that I had failed her. I should have left Chile with her the same night prior to the military coup of 1973 and never returned to this cursed land. She was too young to be left alone by the man who professed to love her. Nothing was preventing me from just leaving Chile except this commitment to my duties to the Foreign Service. "Did I love my Anne less than duty to the government?" I asked myself, and the answer was definitely negative. Then what I was doing here?

Upon returning to my place, I quickly went to bed, anticipating a long boring meeting at the office the following morning, and I was extremely tired. However, shortly after I went to bed, I found myself totally awake and thinking of Anne, who by now was somewhere in the air in her way to the States.

As I recalled, the first time I met Anne was at the campus of the University of California at Riverside, where I was taking post-graduate courses in economics and marketing, which would enhance my incoming duties in the Foreign Service. The year was 1967, fresh from Vietnam and looking for a promising career at the Foreign Service, which I had joined in January of that year.

It was a very hot day of June when I ran into her as I was entering the enrollment office. I guessed that she was probably in her twenties, about 5 feet 5 inches tall, sort of slender, white skin, brown hair, and hazel eyes — sort of an ordinary girl that you meet on an ordinary day. She blushed slightly as she became aware that I was looking at her, managed a faint of a smile, and looked away. After I filled out the enrollment papers, I turned around, and I was surprised to find her standing nearby with her hand extending a paper to me. I came closer and looked at the paper, which was the copy of the enrollment paper which I had just turned in.

"You dropped it," she said smiling, and the ordinary girl that I had looked at earlier had suddenly become no longer ordinary. On the contrary, she was outgoing and pleasant and always carried with her that smile that had gained my heart. We courted for a year, married, and several months later when the register for the Foreign Service assigned me to a position at the American Embassy in Argentina, she took it as an adventurous time, which would probably last for a few years before returning to California to raise a family of our own. She had just turned twenty-two, and I was twenty-eight years old.

Absorbed in my recalling, my tired mind found relief in a sleep that my tired body needed badly. Perhaps it was the notion that the next day would bring an experience of its own and there was nothing that I could not do to experience it — life was an experience in itself.

Part V

It was July 27; a week after Anne had left, Spencer returned from Buenos Aires. It felt good to see him, and he seemed glad to see me. He arrived on a day that would have a deep impact on the United States government. On this day, the House Judiciary Committee recommended the articles of impeachment against Nixon.

Spencer felt bad that he had missed Anne. He had a great deal of affection for her. Many times he had expressed his affection for her by commenting that if there was another Anne, he would waste no time in marrying her. We both took it as a compliment, knowing Spencer's character. Spencer was the type that seemed to not care for female companionship, not that he disliked females, for I knew he had a share in his circles of associates. But not once since I had known him had he thought of someone in a serious way, except for the girl he had lost in Nam. I sensed that now due to his work he could not afford to have a wife. It would tie him down. He was a man on the loose and wanted no responsibilities of that sort.

Upon seeing that I had come to pick him up in an embassy vehicle with a driver and a security guard, both Americans, he smiled showing his approval. On the way to my place, we could not help from expressing our thoughts about the possible impeachment of the president. We both agreed that the thing Nixon was most guilty of was his carelessness in taping the whole affair.

Americans were a smart intelligent people, and they all knew that most of their presidents had committed worse deeds than the Watergate scandal; they just could not stand stupidity. The real thing for us to be concerned about now was the effect that the impeachment of the president would have on us. We knew that even if Nixon was impeached, he could still choose to stay president, but knowing Nixon's character, he would probably step down. Then what? What impact would that have on Chile under another American administration? A liberal U.S. president would be Pinochet's worst nightmare.

After the car left us at my residence, Spencer looked around the surroundings in an approving way. He commented that the complex had a high degree of security. I assured him that it was a well-protected place. Most of the residents were Americans except for two Canadian families living nearby. The place was continuously being patrolled by military security forces, and there also was an outside security perimeter surrounding the complex.

"I guess this place has all kinds of bugs," he said, looking at the surroundings of the small living room. Then he signaled at me to go to the back porch. We both sat looking at the white wood fence separating the yard from the neighbor. Spencer, knowing that most of my neighbors were Americans, asked me who lived across the fence, and I told him that it was the Brown's place. Henry Brown was an educator, and his wife was in communications, and their two small children attended kindergarten at an American missionary school. Spencer knew both of them.

"Good people, the Browns. Too naive to know the mess they are in," Spencer said, looking toward their yard which was as quiet as mine. Unlike most diplomats who spent most evenings and weekends at parties to the tune of cocktails and unending chatter of common knowledge, the Browns chose to live a private, quiet life, away from the seeming glamour of the diplomatic world. They were family-oriented people and not just because of the kids. It was their persona.

"They are very friendly and yet quiet and reserved. I like them, and Anne does as well. When Anne was here, she got to know them better than I did. Of course, my Anne is a real sweetheart," I commented, and Spencer's grin spoke of approval. He knew Anne too well.

I told him about our intentions to begin a new life in the States by the end of the year, and he looked pleased. He expressed his concern for Anne by telling me that it was only right that I should be with her. After a while, the conversation started changing into a different direction. Then after a while, there was this sort of awkward silence that neither one of us wanted to break.

Spencer gave me one of those thoughtful looks of his, like he was trying to read my mind. It was his way to express his trust in me.

"How did it go?" I finally asked.

"For a moment, I thought you would never ask," he said grinning. "It didn't go well. The company will sell this asset before it becomes a liability."

I knew exactly what he meant. General Prats had rejected their proposal, and he had to be killed. At that moment, Spencer stood up and walked toward the shrubbery at the end of the yard, a prudent move as not to be heard. In our world of intrigue, it was just customary. Words seemed to escape me as I walked besides him. "When would this end?" I asked myself. The general was a good man. He was no Marxist, but he was an obstacle to the interested parties. The junta wanted him out, and we did not want another government in exile.

I knew that it had been a blow to Spencer for I knew he liked him. When the military had once tried to bring Allende down, General Prats had persuaded the leaders of the revolt to put their arms down. Those of us who had witnessed that event had come to admire General Prats; he was a brave man.

The tanks had already surrounded the Presidential Palace, and at precisely the time when the coup was gaining momentum, the general walked toward the tank leading the attack and stood alone in front of the tank to demand its surrender. The officer inside the tank could have blown him to pieces. Out of admiration for the general however, he chose to be placed under General Prats command, and the coup was avoided.

I remembered that Spencer, who was accompanied by another CIA agent, managed to get close to the general and had shaken his hand. On that occasion, I was with another associate of mine witnessing the episode from a block away, and I realized at that moment that Spencer had some connections with the higher ups of the military. It seemed to me that Prats knew him. In time I found out that Spencer had frequently visited the general's home and had gained a sort of friendship.

Spencer turned toward me. His eyes were reddish — the long hours and the lack of sleep had taken its toll.

"Damn, John," he said. "The station here wants to liquidate this account immediately. They are only waiting on a confirmation from Panama."

"Panama?" I asked.

"Yeah, we are waiting on Panama," he replied.

"Why are you waiting on Panama? Why can't the station here get it straight from the boss?" I said, referring to the CIA director.

Spencer did not reply. He shrugged his shoulders and grinned as usual, and as usual I would not get an answer.

"Who will be in charge of closing the account?" I asked, hoping that it would be a Chilean hit.

"Sometimes it's better to talk about human affairs in terms of business transactions. Don't you think so?" he said, not responding to my question.

"It's less painful. Numbers have no faces. It is easier to erase them." I said.

"You are damned right. As long as the numbers have no faces, it is easier to close any transaction. But these are not numbers. This is a human being — my friend Don Carlos," he said. "In answer to your question, I am the one assigned to close this account. This is a combined operation between us and DINA."

I felt my throat tighten, and I coughed lightly to ease the sudden pressure. Words were nowhere to be spoken. I looked straight into his eyes, and as on many other occasions, the seconds we spent on this silent exchange were as if we had spent long hours of verbal talk.

"How can I help you?" I asked, sensing his profound aching dilemma.

"Honestly, I want no part of it. Regardless of what Colonel Contreras says or what the State Department thinks, Don Carlos is hardly a threat to us or to Pinochet. But I am obliged to fulfill my duties."

I knew him too well. He needed me. "What do you want me to do?" I asked again.

"I want you to see our friend Percil. I cannot see him at this time. Big Brother is everywhere. We have too many agents at the station here in Santiago, some I don't even know. I want you to tell him that 'The swallow wants to fly north.'"

"I'll get that to him today." I said as we went into the house.

"What about your people at the Valparaiso station. Can any of them help you out?" I asked as he picked up his briefcase

"There is no CIA station at Valparaiso," he responded.

I was sort of puzzled because all this time I really thought that there was a CIA station at Valparaiso. It never occurred to me to ask.
He grinned. "What gave you that idea?"

"Well, you are stationed there. It seemed to me that you were reporting there," I replied.

"Not really. And this time we won't go there. When I return, I'll tell you all about it," he said with a smile, seemingly pleased that he had put something over me all this time.

"I understand," I responded, and I wished him well.

As he departed, I shook his hand and said, "It is sort of funny. In Juan Capistrano, we always waited for the swallows to come from the south."

He managed a smile and thanked me as he closed the door.

A while later, as I got ready to visit Sir Percil at the British Embassy, I realized that there was something more to Spencer receiving his correspondence through the British Embassy; old man Percy had now been thrown into the equation of the clandestine operation. It felt good to know that Spencer had brought me into the game of espionage. He trusted me though at times I had shown some doubts about his friendship.

I knew I would never be part of his world of clandestine work, but the glimpse of it was sort of appealing. Of all the people in the world, it had never crossed my mind that there could be a hint of trust between old man Percy and Spencer. Spencer had flipped another page of his life for me to read and ponder about it. And ponder I did…

Spencer had definitely ruled out the existence of a CIA station at Valparaiso, but he was assigned to the Valparaiso area, which still left questions to be answered. Spencer had not said that he was reporting to the station in Santiago and yet he had access to the station there and to the embassy and received assignments at the station in Santiago. I also knew that he communicated with the British with the full knowledge of the American Embassy and correspondence with his mother was through the British Embassy. To whom did he report to? It was now a question in my mind, and probably I would never get the answer.

When I came from Argentina, it did not surprise me to find Spencer in Chile because we had some sort of correspondence since I had left the service. In his last letter, he had made reference that he was being sent to Chile. By this time, he had given me enough information to assume that he had possibly been recruited by the CIA. The first time I had met Spencer was in Vietnam, and right away I thought that it was sort of odd that being so young he was already a first lieutenant though I knew that he was a college graduate, which gave him an officer rank. Soon that impression changed when I learned from a captain that Spencer, at his young age, already had a master's degree in languages and had mastered several languages and dialects. In Vietnam alone, I witnessed him speaking fluently at least six dialects. But what really caught my attention was the fact that he had come to Vietnam as a military adviser to the South Vietnamese Army in 1961 when he was perhaps twenty years old. "How could a twenty year old be an adviser?" I questioned myself at that time. But as time passed, Spencer did partly answer my question. At 6 feet 3 inches tall and tailored in good muscle tones, he was not only an imposing figure but a fearsome deadly figure in battle. But his coming to Nam as an adviser at that young age still remained a puzzle that I chose not to solve.

I knew he had come to Chile on a special assignment sometime in 1969, two years before I did, as an adviser to the Chilean Army. I also knew we had well seasoned agents prior to 1970 stationed in Chile and some of them were still with us. However, Spencer seemed to be always in charge of a situation or have some of them working as his subordinates. There was the fact of his proximity to Contreras, and I also knew well that he had visited Pinochet on several occasions. He also had some sort of connections with Archbishop Medina, a strong supporter of the military junta. What about his closeness with General Prats and Sofia? All of these would leave interrogatives on anyone's mind, and I was no exception. Definitely Spencer projected a larger figure than he pretended to be. The fact that he was a CIA operative impeded me from asking questions or seeking answers, though at times out of curiosity I would venture in some hunting that took me nowhere for Spencer knew me too well.

Most of the world knew that the United States government had played a crucial role in the military coup of 1973, and since then it was well known that it supported the dictatorship of Pinochet. But the role of the British in the coup had partially been ignored and seldom had ever been questioned, possibly for lack of concrete evidence or for the simple fact that the Chileans of British descent permeated deep through the fibers of the Chilean themselves, thus refusing to pass judgment upon themselves.

It seemed to have passed unnoticed that the coup had begun at the port of Valparaiso by the Chilean Navy, and here were two important factors that had escaped the shrewdness of the American haters. The hatred for the American government had blinded the accusers, and it had escaped the most obvious — the role of the British element in the coup. Perhaps this was not solely due to the world's hate toward the Americans, but there was also the smoothness and suaveness of the British themselves in accomplishing their own goals. The best strategy was to keep a prudent distance from the Chilean government and let occurrences unfold in their behalf and in the interest of the major predator who would lose no time to let the world know that they had captured the prey. Since I had come to Chile, I was very much aware of the British influence in Chile. It was written in its history and culture. While the Germans had a greater influence in the army, the British ethnic element had made its presence felt in the Chilean Navy and others aspects of Chilean society. The British, since the days of Francis Drake and more so during the War of Independence, had left in Chile an undeniable legacy that was to be accentuated by large numbers of Briton immigrants coming to Chile during the 1800s. Valparaiso at one time had the largest British ethnic group, and still today Chilean British or Chileans of British descent dominate most of Valparaiso's affairs.

English names and customs were as common as Chilean wine. On one occasion when working at the embassy, Mario invited me and Anne for onces at his home. I learned that onces meant lunch, which was to have a cup of tea during the afternoon. This was definitely a British custom that had assimilated into all levels of Chilean society when the British had come to Chile centuries earlier.

However, it was in the makeup of the Chilean Navy that the British influence was more apparent, and it was reflected in its heroes being Lord Cochrane, the Father of the Chilean Navy. In 1817, Bernard O'Higgins, the son of an Irishman and the first president of Chile after Chile gained independence from Spain, called on Lord Cochrane, a British Navy officer, to form the Chilean Navy.

Lord Cochrane immediately hired hundreds of British officers and seaman to help him form the Chilean Navy. Their role in Chilean warfare during the late 1800s in the War of the Pacific against the Peruvian and Bolivian Confederation became imbedded in Chile's history. Knowing the role of the British in the history and culture of Chile and that Valparaiso was the base that had propelled the coup, I was now faced with the hard reality of taking a closer look at the relationship that Spencer had with the British.

This was especially true now that he was sending a compromising message to Sir Percil. There was also the inescapable fact that his mother was a Briton — a British agent who during the Second World War had worked for MI5 and later after the war had joined the British MI6. Could it be that Spencer was also working for the British?

Part VI

The news of President Richard Nixon's resignation on August 8, 1974, shocked the world. The persona that Nixon had always projected to the world was his resilience in the face of challenges, his perseverance to thrive in adversity; he had never been a quitter. However, most Americans, even those who hated him, had to recognize that he was an American after all. As president he would have never considered dragging his country through a prolonged political ordeal that could jeopardize the national interest. Expedience was part of the American spirit, and expedience was part of Nixon's character.

Vice President Gerald Ford becoming the president was sort of an ironic twist to the United States — a democracy known to elect its leader through the votes of its people. It was ironic in the sense that no American had ever cast his vote for Ford as a vice president or as president.

In the days that followed Nixon's resignation, a feeling of uncertainty permeated through the embassy. President Ford was practically unknown in the international political arena. President Nixon had cast a giant shadow upon Gerald Ford — as if he had never existed. There was no doubt in my mind that this uncertainty was also affecting the Chilean dictatorship's thinking process.

However, when President Ford issued a full and unconditional pardon of Nixon and Kissinger continued to be Secretary of State, the State Department and Pinochet's government were elated. It was an assurance that the current state of affairs was to continue in Chile.

Pondering the recent events that had taken place in the United States and the seemingly unchanging political mechanism of the Pinochet government, I became somewhat sort of detached from the world I was facing. After Spencer had left, I sent information to a reporter friend of mine working for the Times on the possible assassination of General Prats. I thought that perhaps my information would prompt pressure by the world press on Chile's regime to abort the assassination. I knew that it would mean the end of my career as a diplomat, but it did not matter. I had already sent my resignation, and my assignment would be over by the end of the year.

Anticipating a total change of life in December, I was now constantly thinking of a peaceful life with Anne in the States. Now more than ever, I wanted to leave the Foreign Service — the same feeling I had at the end of my last tour in Vietnam that came to an end in 1967. Too much blood was spilled in Nam, too many deaths. There I had lost friends, but they were soldiers, and I understood it and had accepted it as such.

Here in Chile, my friends were no soldiers. Charles and Frank were ordinary human beings. Mario, his wife, and the children were ordinary people. General Prats, though a soldier, was a decent man. He was an ordinary man who could have been left to enjoy his retirement. Thousands upon thousands were ordinary people — people who only wanted to live, to enjoy life as it was given to them — God's gift to be cherished and to be enjoyed.

In this state of mind, I found myself on a late Friday evening strolling by the park near the American residential compound where I was residing. Then suddenly, sort of strangely, I felt a rushing wind to my ears that made me close my eyes for a second. Instantly I shook my head and looked around. There was no one. Several seconds later I felt a burning sensation on the left side of my temple, which made me touch that particular place on my head thinking that perhaps an insect had stung me. Then unexpectedly my knees buckled, and I started falling as shadows seemed to engulf me. Now I knew that I had been shot for I had gone through the same in the past when my luck had held its own ground; perhaps my luck would still hold, I told myself as I hit the ground.

Lying on the ground, my mind rushed for an answer. I was conscious and aware that I had to stay still and fight my hardest to remain conscious. I thanked the war now. In it I had learned the basics of remaining alive. I had to stay alive. I would not leave Anne alone, not yet.

During the war, I had been shot several times — twice seriously and others of lesser consequences. Once a shot grazed my forehead, but I remained conscious, fully aware of the enemy closing in. Laying on the ground pretending to be dead, I waited for him to come closer, and at the last instant, I killed him.

I avoided the thrust of his bayonet by inches. Now it was no different as I lay motionless on the wet grass waiting and waiting for what seemed like a long, long time. I thought of my Anne in the States and wondered what she was doing at this very moment. It would be unthinkable for me to leave her now when our dream would soon be realized. I had to live. I had to survive this dreadful moment. I would not leave Anne alone.

Moments later I heard the engine of a vehicle coming closer. The vehicle's idling and the slight squeak of the brakes made me guess that it had stopped by the curb to check the results of the shooting. I knew that soon I was to hear the sound of the car's door being opened. In my mind, there was no doubt of the shooter's intention of making sure I was dead. A door being opened meant death. This moment was as deadly as death itself — all depended on hesitation. If my killer-to-be had no hesitation to give me a final shot, my life would end at that moment. But if I did not hesitate on playing death to the last second to fool my would-be killer, then I would live.

I waited for the outcome, and as always in moments like these, time drags and instants are eternal and still. There was no sound of the door being opened. As I lay with my cheek on the wet grass, I could partially see the car at the curb, which gave me some relief, and yet the car would not move. Again it became a guessing game, and again instants became unending moments as the vehicle remained as it was, not moving at all. I only could hope that the shooter was so sure of his skill that he was just contemplating his kill. These seemingly long moments of guessing, such as the one I was experiencing, were agonizing.

The car started to move, hardly making a sound. I chose to lay there for a while to make certain that the vehicle was gone. After a while, I got up and pressed my hand on the wound to stop any bleeding, if there was any. By the street lamp light, I looked at my fingers to see the blood. There was hardly any. It was like a scratch, but still too close for comfort. I assumed I had been shot by some insurgents. The military would not have missed.

Hurrying to my place, I cursed myself for being so careless. Looking at the wound, I considered myself lucky. It was hardly a scratch. By Monday it would not be too visible. Again I cursed myself for being so careless. No diplomat in his right mind would take a leisurely walk on his own — not at night anyway. Several weeks earlier at the embassy, we had been warned about going places outside the embassy or the American security compounds on our own.

Usually on weekends I would call Spencer to spend time together watching a soccer game, but lately, considering the situation, a soccer match was not an inviting event, though there were some games of lesser notoriety still playing around the city. All that was left were the cabarets, night clubs, and movie theaters, but all of these were not on my agenda. Sometimes I would join Spencer for a drink or two, but lately we chose to have drinks at my place. In a sense, I was glad that Spencer was not in town this weekend or he would have probably stopped at my place and have noticed the scratch on my temple. I knew Spencer well —things would seldom escape his attention.

On Saturday late in the evening, I called Anne. The sound of her voice brought me a deep sense of security that assured me that I was to survive my stay in Chile — nothing would stop me from returning to the States to stay with her. She told me she had spent most of the day visiting her folks and shopping. When I asked what she had bought, she sort of laughed and told me that it was just women's clothing. We talked for at least an hour, and we were both eager for the month of December to come, and for an instant, I nearly mentioned my recent escape from death. We said goodbye, and as always, she told me that she had me constantly in her prayers. I thanked her, and again I stopped short from telling her that it was her prayers that had spared my life.

On Monday when I returned to work, the scratch was not noticeable, and business continued as usual. I chose not to tell anyone about the incident; I would wait until Spencer's return. Meanwhile I would have to be extremely careful. MIR still had some insurgents around.

Sometime in the morning, I learned through James that Spencer had flown to the States to visit his mother, who had suffered a stroke. The swallow had flown north. Immediately I saw old man Percil's hand in this. It was a stroke of genius by one of the masters of deception and a friendly gesture by the British to the son of one of their faithful servants, Stella Truman. Spencer had skillfully avoided the unpleasant assignment to liquidate General Prats.

It was now September 24, 1974, more than a year since the military had taken over the country. General Augusto Pinochet, who had become the president of the junta, was now in total control of Chile.

On this particular morning of late September, James confronted me with the papers that I had sent out of the country. My mail had been intercepted by the military. My efforts to bring attention to the planned assassination of General Prats had now been halted. The General would be killed, and it would probably cut my stay in Chile short.

James was definitely upset but not angry. He seemed more concerned about my safety. He pointed out that DINA demanded some answers on how

I had obtained information that was only known to DINA and the CIA. He also let me know that the correspondent for the Times, whom I had tried to contact, had been killed in Nicaragua while covering the elections there. James told me that it would not have helped me anyway, being that the reporter was a CIA agent. James also let me know that he as well did not like the idea of getting rid of the general. He pointed out that all things led to the general's well-known intention of heading a government in exile in Buenos Aires and that Pinochet, as well as the United States, would not allow it.

He informed me that President Ford had endorsed Nixon's doctrine. Chile and the State Department were to continue the current policy on Chile, giving Pinochet's government full support on establishing a sound, stable government.

The month of September 1973 was ending on a bad note. On September 30, Chile was shaken by what I had feared and yet expected. In Buenos Aires, General Prats had been assassinated. But what was more revolting to me was that his wife Sofia had also been killed. Both had met a violent death in a car bomb explosion. Though I had expected the general's death, it never occurred to me that his wife would also die. At that moment, I could not come to terms with the CIA's participation in this horrendous act, though I knew that a single death in the pages of any intelligence agency practically amounted to nothing. Yet some of us who are part of the government, in an effort to distance ourselves from our own guilt, do cry out "Fault!" to ease our guilt.

The only consolation I had was to know that Spencer had not been a participant. I did wonder what Spencer was thinking for he, like myself, would have never figured that Sofia would be killed. Spencer cared for them; otherwise he would have taken the assignment just to spare Sofia.

As expected the United States and the Chilean government denounced their deaths as a leftist ploy to discredit the government headed by President Pinochet. Locally and outside of Chile, the skepticism of no American involvement was loudly expressed. The only good news coming from Chile was that Pinochet had agreed to release Orlando Letelier, who had been in prison since the coup had taken place. The news of Letelier's release was good news, but it also had a negative impact in the world community because it was seen as a peace offering for the death of the Prats.

At the embassy, the death of the general was met with some reservation but reluctantly accepted as a matter of expediency. But the death of his wife, Sofia, had a profound negative impact on most of us; her death was not acceptable. Again the agency seemed to be run by another incompetent director. From the fiasco at Bay of Pigs to Watergate, the credibility of the professionalism of the agency had not improved. Although the assassination had been a combined action of the CIA and DINA, the CIA would have to share culpability.

Our own credibility as an ethical American presence suffered. The United States foreign policy felt the negative impact of world criticism. But time would pass, and though people and countries do not forget, they tend to ignore the obvious when dealing with a superpower. It is Darwinism at its best — in the struggle for political survival, the most abiding of the smaller countries will survive by seeking the protection of the strongest.

As days went by in this political upheaval, I grew uneasy because James and the ambassador's office had not given me an official warning notice on willfully breaking the diplomatic protocol on directly interfering on matters related to the Central Intelligence Agency. I had expected to be called to the office of the ambassador or to be placed on restriction, but nothing happened.

Then Spencer returned, and we agreed to meet at a place away from the watchful eyes of the American and Chilean intelligence for we wanted to distance ourselves from each other in the eyes of those who were aware of our friendship.

We met on a Sunday afternoon at Cerro San Cristobal Park, located on the highest hill in Santiago. This public park offers a magnificent view of the city. From where we were, we could see most of the city. On a clear, sunny day when Santiago is free of smog and the Cordillera of the Andes and its white snowy peaks are in the background, Santiago is a beautiful city.

Though the scenery was beautiful and pleasant, there was no joviality or tranquility in the exchange between us. Each word was definite and revealing, and I could tell that there was something in the making. The death of the general and his wife had affected Spencer deeply, and now Spencer was a man on a mission. He was extending his hand to me, and yet there were reservations holding me to the pier as I stared at a fragile boat being tossed by a menacing sea. I just could not embark, not now. My Anne was inland waiting in the security of our home.

As I listened to him, I grew afraid for it reached my sense of fairness. Unexpectedly I was now contemplating something that I had always rejected. However, my love for my wife would not allow it and yet...I was thinking about it — not fully thinking, but the notion was there.

"John... *just think* about it," he said. "We both took this job — you in the academics and myself in the execution of it. We both did it for the same reason; we wanted to make a difference.

He looked at me intently; his steel blue eyes dug into mine fiercely and demandingly.

"We did not get into the Foreign Service for money or prestige; we just wanted to make a difference, but…now? Damn! Now someone else is making the difference. And the difference will eventually deal us a death blow by bringing back Marxism to this country, and everything that we have done will be for nothing,"

At that moment, I had a glimpse of past days when we had talked about things that mattered. Six years earlier, at the peak of the fighting in the Tet Offensive when the whole complex of the American presence seemed overwhelmed by the North Vietnamese, the free spirit of the American soldier had made the difference. Not the politicians at home, not the conservatives, neither the liberals nor Joan Baez nor Jane Fonda, neither the sad lingering songs of Bob Dylan which we had learned to love had made any difference. It was the American soldier on the battlefield that made the difference that gave us victory over the North Vietnamese. It was that little something inculcated in us at home — not to give up without a fight to the finish. You do not solely learn that at home or at the church or at work. It was that something that you breathe everywhere in the American habitat. It was that "John Wayne sense of Americanism" that was imbedded in us.

In Vietnam we had talked about what making a difference meant. Now Spencer was again talking about making a difference, and as he spoke, it did make sense. The death of General Prats and Sofia had placed him where he was now, questioning and demanding action. Spencer was convinced that the general would have made little difference at all. Pinochet already had a firm grip on the Chilean Armed Forces.

"The general was of no danger to us, neither to Pinochet. He could have been neutralized. The general loved his wife and daughters; he could have been persuaded to live in the States. He used to live there, you know," he said and paused. "And Sofia? ….Damn! When I heard that she had also been killed, I blamed myself for not being there. It shouldn't have happened, at least not this way."

"There was nothing that you could have done. It is done," I said. Stopping in my tracks, I placed my hand on his arm to give him some consolation.

He did not reply, and for a while, we walked without saying a word. We stopped at one point and looked at the city below; it looked restful at the foot of the Andes. After a while, he continued to speak about what it meant to make a difference.

"We are not like them," he said. "Take for instance Michael Kenner. Here is a guy who kills for recognition. He really thinks that Pinochet will pin on him some sort of national recognition, like the Medal of Honor. Far from it! The moment Pinochet or Contreras gets tired of him, they'll dump him."

I kept silent. All I knew was that at one time Michael had been in charge of some of the Peace Corps stations that were serving as umbrellas for the CIA. I knew Spencer did not care for Michael. I considered Michael a flamboyant character who liked to be seen as part of the agency, though Spencer had told me that he worked for DINA and at times the CIA would use him, but he was not a true CIA operative. Being acknowledged as part of the agency gave him some prestige among the Chilean high society.

I grinned at the thought of Michael trying so hard to be noticed by the high social circles, for in our own circles, he was a parasite, living off his rich Chilean wife and off Pinochet's table, getting the crumbs and waste. Michael was the son of an American businessman and had come to Chile to work for his father, and in time he had renounced his American citizenship by becoming a Chilean citizen. Michael claimed to have a dual citizenship, but in our eyes, he was a traitor to our country by given up his American citizenship.

"I hardly know the guy, but you do," I said. "I heard that his wife throws lavish parties."

"Yeah, Maria likes to be notorious just like Michael, not because of her writing ability, which she has." Spencer paused briefly and reassured me that she was indeed a published writer. All I knew about her was through others who had been to her parties.

He continued, "She is well educated, but her mind revolves around her heavy drinking of hard liquor and sex. I went a couple of times to her parties, and each time Michael was not there. There were, however, lots of men and good-looking women for the taking. To tell the truth, it reminded me of those aspiring Vietnamese middle class families in Saigon who wanted so badly to be part of the established upper class but they did not have what that Vietnamese society had, which happened to be class. You must be classy to have class. In reality their gathering had the atmosphere of a whorehouse…sort of a bordello."

He took a brief pause. "But don't let appearances fool you. She may be good looking and seemingly pleasant, but she is a cold killer. Contreras told me that Michael had taken her to Argentina, and she was with him when the bomb exploded."

Spencer paused and looked at me, expecting some sort of reaction. There was none; nothing surprised me anymore. He then briefed me on the killing of the general. It had started as a joint operation by the Agency and DINA, but as soon as Michael and Maria had touched Argentina's soil, the agency had left DINA alone to execute the task. It was obvious to him that Michael, Maria, and some Argentinians had done the job — perhaps other DINA agents were also involved.

Then Spencer changed the subject. It was obvious to me that the Prats incident bothered him. He brought the conversation to our present situation in Chilean politics; there was no denial that we were part of their political reality. Listening to him, I realized the degree of his rhetoric — he did not have to go after the fish; they all came to him. I was one of them and I listened.

It had been my willingness to listen to him that had gained his confidence in me. In his world of espionage, trust was a rare commodity. It could kill you. He proceeded to tell me that at the heart of his dilemma was Kissinger, the American Secretary of State, and his friendship with Orlando Letelier, the former Allende ministry of defense. Spencer felt their friendship had blinded Kissinger. We all knew Kissinger had played an instrumental part in the release of Letelier, who was now living in Caracas, Venezuela.

"The general would not have made a great difference, but Letelier does. He should have been tried and shot," Spencer said. His words affected me. I had never met Letelier, and I did not want him dead. Letelier was a well-known diplomat whose figure demanded respect.

As if he had read my thoughts he said, "Don't ever let your personal feelings interfere with expedience. I liked the general, and he was my friend, but in the final analysis I had to recognize that, though he was not a real threat to us, he was an inconvenience to the State Department. Because I did allow my personal feelings to interfere in the performance of my duties, I was not able to do the job I was supposed to do." He paused and grinned as he continued. "To tell you the truth, I would have done it like the mafia does...with a kiss and the sign of the cross." He stopped talking, seemingly disgusted by his own words. "Sorry. I shouldn't have said that. But it would have been a clean hit. Sofia would still be alive." Again he paused. "Regardless, in retrospect, the general was a lesser threat than Letelier. The general could have raised some sympathy, not only from the dissidents but some from the populace. We have to remember that he was a well-liked person by the ordinary citizen. One thing we have to recognize — in general the Chileans are a fair people. And yet the general still would not have the pull that Letelier has on the Chileans."

I had kept quiet while he was talking, but my mind was absorbing each word he had said. Spencer should have been a diplomat. His choice of words had always attracted my attention. Spencer was correct: Letelier was an obstacle. He had been instrumental in the denial of European loans to Chile that I had helped in trying to obtain.

I had to agree with him. I knew that Letelier had already been contacting some of his liberal friends in Washington, D.C., trying to persuade Congress to deny further aid to Chile. We simply could not afford to have him in Washington. But to kill him? The thought of it was frightening. Killing Letelier was not on my agenda.

As a way to soothe the conversation I said, "Yeah, if he was in the States, but he resides in Caracas. What can he do from Venezuela?"

"For the time being maybe, but he will end up in the States. Kissinger wants him near so that he can enjoy his social life. Letelier is a well-liked diplomat, and his style pleases the likes of Kissinger," he responded, sort of annoyed at Kissinger, whom he had always considered an American political aberration. Spencer would not accept the idea of someone from German descent running the American State Department, especially someone whom he considered a Nazi.

"Has it ever occurred to you that by having Letelier under the American umbrella he could be well guarded? Maybe that is in the mind of Kissinger," I finally replied.

He shook his head. "No my friend, what is in the mind of Kissinger is to appease his political foes, here and abroad. He thinks that Letelier is just a misguided friend in need of his help. Being Kissinger is all that he cares about. Whether he was under Nixon or under Ford, it does not make any difference to his character. He will continue to be Kissinger, a Nazi bastard."

"Well then tell me, what is on your mind? It seems to me that you are telling me all of this for a reason," I asked. "You know how disappointed I am with our policy here. When I came here I was like you — I was an idealist but no longer. That is why I called it quits." I paused, and seeing that I had his total attention, I asked, "What do you propose to do and what do you want from me?" I expected a response, but he did not answer.

The awkwardness of his silence bothered me for I felt that he was measuring my sense of commitment, and I bluntly tried to make him uncomfortable with my own digging. "Sometimes I do not really know your position on some issues which are very questionable. You hate the Nazis, and it seems to me that you contradict yourself with your actions," I said, expecting a burst of cussing in response. But he ignored me by glancing at me without a word and no change of expression in his face.

"Let's take your role in the killing of these people. Most of these army bastards are Nazi oriented. It is a fact that Colonia Dignidad is being run by a well-known Nazi, a German Nazi, and also Colonia Grimaldi is run by Berrios, another self-declared Nazi. And let us not forget our friend Michael. You may not be their friends, but you do nothing to stop them," I said with tones of sarcasm in my voice, determined to bring him out of his impassive silence. "You call Kissinger a Nazi. What about you and your lot? You are nuts!" Seeing that I was going nowhere with my outburst of sarcasm, I kept silent and waited for him to speak.

At a clearance along the path, we stopped and looked at the tall statue of Saint Cristobal towering over the top of the hill. Finally Spencer broke the silence and made the comment that it took a great effort for the Chileans to erect the massive statue. It made no difference to him though. In all probability, it had made a difference to those who worshiped the stone.

He kept his eyes on the statue for several moments. He then turned his attention toward me. Thoughtfully he placed his hands on my shoulders and said, "That was a great tirade of frustration that you threw at me, my friend. Most of it is true, but I think that deep inside your wondering mind you know I am not a Nazi. There is something that we Americans call expedience, especially in what I do." Keeping his eyes on mine, he added, "I still do trust you. You must believe it. There is no one else who can help me with what I am trying to do. You must keep it to yourself, whether you help me or not."

As always I told him that there was nothing to worry about and that regardless of our differences we were friends, and confidentiality was an important part of trust between friends. As always when feelings were being expressed, he was not at ease and was a little uncomfortable.

"John..I only ask you to keep it to yourself, and you come out with all this sweetness. But I do appreciate it," he said smiling and added, "Letelier can make a difference in the future of this country, and we have to make it possible for this difference to disappear. Or eliminate what makes this difference possible."

He kept his eyes on mine for a second to find a reply. He then gave me a gentle pat on the shoulder and moved away. I grabbed his arm, and this time I was the one giving a meaningful look into his eyes, probing deep into his heart. My eyes were of a man trying to reveal the thought of his mind and the intention of his heart. Finally I burst out, sort of muttering as if I was talking not in reality but in a dreamlike scenario. "You mean Kissinger?...You do mean Kissinger...Right?!...Are you mad?...Spencer!...Kill Kissinger?"

Spencer's eyes were as clear as the sky above, too clean. There was no cloudiness to hide anything; there was total truthfulness. I turned to the city below. It seemed unreal to me from that distance, like a picture. I felt detached from everything, even myself. "Killing Letelier?...Killing Kissinger?" I muttered, questioning, probing into what had never even entered my thoughts.

We continued walking the narrow path along the shrubberies and gardens of the park. Everything was quiet and peaceful. There was a certain silence intruding into the deepest part of me, cutting and cutting. Spencer did not talk. He walked along in silence, respecting my own silence. He would not interrupt.

It then came time to depart. Spencer assured me that if Letelier could be eliminated then there was no need to kill Kissinger. He also reminded me that our talk was based only on the presumption of my own commitment to it. As for that commitment, at this time, it was still in the air, and it did worry me for I had not given him an answer, thus showing that I was thinking about it.

As he was leaving, he said with a grin in his face, "What about this people that you are defending so much? A large segment of them, whether poor or rich, hold Hitler and his Nazis in great regard, and don't forget that in World War II, Chile was neutral and after the war it became a haven for Nazis escaping Germany, and it is evident in all segments of its army."

I did not respond for he was right. I had seen it with my own eyes. Nazism was detestable to us but acceptable to some Chileans. A college teacher once told me that considering what the Jews had done to the German people, it had been just retribution. But he was fast to add that Nazism would not happen in Chile.

Several hours later, I thought about what Spencer had asked me — to commit myself to the killing of Letelier, something that had never entered my mind. Just the thought of it was shocking. I would not consider it, and I would never do it. Spencer knew me well, and he knew that if I ever consented to Letelier's death I would not deter from it for he knew my feelings about commitment.

Spencer was right. A sense of commitment was something special to me. In my life, it had a sacred connotation. My parents had taught me the meaning of commitment as total devotion to my words as a free man. Commitments were to last a lifetime as long as you truly believed it. In the same respect, I committed to spending the rest of my life with Anne, and I was looking forward to being with her in California.

There was a time that the diplomatic world seemed a good choice for an idealist, but Chile had brought that to an end. Spencer's world, though it seemed inviting in its challenges, could never be mine. I could not commit myself to his world of concreteness and coldness, a world devoid of feelings. It was a world where death was sudden and as common as breathing. It was a cold, brutal world where men were engaged in wars that knew no endings and that was not the world I had envisioned.

Spencer had talked about making a difference but differences on whose behalf? Letelier could make a difference in the future of Chile, but to what ends? Maybe Letelier would not bring a Communist government into existence even though he had embraced Marxism. The lessons learned from Allende's failures could prompt him to turn in a different direction. He was a politician like Allende, but unlike Allende, he was also a diplomat and that could make a difference of sorts.

Thinking about it, I could not help from laughing as I recalled a Bible scripture that Anne had read to me. It was something about us being a grotesque spectacle to the angels. If angels were watching us, they would laugh at us, seeing how tragic we were. Human beings were at times a laughable spectacle. And I was one of those insignificant miserable beings who wanted to change the world at the cost of pain, suffering, and death and would not consider the killing of one man in order to stop the killing of many. I was a hypocrite. Who was I kidding? Here we were bringing to our own backyard a man whose thinking we had traveled a great distance to kill. To allow Letelier to preach Marxism at home while thousands upon thousands of Americans had fought, and still were fighting and dying on foreign soil, to prevent the expansion of Marxism was absolute madness, and in the midst of it, I was being scrupulously minded. I was wrong, and Spencer was right after all — it was our duty to the American people to stop Marxism abroad before it could reach our land.

Part VII

December 7 is considered by most Americans a day to remember. It is a day which President Franklin D. Roosevelt called "a day of infamy." It was on this day when Japan, without warning, attacked Pearl Harbor. This propelled the United States into the Second World War in 1941.

December 7 would also be for me a day to remember — rightfully stated, a day of infamy. On this seventh day of December in 1974, my wife Anne was killed. It happened at Pudahuel Airport just outside of Santiago by a mortar attack on the car that was picking her up. Also my boss James, the chauffer, and a security man were killed. Anne was gone, forever gone from my life. Our expectations, dreams, and hopes had suddenly come to an end. What was supposed to be no longer would be. My Anne was dead. The new life I had come to know a few years earlier had abruptly come to a halt, motionless in the passing of time. It was now buried in the cold harshness of reality, perhaps for a lifetime until that world in which she had deeply believed would return, not only in my life but also in the life of my beloved wife.

Spencer was the first to inform me about Anne's death, and my reaction to it was complete denial. It just was not true; it could not have happened. My Anne was in the States, I kept telling myself. Although seemingly there was concrete evidence that she was in the car with James and the others who had been killed and her name was on the airline passengers list, I would not accept her death. In those moments, it was logical for me to assume that she was in the States, where she was to wait for me until New Year's Day, for I had already scheduled a flight for December 31.

The attack at Pudahuel had occurred on Saturday morning at around noon, and as soon as I was informed that James and his security people had been killed, I started to leave for the embassy. I was told by the American security people to stay put due to fears that the perpetrators were after embassy personnel. As James was my immediate superior, it was conceivable that I could be next on the agenda of the killers. Two agents stayed with me as a precaution.

At around four in the afternoon, Spencer arrived at my place and told us that the situation at Pudahuel was under control and assured the agents that there was nothing to fear, that the compound where I was staying had enough security. After the agents left, Spencer asked me to sit down because he had something to tell me, and at that very instant, though he had not said a word, I felt as if something hard had hit me in the stomach. I felt a nauseating sensation overpowering me. It was strange for at that moment I did not have the faintest thought of what he was going to tell me.

As he unfolded the chain of events that had taken place at Pudahuel, he told me about the unidentified fourth person found in the car. She was a female, and by the list of passengers who were aboard the plane in which James had arrived, she had been identified as Anne Mary Curtis, my wife.

Spencer himself had taken over the investigation, and in his mind there was no doubt that Anne had been the fourth casualty in the attack. He guessed that James had probably found out that she was travelling in the same plane that was bringing him from Washington, D.C., and had offered her a ride to the embassy.

Because I had talked to Anne a day earlier and she had given me no indication of coming to see me (although she had commented that she really wanted to spend Christmas with me), my first reaction was denial. The time frame for her to leave the States and be at Santiago within the following day was too narrow. It just did not happen. How could it be possible? I just had talked to her on Thursday.

I immediately reached for the phone and called her and then her parents, but there was no answer. Then I remembered that this was the night that she and her parents attended services at their church, and a glimpse of hope shone ever brighter, an assurance that my Anne was alive and that the woman found at the car was someone else. Expectantly I left a message on the voice mail for them to call me as soon they were home. And yet in my mind there was this thread of fear hanging there for I knew my Anne and her liking for the unexpected — for only last year she had come to Chile when I had not expected her at all — and also there next to the phone was this passenger list from the airline that Spencer had given me. I looked at the list and told myself that it was a coincidence; it had to be a coincidence. Anne Curtis could have been someone else's name. It could happen; it happened all the time. "But how coincidental was it to find another Anne Mary Curtis?" I asked myself. I had no answer. I would not answer.

Spencer, fully aware of my distressful situation, stayed with me, which I did appreciate because in those moments I could not truly dissipate a strange fear that was taking hold of me. It was not clear to me what really was transpiring, I only knew that the incident at Pudahuel had raised the possibility of my Anne being dead even though my denial was as strong as the raising of that possibility. There was this fear, the fear of really knowing.

As I waited for a call from Anne or her parents, he made coffee and prepared some sandwiches, which I did not touch, having no appetite at all. Spencer talked to me about some of the things that he had been working on and made some casual references to the possible replacements to fill James' position. He mentioned there was an ongoing investigation of the incident at Pudahuel but refrained from getting into the details. He just said that the CIA and DINA were conducting a thorough investigation of the incident, which seemed to have been well planned.

He also informed me that the State Department had received word from the junta that General Augusto Pinochet was to be appointed president of Chile by a junta joint decree declaration within two weeks. This move would legitimize the military government and would place Chile among the rest of the nations as equal. The State Department was to recognize immediately Pinochet as president of Chile, and the papal nuncio in Santiago was to legitimize Pinochet's position as the head of the Chilean government. The junta trusted that the rest of the nations were to follow the United States' position if their embassies were to stay in Chile.

As I listened to Spencer, I realized that all that he was telling me at this time had become meaningless. At that moment, if one of Chile's volcanoes were to erupt, it might as well swallow the whole country and I could care less. Anne was all that I cared about. Time was taking a nap — it seemed to pass at an incredibly crawling pace, the instants forever turning into seconds and seconds into minutes as equal in its pacing.

From Santiago to San Jacinto in California, there was about a four-hour time difference. It was now going on 1:00 A.M., and they should been at home by now, and the phone was still silent. I waited half an hour and called Anne, but there was no answer. I called her again and no answer. I told myself that she was probably staying with her folks. I called them, and Carl, my father-in-law, answered, filling me with a sense of gladness. I just knew that Anne was with them. But then there was this long pause as Carl called Mary, his wife, to the phone. She sounded very excited and repeated what Carl had told me that in my denial I had refused to accept: Anne had left for Chile on Friday and should have arrived at Pudahuel around 8:00 this morning. Anne had been killed at 11:30 on the morning of her arrival.

As I had suspected, Anne thought of surprising me so both of us could spend Christmas together and also to tell me that she was expecting a girl, whom she was to name Ruth after my mother. I remembered that in July she had jokingly expressed that in the possibility of getting pregnant, if it was a boy she would name him John after me. I quickly responded by saying that there were too many Johns around and that she had to be more original. She laughed and proceeded to tell me that if the baby was a girl she would call her Ruth after my mother. I remembered saying nothing. I just looked at her. She looked so young.

At that moment, I did not think that she would get pregnant because we had talked about waiting another year, but in retrospect, maybe she had others things in mind. This was my Anne, always doing the unexpected. Mary told me on the phone that Anne was already five months pregnant, but she wanted to keep it a secret from me and that on Christmas Day, she was really going to give me a meaningful gift: the news of being father to a baby girl.

Unable to contend with the grief that suddenly rushed in and took complete hold of me, I motioned to Spencer, who picked up the receiver and talked to them. I left my place and passed the guard station. The guard strangely enough did not stop or question me; he just waved as I went outside the compound.

Moments later I walked the empty sidewalks, street after street. An intense pain I had never felt, not even when I lost my parents, tore my flesh and broke down my spirit. In those moments, I was a broken down man. Tears came and left as the sobbing became lesser and lesser, and finally there was nothing left. I felt exhausted and completely dried out. I sought the inviting restfulness of an empty bench and sat. Nearby a car slowed down as its lights died out. Moments later the car's door opened, and Spencer came out. He came toward where I was and sat beside me.

I hardly remember the rest of that night, but I do remember that Spencer stayed with me. In those moments of intense grief, Spencer showed his friendship. He stayed close by, and later he was instrumental in securing a flight that allowed me to take the cremated remains of my Anne back to the States for proper burial. I left Chile on December 16, the day prior to the inauguration of Pinochet as president of the Republic of Chile.

In California the memorial service was held at a small Presbyterian church at a place called Hemet, not too far away from Idyllwild where Anne had bought a house which was to be our future home. It was now December 21.

The service was modest, and the well-wishers were all strangers to me except for my in-laws. They all paid their respects to me. Most of them were older, and I felt their caring, loving spirit inside of me. At the end of the service, the minister gave Anne's ashes to me. In turn I gave the ashes to her folks. At the moment, I had not yet visualized my life ahead.

Everything around me seemed unreal. Each moment seemed rehearsed, as if I had gone through the same episodes sometime in the past. Each scene was neatly being played, each change of scene carefully unfolding to my needs: the well wishes, the meaningful handshakes, the words of encouragement. It felt good, but far away it seemed that all of these were taking place in a distant place. For inside of me, the memories of my Anne kept flashing endlessly in my mind, and I totally rejected all sense of reality. Each moment I was telling myself that this was not happening, that it was a nightmare from which I wanted so desperately to wake up.

After the service, Anne's parents took me to Idyllwild to visit the home which was to be our home. I was dumfounded when I saw the house partially covered with the snow of the prior day and the tall pine and cedar trees and large rocks; it was exactly as she had described to me. It was a beautiful place and reminded me of some of the houses we had seen in Osorno.

At the porch, I stood for several moments staring at the door. I could not help from thinking that through this door my Anne had gone inside the house as I was doing now. For several moments, I held the key in the lock, unable to turn the key for I felt that behind the door was the tangible world that Anne had envisioned for both of us. As I stood staring at the door, I glanced to the side and saw Anne's parents standing by the trunk of a large tree holding each other. Carl and Mary Morris, now in their sixties, looked so fragile and so small against the large trees and giant boulders where giant streaks of snow had now become long icy tears suspended in air.

Their grief and pain reached my heart, overcoming momentarily my own grief. I remember Anne telling me how devastated they were when their only son, five years older than she, had fallen to cancer at a very early age. And now their only daughter was gone, and the little baby girl they had anticipated to hold was also gone. They were now facing their old age alone, but not totally alone because they still had me.

Reassuring myself that I would be there for them, I turned the key and went into the house to face what I had imagined to be. In her letters, Anne had told me the things that she had done in some of the rooms — all the decorations and things that she thought I would like and in particular a painting that she had hung in the bedroom's wall. It was of a young couple sitting on a bench looking across a lake to the last colorful vestiges of a dying day. It was a beautiful painting, and it was exactly as she had described.

As my eyes glanced from place to place afraid to rest — afraid to stop and feel the full impact of a past reality that in these very rooms could have been my own reality — I paced the wooden floors just contemplating and devouring the surroundings. My Anne's touch was everywhere. I felt it deep inside of me. Then I caught the picture of both of us on top of a glass table in the living room. Unable to contain the pain, I broke down and asked over and over why — why had death come to her so early in her life? The most intense of these moments was when I went to the bedroom, and strangely on one side of the bed, the covers were carefully folded as when one gets ready to go to bed. It seemed as if this side was waiting to be occupied. As I kept looking at it, I became aware that this was not Anne's favorite side — she always liked the left side of the bed. This was my favorite side, and it was apparent to me that she had left it prepared for me before taking her last departure to Chile. Standing by the bed, I could not contain the flood of grief coming from the deepest part of me, and I openly sobbed.

If the pain had been excruciatingly intense until that moment, I was not prepared for what came next. As I looked toward another room where the door was partially opened, I saw the white form of a baby crib. I went to the room and looked inside — this was my daughter's room. Suddenly I felt strangely light, as if I had no weight at all. It seemed unreal, like I was in a sort of a dream state. I felt detached from myself, as if my eyes were seeing everything from everywhere and at times I could look down from the room's ceiling at what was below. I was not flesh at that moment; I was what I was inside, a floating desperate spirit in pain.

Reality returned, and I found myself standing near the crib looking at the many decorations that my wife had placed around the room. Strange as it may have been, a peaceful calm came upon me. I looked toward the open door, and for moments I imagined a little girl waving and smiling at me as she turned around and left the room. Then it was nothing — total emptiness and a pain I had never experienced came upon me. Reaching for the crib, I kneeled down as the tears flooded my eyes. At that moment, I realized that I had lost two persons, two precious human beings: my Anne and Ruth.

I knelt down for I do not remember how long. Memories came and went by the hundreds, questions by the thousands, and nowhere were there answers. I wanted so badly to die, to just go and join my loved ones. On top of a nearby dresser, two pairs of blue, tiny booties called my attention, and raising up I went forward. I picked up the tiny booties and just looked at them as a feeling of profound tenderness, such as that I had felt when I was with my Anne, started to fill my whole being.

I got up, and for several moments, I just looked at the empty crib. It was to remain empty and stay empty, I told myself, but then I recalled that Anne had believed in a new world soon to come — not a paradise in heaven but right here on this earth. If she had been right, maybe in time, Anne, the baby, and I were also to be together again in that peaceful world. Somehow that glimpse of hope gave me the needed strength to leave the room and return to the bedroom to see again everything that was there, everything that was Anne.

I looked at the things in the bedroom, and though I had gained some peace of mind, the very thought that Anne was dead again sent excruciating pain across my chest, and uncontrollable tears flooded my eyes. And yet I still felt through the pain a sense of reassurance that denied my own sense of death, that death was not final, that death was just a coma in a sentence that had no ending.

After a while, my pain subsided, and I sat dawn on the edge of the bed. Again I looked at the picture hanging on the wall of the young lovers peacefully looking at a sunset. Earlier when I had looked at it, it was just a beautiful picture. Now I could sense Anne's peaceful, tranquil nature, and at that very moment, a soothing peace filled my being, a similar feeling that I had experienced in my daughter's bedroom. Again the soothing peacefulness that I was experiencing overcame my broken spirit, and a while later I was able to regain the strength that I needed to leave the house.

Outside the coolness of the day received me with open arms; it was a beautiful day. Not far from the house, I saw my in-laws seated by a small boulder. Seeing me they stood up and walked toward me. They seemed so small and lonely though they had each other, but both had become one, and their oneness spoke of loneliness. Extending my arms, I held them against me for a long while, and the three of us shared the pain of Anne's and our little girl's departure.

On Christmas Eve, we were back to Anne's place — that was what I thought of the house. It was her place although I knew that I was part of it. On this day Anne had been born; she would have been twenty-nine years old. Mary brought some picture albums and several short reels of movies that they had. It was a new experience for me. As I looked at the photos and movies, I was fulfilled with the feeling of family love. It was so overwhelming, this feeling that came over me as I saw Anne growing through the years until she had become a young woman.

As the minutes passed, we all became aware that though we were openly crying for our loved one, there was also this joy of having been part of her life. At the end, Carl showed a video that Anne and I had shot in Argentina while we had spent time with the gauchos on Argentina's great plains. This last remembrance brought some silence as we looked at each other. We all knew that Anne's life was for us an open book that we were to read the rest of our lives. Death had not closed the book of her life; instead it had opened, and as long as we were alive, there would be no last chapter.

Though I was returning to Chile within a week, I assured them that they were not alone and that when my assignment ended, I would return. I asked them to be the caretakers of the house for I had decided to keep it.

Later in the day, we left the house to return to their place, where I was staying. We had lunch at a coffee shop in the center of the town, and then we drove to Hemet Lake not too far from Idyllwild. Hemet Lake was one of Anne's favorite places.

Standing by the shores of the lake and looking toward the green pine forest running all along the other side of the lake, I knew why Anne loved this place. I thought of the picture in the bedroom where the young couple was contemplating the sunset across a lake, a lake just like this lake. Again I thought of my Anne, and I imagined her being here contemplating the serene, peaceful surroundings, and I thought of the many times that she had told me of this restful place. I felt bad for I did remember that in those moments she had spoken from her heart while I remained a casual listener. A feeling of guilt came upon me, but I managed a smile, which did not escape the attention of Mary, and seeing her wondering expression, I told her what I was actually thinking.

"Don't feel bad, son. It is the nature of man to seem uncaring, but they do care. My Carl is the same way," she said, reaching for Carl's hand.

I looked at them, and again I reassured them that I would return and stay with them. They reminded me of the teaching position at the college waiting for me, and I politely told them that because of Anne's death, there would be an investigation. It was my duty and responsibility to find out what had really happened that had caused the death of Anne and some embassy personnel. Again I reassured them that I would return. It would not be soon, for it could take several months.

On Christmas Day, we attended services, but before leaving for the church, I noticed that some of the ornaments that my in-laws had displayed at their home when I had arrived from Chile had been taken off. Mary told me that during the night Carl had gotten up and taken them down. She asked for no explanation; neither did I.

During the service, I became more aware of the pain they were experiencing. Perhaps it became more apparent now that I had come to terms with dealing with my own sorrow and my pain had been pushed a little deeper inside of me. At this point it did not matter if it was for better or for worse, I just wanted to live a little longer. I wanted desperately to return to Chile.

I knew that in all probability I was not to return here for quite a while and maybe I would never return. I was determined to find the killers of my Anne and my baby girl. Now I was feeling what Spencer had felt when the gooks had brutalized and killed his girlfriend. Now I could understand why Spencer had embarked on a quest for revenge against those who had taken his woman. The brutality of my loved one's death now demanded from me retribution — a sort of retribution that could easily end my own life, and this was a comforting thought. Life without Anne was no life at all.

It was obvious, from my perspective, that Anne's presence in those tragic moments must have been a coincidence. It did not, however, excuse the fact that the Marxists were guilty of the act. They would have to pay. The target had been James, who had been returning on the same plane that Anne was travelling on from a trip to Washington, DC. James had been there to testify before a Senate committee — not as a diplomat, but as a highly regarded CIA agent. This information was revealed to me by Spencer, who asked for the utmost secrecy due to its extreme confidentiality. Only key people in the State Department were aware of James being a senior CIA agent who reported directly to the director and to the president of the United States.

Now it was clear to me the role of James at the stadium when he and Contreras saved my life. Since then I had wondered why a diplomat had personally come to my rescue. Diplomats do not confront any place of death, such as the stadium. That role was for the operatives or CIA senior officials.

As the sudden death of James had altered somehow the CIA apparatus and his front position at the embassy, the status of my diplomatic position was immediately extended to fill in for James until a replacement was found. It did not take long for the position to be filled — and this time by a career diplomat, not a CIA operative pretending to be a diplomat. James' replacement was Elmer Defreese, an elderly gentleman whom I had known while I was attached to the embassy at Buenos Aires.

Knowing of my intentions to join the CIA, Spencer had already sent my military files to Virginia for approval. He felt that because of the years I had spent in the service and in the diplomatic field that an appointment was possible considering the precarious situation in Chile. Aware of Spencer's position within the CIA, I had no doubts that soon I was to join the agency, whether on an official or non-official capacity. At this point I did not care. All that mattered was to avenge Anne's and Ruth's deaths. My sole purpose in joining the agency was to get rid of all the Marxists and Communists in Chile. I was joining Spencer's crusade.

On an afternoon in the third week of January, while I was at my desk going through some documents, Spencer walked in. He told me it was time to leave and proceeded to tell me that he had straightened out the situation with Mr. Defreese. On the way out of the embassy, he told me that I was not on the agency's payroll yet, but I was now part of it.

"Hell John, with all the dough that you have stored away, you don't need their money," he said. "Are you packing?"

"Not now, but I left it in my desk. Thanks for reminding me. I just didn't think about," I replied as I turned toward the embassy.

He grabbed me by the arm and said, "Let it go. From now on you have to go back to improvising as we did in Nam." Seeing my puzzled expression, he added, "In our field, the smart ones are the ones who seldom carry a weapon. Diplomats can do it because they are not subject to be searched due to their diplomatic immunity, but hell if we ever are caught by the locals with a gun, unless you are on official business, they will skin you alive before they let you go… if they let you go."

"That's a hell of a way to start a new job. No tools provided," I responded as I kept pace with him on the way to the waiting car.

In the months to come, I realized the complexity of the CIA. It was an obscure entity filled with unexpected expectations. It was an animal constantly on the move. But what was most intriguing was the blurred sense of direction. It seemed that some agents were independent cells within cells — even Spencer had been evasive when on some occasions I had asked him for his base of operation and he had not given me a clear answer. I stayed in Santiago, and I would report to the station there. Most of the time Spencer took me with him on several assignments so I could get familiar with what was really occurring behind the curtains, and I was surprised by the things that at one time were occurring right in front of me and I did not have a clue. This was an entirely different world, and like Spencer had told me, I quickly learned to improvise in my skills as an operative. Definitely there was no glamour at all like in the 007 James Bond movies.

I was not too sure, but in time I figured that Spencer was independent from the CIA station at Santiago. His reporting was seemingly at Valparaiso, which made me think at times that he was probably working with the U.S. Navy Intelligence, which had been very active during September 1973. This was not a new thought for after the coup, Spencer had spent some time securing Valparaiso with Chilean Navy Intelligence and U.S. Navy personnel, which led me to believe that he could also be a U.S. Navy agent. However, this thought came to a halt after learning that he was communicating directly with the army station at the Panama Canal Zone and also with someone else in the States. Spencer was as complex as the agency itself.

Action came soon. In no time I participated in several night raids in the Conception zone, where some subversives were still active. By the end of January 1975, I was part of DINA and rubbed elbows with some of the most vicious and very intelligent agents of DINA, who were mostly army intelligence officers. They were highly educated and extreme professionals in their particular field.

Soon I was to find that killing did not come easy for me; in the midst of some encounters with the subversives, I would rather take prisoners than just kill them as most DINA agents did. DINA's agents complained to Spencer that I was too soft with the enemy, but he did not say anything to me.

In the months of April and May, I was part of a joint effort by DINA and its Argentinian counterpart SIDE in the total elimination of the Uruguayan resistance leaders in Buenos Aires. At this time, I was surprised at the large numbers of operatives working for DINA, including many women and some extremely young.

The raid on the subversives was to take place on a small factory located on the outskirts of Buenos Aires, an area familiar to me since the days I had worked at the American Embassy. The factory was owned by a Uruguayan family well known for their leftist activity in Uruguay and Argentina. The owner, Don Demetrio Silva, had recently been killed in Uruguay by Uruguayan military security forces, and now the factory was being run by his two sons, well-known leftists with links to the Uruguayan OPR–33, a strong leftist organization, and to the Argentinian People's Revolutionary Army. It was well known that the factory hired workers from leftist cells with the exception of some office personnel.

We knew that a meeting was to take place at the factory after closing time, which was at 3:00 P.M. and that Francisco Torres, one of the leaders of the OPR, and others from the People's Army would be attending. Prior to dawn, we had stationed our agents and a military contingent of forty soldiers on several empty buildings around the factory. It was a touch of luck for we really had not expected that several of those buildings would be emptied, perhaps due to the poor economy of the country.

Throughout the early hours of the morning and prior to the attack (which was to take place at exactly 4:30 P.M.) we kept close surveillance on the building, and it surprised me that they kept so busied considering the state of Argentina's economy. Commercial trucks of all sizes kept coming and going through the gates of the building for most of the day. Then exactly at 3:00 P.M., the sound of the company's siren stirred the air, bringing the working day to an end. Shortly afterward the office personnel and some of the workers started to leave, and finally at 3:30 P.M., the workers traffic stopped. A large number of vehicles, however, stayed in the parking lot. As one of the workers closed the gate and went inside, I asked Carlos, a Paraguayan agent, for his radio transmitter, and I called Spencer, who was in another building, and told him that thirty-five cars were still in the parking area. He told me that he was aware that there were perhaps forty people inside and that the raid was to be delayed for another half hour to make sure that those not affiliated with the group would leave.

As I was talking to him, my attention was diverted through the window by two young people riding bicycles and stopping by the offices. I noticed that the boy had a briefcase, and the girl had what seemed to be a large purse. After having some sort of a discussion, they went inside, which alarmed me for I figured that the office was closed. Spencer told me that those two youngsters were perhaps couriers for the subversives, and I grew alarmed for they seemed awfully young. Spencer reminded me that in Nam couriers for the goons were much younger.

At 4:45 P.M. we started moving toward the building. Then at 5:00 P.M. we stormed the building. A larger group moved from the warehouse in toward the main building and others came from the side as my group went through the front, which was deserted. The offices were nearly empty, and we found two middle-aged men in suits who offered no resistance and were taken prisoner. As an agent started to ask them questions, the rapid fire of semi-automatic weapons coming from the factory and warehouse area filled the air, forcing us to move forward. At that very moment, two shots were delivered close to me, and turning around I saw that our prisoners had been shot by the agent who was interrogating them. The intensity of the fighting ahead left no time for wondering, and I continued moving forward with my .45 in my hand.

In seconds I became aware that M16s were being used but not by us, and several of my men fell in an opening between the offices and the factory. However, our larger force of soldiers led by Spencer had inflicted many casualties and was systematically advancing toward where we were. In the continuous fighting, among screams of defiance and pain, desperate men and women determined to kill or to die exchanged bullets and bullets, cursing and damning each other, cussing each other's mothers to the very end. And through all this deadly, sinful encounter, I told myself that God was nowhere near and that it was our own doing and we deserved whatever the outcome would be. It was justification at its best and the easiest way out of the guilt that was already ravaging my spirit. Constantly I kept asking myself if this was what Anne would have liked for me to do, and the answer was always the same: a definite no. She would have been totally disgusted.

The outcome of this encounter was in our favor but at a heavy price — not only in lives but in our human make up, especially my own. In time it could determine the course of my life. Gradually my resolve to avenge the killing of Anne was eroding away due to the nature of this work which called for what I was not willing to freely give. By this time, I knew that the killing of a human being was not part of me. I was no longer willing to kill, and to be an operative, one must have this willingness to kill.

It had been carnage with more than twenty guerrillas killed out of a force of thirty while we lost ten of ours. There were many wounded on each side, but I knew well that their wounded would not last. While I was attending to some of the wounded, Spencer several times told me to get rid of the wounded leftists. Seeing them in pain and laying helpless on the concrete floor of the factory, I was unable to follow his order.

Seemingly annoyed at my unwillingness, Spencer walked up to a young wounded girl and shot her in the head.

"It is better this way than to let her fall into the hands of the Argentinians," he said, showing no emotion at all.

Though I had seen Spencer kill and execute people in the battlefield, I had never seen Spencer as in this occasion. He was a different Spencer; he was cold, indifferent and totally detached from any feeling of compassion or pity as he went on executing the wounded. Other agents and soldiers followed him. At the end of the ordeal, thirty leftists lay dead.

There was a young boy, about fifteen years old, who was to leave another impression on my tired mind, a solid unerasable imprint of our inhumanity toward other human beings. There was no doubt in my mind that he was part of the subversives; otherwise he would not be here. I recalled that he was one of the youngsters who at closing time had arrived on bicycles, and looking toward the girl who Spencer had killed, I also recognized her by the color of her dress — a bright violet color which now was soaked in blood, tinting the dress to a rustic color of blood being dried out.

The boy, who was now being cornered by one of the agents, looked like a helpless, scared animal, and seeing him closer I was taken aback by his youthful appearance. He couldn't be over fifteen. He was not armed; instead he held a black book close to his chest as protection. I assumed he was probably an office boy that the subversives hired to carry messages, sort of a courier as Spencer had said.

He was well-dressed (blue suit, white shirt, blue tie, and shiny black shoes). A SIDE agent grabbed him by the hair and viciously pushed him against the wall. I protested and asked Spencer to tell the Argentinian to let him go, but Spencer pushed me aside, and seconds later the boy was shot. I looked at the young figure lying now on the floor as blood surrounded his head and flowed down his neck to his shoulder. His white shirt was now crimson red. He still held the book in his hands, giving the impression that it was his most valuable possession. Perhaps it contained some information useful to us. I held my breath, feeling nauseated. Instantly my mind jumped to another time where I stood looking at Frank's corpse. Had I been living a nightmare all this time? "Maybe my life had stopped somewhere and all of these have been a bad dream," I said to myself, seeking relief. But there was none given — this was my reality.

The agent who had killed the boy bent over his body and took the book off his hand and glanced through its pages. Then strangely he lowered his head, as if he was tired, and after a few seconds, he proceeded to remove the boy's belongings. I could see in his hands a wallet, a small notebook, and what appeared to be two pamphlets. Then he gave a loud cursing as he got up and walked to Spencer. He gave the boy's belongings to him and walked away seemingly disgusted. Spencer looked at the things retrieved from the boy's body and looked toward the body for several moments. Afterward he joined the rest of the agents who were retrieving identifications and information from the dead bodies.

I looked at the agent who had shot the boy. He was leaning against a large piece of equipment looking at the bodies sprawled on the concrete floor, but his eyes constantly focused on the boy's body that was now being carried away by soldiers. I wondered if the coldness of his act had suddenly reached his conscience, or perhaps it had something to do with the book that the boy was carrying.

Nothing seemed to make sense in this madness. I told myself over and over that I was no part of this madness, and it just could not be happening to me. True, there was blood on my hands, and I was guilty of sending many men to an early grave, but that was war, and in war soldiers must kill in order to survive. Here in Chile, I was not fighting for my country but for the wants of a powerful country that year after year was stripping Chile of its wealth in order to increase the profits of American corporations — corporations that were detached from the needs of the common American workers, workers like these who had died to achieve some sort of change in their lives, just a small change that could improve their lot. But my own reality was also hiding behind my own excuses because I was not really fighting for my country. I was here to avenge the death of my wife and my daughter, and in the process, innocent ones had fallen to my zeal for revenge.

Still with my eyes on the young dead boy, I stepped in between the dead bodies, and I went to the young girl Spencer had shot. Her blond hair partly covered the side of her face while the rest was now crimson. I leaned over her, and I touched her face. It was warm, and I wished she was still alive though I knew she was dead. She was very young, maybe sixteen. I felt a hand on my shoulder. Someone was giving me strength to get up. My knees felt weak. I looked up, and I saw Spencer, who told me to gather my men so we could leave. As I started to leave, I looked at the girl whose body was being taken away by the soldiers, and I could not repress the tears. I did not hide them either as I called those of my group.

That night at the military barracks where we were staying, the scenes of the girl's and the young boy's deaths kept passing through my mind. I wondered about the book he was carrying. It seemed very important to him, and he never let it go out of his hand. Perhaps it contained extreme information too valuable for their cause. I was not only physically but also emotionally exhausted, and I was not able to sleep for several hours. It was probably after midnight that I succumbed to sleep to shortly wake up from a bad dream where I saw myself staring at Spencer, who was pointing a gun at me at close range. Seeing his determination to kill me, I closed my eyes, sensing the inevitable. After waking up, I lay awake several hours until Spencer shook me and told me to get up.

At the cafeteria, as agents and soldiers passed along the coffee and the plates with biscuits and fried eggs, I found myself looking at Spencer, who sat further down across the table. Still having the dream fresh in my mind, I wondered if my life would end at the point of his gun.

During breakfast the conversation centered mainly on the elimination of the Uruguayan subversives the prior day and the loss of several of our men. But there was also the news that one of our men, an Argentinian, had committed suicide shortly after the raid. It seemed that nobody had a definite answer for his act, and some wondered if when returning home he had found his wife with another man. But most of his friends agreed that the agent had no scruples and would not kill himself for a dame. On the contrary, he would have killed the wife instead. According to them, the agent also had a young son whom he worshipped, and he would not leave him alone in this world by himself. I knew then that he was the agent whom I had seen kill the boy. Could the boy's death have driven him to kill himself? What was in that book that seemingly had bothered him? Now I was hearing that he had been a seasoned agent, a man used to killing. It did not make sense; it was unlikely that he had killed himself for just one boy.

After breakfast the commander of the Paraguayans asked for everyone to stay for a brief meeting. Though it had been an strenuous ordeal, it was business as usual for the group. The leaders representing the different nationalities addressed the group and thanked everyone for the sacrifices made in the name of freedom. Spencer then took over the meeting and pointed out some of the weak points in the attack, and it did surprise me that everyone paid more than the usual attention to him than I would have expected. While the other leaders had addressed us, I was aware that some of those present had some small talk among themselves, and more than once someone had called for a cease to the interruptions. However, when Spencer talked, there was complete attention to what he was saying.

There was no doubt that Spencer was in charge of the group even though there was an Argentinian captain, the head of the Uruguayan secret service and a Paraguayan commander present. I thought that it was probably because DINA was the leader of the intelligent secret agencies of the countries of the Southern Cone and Spencer was DINA's commander in the field service, which had been obvious the prior day when he outlined the attack on the subversive camp.

After the meeting, we exchanged well-expressed wishes, shakings of hands and embraces as most friends or families do. Spencer and I found ourselves travelling further north to a border checkpoint between Argentina and Paraguay. It was at this check point that the Paraguayan military forces had captured Jorge Fuentes, a most sought-out leader of what was left of MIR. Fuentes being a Chilean, he was kept at the border station until he could be interrogated by DINA. It was the first time that I had met Fuentes, a man who in his early thirties looked too frail to resist the hard punishment waiting at Paraguay.

Fuentes was of special interest to me. He had been linked to the Pudahuel attack which had killed Anne and Ruth. This time I chose not to question him. Spencer and another DINA agent interrogated him. I was not present during the interrogation, but it was evident from what Spencer told me later that Fuentes had told them all that they needed to know. Fuentes was to be kept in Paraguay for several months for interrogation purposes before being brought to Chile for further interrogation. During all this time, I could not shake off the face of the youngsters we had killed the prior day and how cold-blooded Spencer was in the killing of the young girl. Although the killing of the young boy had been gruesome to see, seeing Spencer as a cold killer had left a greater impression on my mind. At that moment, I could not understand it for in the past I had seen Spencer in the act of killing, and it had not bothered me as it had now.

On the way to the airport where we were to take a plane back to Chile, there were too many quiet moments between Spencer and me. I knew he was not pleased with my performance, and I could care less at that moment, for witnessing him killing that young girl and that boy being brutally killed overshadowed everything else in my life. I was still cordial to him; perhaps it was my sense of containment, something that I had learned in the diplomatic field. Against any adversity, you must contain your own feelings for the sake of normality. At one point just to break the ice, I asked about the Argentinian who had committed suicide, and he told me that it was perhaps due to the killing of the young boy during the raid.

It was unusual, he said, for a supposedly seasoned agent to have gone the way he did. It should not have affected him, but it did. He told me that this experience should be sort of a learning experience for me. He emphasized the need to learn how to detach oneself from personal feelings during an encounter such as the one we had just experienced. It was of extreme importance to constantly remind yourself that we were there to kill the enemy. As I listened to him, the pictures of the girl and the boy kept flashing through my mind. They were so young, and the boy looked so scared. The girl was already on the floor wounded when Spencer had shot her. She needed medical attention, not a bullet in her head.

Unexpectedly he said, "We screwed up with those two. They shouldn't have been there. But hell! How were we supposed to know that they were not part of the group?"

"What are you talking about? Who?" I asked, startled because his comment had come out suddenly after he had just finished giving me some points on what was expected from me on assignments such as the one we had just finished.

He did not respond. Instead he reached for his briefcase and brought out two books — one with a black cover and the other of a maroon color — and several brochures. These were Bibles and religious brochures. Immediately I recognized the black Bible. It was the same book that the boy was holding. Without saying a word, Spencer gave them to me and kept a stern look at the passing road.

As I went through the Bibles and brochures, I realized that these were Jehovah's Witnesses literature, and I became disconcerted. I glanced at Spencer, who was now watching me and expecting my reaction.
"Yeah, they were Jehovah's Witnesses...but I can't figure out...what were they doing there? It doesn't make any sense," he said, showing his displeasure — not with himself or the event itself but against the two young victims. "Jehovah's Witnesses do not get involved in politics. In war time, they are neutral, and they only recognize Jehovah as their God and Jesus Christ as the ruler of the Messianic Kingdom. What were they doing there? It doesn't make any sense. What do you think?"

I moved my head negatively for I had no answer either. I felt a tightening of the throat, and I looked at him seeking some sort of an answer. He looked away somewhere but not at the surroundings — farther away, perhaps looking for what I was also looking, searching for answers that would never be there. These were two young Jehovah's Witnesses, and both had the same last name

— perhaps brother and sister or maybe cousins. The same question that Spencer had asked earlier came to my lips: What in the world were they doing there?

As we reached the airport, I returned the books and brochures to him. He told me to keep them and that he had left words with Martinez, the Argentinian captain, to find their addresses and find out the reason why they were there in a factory known to be run by a leftist organization, something well known in that community. He became silent and remained silent until we landed in Santiago. I went along with his silence, for his silence matched my own silence. That is what guilt does to most men who do not seek forgiveness but instead seek answers on their own to justify their unjustified deeds. Against the background of my guilt, my thoughts were on those young lives and on my Anne and how disappointed she would have been with me.

After checking out at the customs service, we came out of the building to meet a cool May's early evening, which felt good. It had a refreshing effect on us. Spencer signaled a taxi and told me that he was going directly to Valparaiso and for me to stay put at my apartment until he could get in touch with me. He gave me a brief smile, sort of a grin, and got inside the cab that immediately took off. I did not call a cab. Instead I walked along the sidewalk for I needed time to bring myself up to normality.

Still fresh in my mind was the book and the brochures that now were in my small suitcase. Then unexpectedly I caught sight of the gate in the far distance where Anne and Ruth had been killed, and I stood there for a very long time, just looking and remembering my Anne. I signaled for a cab among the many waiting at the curb to serve arriving passengers, and the first in the line immediately took off toward me. I told myself as I boarded the cab that was to take me to my place that Pudahuel was to stay in my mind the rest of my life.

At my apartment, I went through the youngster's belongings and seeing especially in the girl's Bible so many scriptures underlined in many colors it reminded me of Anne, who always underlined in color the scriptures that were important to her. I could not resist the impact of my deed for their deaths were also my deed — I had been there and participated in the killing of so many. Pudahuel in these moments retreated to the inner chambers of my mind as I broke down in tears. I wept for the two youngsters that we had so brutally killed. It was brutal because they knew that they were being killed. I knew because I had seen in the boy's face the face of fear.

It took me several days to come to terms with myself, and I was fortunate for Spencer did not contact me for nearly a week. Otherwise I would have had a tough time in dealing with him. It seemed that seeing Spencer as a cold killer was now a factor in my assessment of him as a person, though as earlier, I kept wondering why his coldness in the killing of a human being was bothering me now when I had known it all along. As I thought of him as a cold killer, the same unavoidable question came to me again, but this time it had gained some momentum. Had the CIA or DINA been involved in the killing of my Anne? Was Spencer part of it? Again Pudahuel came to the front of my mind — wondering, questioning, and accusing.

The attack at Pudahuel had left many questions unanswered. I needed them to be answered. At the time of the attack, MIR had seemingly been erased as a fighting force, thus eliminating its capability as a striking force. Yet somehow the attack had a degree of military sophistication. The military coordination and the gathering of information on the movement of the diplomatic agenda were evident. However, at this time, I chose not to openly question the CIA report on the incident nor the Chilean version of the attack. But as time went by, questions kept surging in my mind for which I had no answers, not yet.

MIR and its elements could have done it, but what if the Chilean Army or DINA was involved? Was the CIA also involved? What was the reason behind killing one of their own? If the Senate committee hearings were a factor, James should have been eliminated before the hearing. James' death did not make any sense. That was the deceptive nature of the agency.

It was not only deceptive, but it had a sinister ring. What I knew about the CIA years earlier was its coldness on dealing with its own operatives. Several years prior to the Tet Offensive in 1968 when CIA agents were trying to alert President Johnson about the reality of the situation in Vietnam, they were killed by U.S. Army intelligent units practically on the lawn of the White House. What these CIA agents knew about the incoming Tet Offensive was not in the best of interest of the army, and the agents had to be stopped. The agency had not been able to dissuade these dedicated Americans from going directly to President Johnson. In all probability, the agency had alerted the army, which prompted army intelligence units to kill them. It was a frightening thought, and I chose to leave it just as it was, a thought.

Being part of the CIA and working with DINA's agents, the interrogatives about Pudahuel kept pressing on my mind for answers. Working with the Chileans, I learned that they themselves also had some doubts about the role of MIR in the Pudahuel affair. Besides agents on our side, there was one man who could give me an answer, and that was Fuentes, who was now a prisoner in Paraguay.

However, it was not long after I had returned from Argentina that I found out that Fuentes, the leader of the subversives who had been apprehended in Paraguay, had suddenly been brought to Chile from Paraguay. He was being kept at Villa Grimaldi, a DINA detention center located at Penalolen on the outskirts of Santiago. And no sooner afterward, I found myself driving to Penalolen to the infamous detention center of Villa Grimaldi in an effort to find the answer to Pudahuel.

Several hours later, I parked at the villa's parking lot and faced the dreaded front wall of Villa Grimaldi, where soldiers guarded the main gate. The guards, seeing my credentials, opened the large iron gate and let me in. One of them led me to a small building.

Once there, I met Michael, who I already knew was in charge of the interrogation of Fuentes. He was surprised to see me. It did not, however, surprise me to find him there. I knew that DINA was using him at most detention centers as an interrogator. Spencer knew him well and had filled me with other details of his activities within the agency. I had only known him as an agent in charge of some of the Peace Corps stations, and I was aware of some of his other CIA activities, but I did not know him well. Spencer had told me that Michael was the American who had sealed the death of Frank and Charles, though at that particular time it seemed that the fate of both men had already been decided by the military. He had also told me that Michael enjoyed inflicting pain on prisoners. Immediately I could tell that Michael did not welcome my presence, and he questioned the motives of my visit.

To ease Michael's apprehension, I played on his skills as an interrogator. I told him that I wanted to question the man who had probably ordered the attack on Pudahuel, where my wife had been killed. I told Michael that in Paraguay I had spent little time with Fuentes because the Paraguayans had taken him immediately after they arrested him at the border station at Argentina. This seemed to appease Michael, and he told me he had no objections. He warned me that Fuentes was in a deplorable state, alleging that he had probably contracted an infectious disease.

Further he stated that Fuentes would most likely deny any involvement with Pudahuel. According to Michael, the attack had been perpetrated by an isolated MIR cell unit that had since been destroyed.

He took me through several barracks, where I saw dozens of prisoners who looked like they had been starved and tortured. Inside one of the barracks that had been divided into several cells, we came to a room where a man sat on the edge of a bed.

He was sitting on the metal straps; the bed lacked a mattress. I turned to Michael in silence, questioning him. The precarious figure of the man spoke of a much older man. It seemed to me that this was not Fuentes. Though our encounter had been brief, he was not the Fuentes I remembered.

The only thing he had on him was a short, dirty towel covering just his head. The rest of his exposed body was covered with sores and open wounds. Around his ankles and wrists, bluish lacerations left by electric shocks were visible. Electric techniques were now accepted as standard procedures in the CIA for interrogation purposes.

Michael grinned and shrugged his shoulders. He assured me that he was Fuentes. As I reached out to touch the prisoner to get his attention, Michael warned me that the man could be contagious, and after looking at him in a seemingly compassionate way, he left. I was not buying it; I already knew the man, and what I knew about him was evil. My eyes scanned the prisoner several times. I glanced at the guard Michael had left nearby, but the guard looked away. I was searching for some trace of confirmation. I still felt that he was not Fuentes. The prisoner, who had been sitting motionless with his hands on his knees and his face partially covered with the grayish towel, now moved his head sideways.

Putting great effort in raising his hand, he removed the towel covering his face. The sight of what was underneath startled me; in fact, it filled me with revulsion. If there had been any intentions from me to get even with the man who had masterminded the attack at Pudahuel, it died there. Standing before this man, there was no thought of revenge — just sadness and pity. I now realized that Michael's objections had been a pretense. He knew well the physical and mental state of Fuentes.

Somewhere now in the minor glimpses of life still emanating off his face, I recognized Fuentes. This was not the face of the young man I recalled. He had aged in the bosom of inhumanity. His waned appearance, the paleness of flesh on its way to the grave, his sunken eyes where two tiny stars faintly shined away, the premature gray hair hanging off his forehead down to his beard, his lips covered with open sores and abrasions — there was so little life left in him. The sight of him weakened my legs, and one of my knees touched the concrete floor. My shaking hands fell lightly on his bony arms.

We looked at each other for seemingly long moments, questioning each other in silence. I was desperately trying to understand. I knew that, like in the cases of Anne's and Frank's deaths, there would be no understanding. This was reality — crude and brutal. Reality did not need to be understood....It had to be accepted as such.

Finally I spoke and told him the truth about myself: I was the husband of the woman who had been killed at Pudahuel, and I needed to know the truth about Pudahuel. Was or was not Pudahuel a MIR hit?

He opened his mouth, but there was no sound. I could see that most of his teeth were missing. His whole mouth was an open wound. After several efforts, he managed to get some sound into his voice. The words were not clear, and I leaned closer and heard him saying, "So odd that you are asking about Pudahuel." With intense pain, he managed to lift his head to look into my eyes. I was at odds with myself; I should not be here asking questions of a dying man.

He muttered something, and I got closer, my face feeling his beard. "Think about it," he said, his voice faint and in his throat. I put my hand on his shoulder — or the bone that was there. All I could feel was bone. A hoarse sound came from his mouth, followed by his voice, now just murmurs.
"Why is it that DINA...or the doctor," he paused. I pressed my hands gently on his shoulder, silently begging him to continue. "Or El Gringo has not asked about Pudahuel?" Now his words became incoherent as he burst into an incontrollable cough. He laid his face down on the naked steel bed frame. After a while, he stopped coughing. He did not move.

In all this time, I had not been aware that I had been on my knees. When I did become aware that I was practically kneeling in front of him, I made no attempt to stand. I just looked at him. The back of his neck seemed unusually clean and untouched — the skin was young.

I stood up and glanced at the guard, who now had his back turned to us. I observed Fuentes' motionless, naked body. I brushed away some unexpected tears that flooded my eyes. Again, as with Frank, I asked myself if this young man had any family left. Somewhere a mother was perhaps praying for him or a young wife was waiting for him. Fuentes was now on the way to the bottomless graveyard of the "Desaparecidos" or "the Missing Ones," the ones whose fate would never be known.

He was dying. They were starving him. I could see that most of his flesh was attaching itself to the bones. Seeing him in such a deplorable state, I asked myself why he was still being tortured; by all reliable accounts, he was no longer a threat to DINA. He was already a dead man.

Moments later I was escorted by one of the guards to where Michael was waiting. Accompanying him was a shorter man dressed in a white smock. Michael introduced him as Dr. Eugenio Berrios. He was in charge of the bacteriological aspects of the facility. Berrios took pride in being very helpful in the development of serums that accelerated the breaking point of any human being.

According to him, sodium pentothal was not as effective as some of the other serums that he was creating. He believed that under sodium pentothal some patients who were familiar with the drug were able to fabricate a lie as a response instead of telling the truth. This was something I already knew. In the war, I had been trained on interrogation tactics, and I would plant false information in my mind as true facts. Under drugs the truth was distorted and effectively confused the enemy. That was the theory. Under practice I still did not know if it would work. Lucky for me, I had never been put under that sort of interrogation.

Michael asked me if Fuentes had said anything of interest, and I told him that the man was on the verge of dying and that it had been a waste of time. He agreed, saying that the Paraguayans had taken all the life out of him.

After visiting Villa Grimaldi, Spencer took me to Argentina, where he kept me occupied for several weeks to gather information on the OPR-33 that was operating from Montevideo and helping the Argentinian People's Revolutionary Army. It seemed that we had not eliminated all Uruguayans operating in Argentina. The raid had nearly wiped out the Uruguayans, but there were still some other cells left. It was not a pleasant trip to go back to Argentina for what I had feared the most happened — the memories of those young lives we had killed months earlier were constantly in my mind.

After a while, I returned to Chile, and Spencer stayed in Buenos Aires for a last sweep on the Uruguayans. Before I left, Captain Martinez informed me that there was an ongoing investigation on the Jehovah's Witness youngsters and promised me that as soon as the findings were available to him he would send them to us.

When I returned to Santiago, I found out my time was limited on searching for answers on Pudahuel because the rapidly unfolding events related to my work with DINA kept me busy, allowing no time at all to focus totally on the Pudahuel attack. However, regardless of my limited time, Pudahuel stayed in my mind, and the doubts kept surging, leading to a definite question: Was Pudahuel a MIR operation?

Fuentes had made sense. He had not been asked about Pudahuel. It was obvious that his interrogators knew he had not been involved in the attack. It was also clear that Michael, who was also referred to as El Gringo, was part of the puzzle. But also it could have been Spencer. He was no better than Michael — both of them were killers. Spencer had interrogated Fuentes when we were at the Paraguayan checkpoint several months earlier, and that was an unavoidable fact that made me wonder.

I had to find out if Pudahuel had been a DINA or CIA operation or a combination of both. I needed to find the reason behind the killing of James, which had resulted in my wife's death. There were admitted obstacles in my effort to find the truth. At this time, these obstacles seemed insurmountable, but I realized that time would reveal the truth, and there was ample time ahead. At the same time, I feared that time was running out on me because the killing and torture of those being caught by us continued, and my heart was in great pain. The face of my Anne was now constantly in my mind and also the memories of Frank, Mario, Julia, their kids, Fuentes, and the faces of the youngsters that we had recently killed in Buenos Aires. All of them were as fresh in my mind as when it happened.

That night I had one of the strangest and most pleasurable dreams I ever had. I dreamed I was standing surrounded by the greenery of a forest in bloom. Nearby was a large pond that was receiving crystalline clear water falling from springs located in the higher terrain. There were all sorts of trees, and some had fruits, and a great colorful diversity of flowers bloomed everywhere. Animals of all kinds roamed the surroundings, and a family of deer stopped nearby to drink water. What was odd was the sense of nearness that I seemed to have with them for I saw myself petting them and the deer were not afraid of me. Then I saw Anne and a little girl coming toward me, and Anne said something that I could not hear clearly, but it did not seem important for I just joined them as I kept looking at the little girl who offered her hand to me. As I grabbed her tiny hand, she smiled. She was a happy little girl.

When I woke up, I lay awake for a very long time wondering about the dream, which as some dreams are, was too real to just let go. I went back to sleep with the hope of returning to the same dream.

Part VIII

In November of 1975, the heads of the military secret services of the countries of the Southern Cone met at Santiago and formed a secret military alliance to be known as Operation Condor. Operation Condor was set in place to be a deterrent to the Soviet and Cuban expansion in Latin America. It would eradicate and eliminate all Marxist and Communist elements by any means necessary in the countries of the Southern Cone. This would include the kidnapping, torturing, and killing of any subversive element, regardless of position or social status or whether they were military or civilian.

There was also an understanding within Operation Condor itself, not necessarily fully shared by the United States government, that its operatives could at times work outside the boundaries of the countries of the Southern Cone. This implied that Operation Condor had the prerogative to reach and kill anywhere in the world any known Marxist or Communist leader who escaped the countries of the Southern Cone and to eliminate any leftist leader of the countries bordering its sovereignty.

Sponsored by the military high commands of Chile, Argentina, Uruguay, and Paraguay, and having the support of the American government, Operation Condor was to be a lethal force to accomplish the wants of the United States in its quest to stop Soviet expansion in the Americas. DINA, the feared Chilean military secret agency headed by Colonel Manuel Contreras, was to take the lead among the repressive military secret organizations of Argentina, Uruguay and Paraguay.

Operation Condor referred to the condor, the bird of prey symbolized in the national emblem of Chile. As Spencer put it, Operation Condor was like the condor — the most powerful and largest bird of prey in existence. It reigned since prehistoric times — unopposed over the Andean Mountains — and chose its prey at will in any of the countries of the Southern Cone and had the capabilities to fly beyond its domain.

What made Operation Condor formidable was its limitless scope of operations; it was to operate independently from the established military structure. At the same time, it would act as a cleanser for the military apparatus itself. It had the power to arrest and eliminate any high official found to be friendly to any leftist regime and would only report to DINA.

Immediately after Operation Condor was established, Spencer and I and two other CIA agents were attached to DINA to be part of Condor. It was a CIA effort to gain inside information on Operation Condor, though DINA had made it clear that Condor was to operate free from CIA interference.

Since the very beginning of Operation Condor, Spencer told me that I was not to share any information with the CIA agent at the local station; Spencer himself was my only link to the agency. Michael was also part of Operation Condor, and yet I was also not to disclose to him any information received from Spencer. Michael, having the status of being a double agent, did not have the agency's trust or DINA's either. By this time, I had learned that Michael was not officially recognized by the CIA as one of its own. As Spencer put it, Michael could be useful at times.

Spencer's group would not report to the local CIA station, thus denying important information to the State Department at the embassy level. Any crucial information to them would trickle from the top. Those of us who were part of Operation Condor were, in a sense, operatives in a cell within cells. We operated independently from the watchful eyes of the State Department, and yet there was still accountability. We all knew we had the approval of the director, Kissinger, and President Ford. One thing was for sure: We reported all our activities to Spencer.

Several months later after Operation Condor was established, on March 24, 1976, the military coup in Argentina brought down the government of Isabel Peron. General Videla was now in power. The Argentinian military being in control of the government meant that DINA and SIDE no longer had to bother with the civilians. This enhanced and facilitated Operation Condor's resolve to get rid of Marxism in the countries that made up the Southern Cone. Before the coup, SIDE (the Argentinian secret police) had at times been at odds with the civilian government of Isabel, which had openly questioned the repressive policy of SIDE.

The military now controlled the government in Argentina, giving SIDE the same power that DINA had in Chile. In Argentina, Operation Condor was now in a position to dictate and execute its own agenda, totally free from the local civilian government interference.

Condor was now flying unopposed by the frontiers of all the countries of the Southern Cone. DINA, the most repressive of all secret military agencies ever to operate in the Americas, was taking the lead. Operation Condor's internal code was: Condor 1 - Chile, Condor 2 - Argentina, Condor 3 - Uruguay, and Condor 4 - Paraguay. Panama again came into play. As far as I knew, all correspondence among the Condor countries would go through Panama. I was not sure if it was a CIA station or a U.S. military station.

In less than a year after Condor's conception, Spencer had managed, with the approval of General Contreras, to take over all functions of Operation Condor, and in doing so, several of DINA's agents whose allegiances to Pinochet were well known were taken out, their whereabouts never to be found out.

It was now July 1976, nearly two years after Anne's death and seven months after the formation of Operation Condor. I was at a military compound in Santiago waiting on Spencer for an assignment from Operation Condor.

On this early, rainy morning of July, I stood leaning against the concrete support pillars of one of the military barracks facing several armored vehicles stationed at the yard. This was the same army post where I had been detained three years earlier. At that time, I was an unwilling detainee. Now I was a willing part of it.

Because I was serving with DINA, a part of Operation Condor, and a friend of Spencer, I had become part of Contreras' close circle. According to Spencer, Contreras thought I was a good man to have around and liked my willingness to listen. Contreras disliked Michael, who naively thought he was close to Contreras. More than once, Contreras had expressed his disapproval of Michael's performance on the Prats issue. According to Spencer, since the deaths of Prats and his wife, Contreras had distanced himself from Michael. The only thing that kept Michael within the Contreras circle was the general's soft spot for Maria, Michael's wife.

Maria, a loyalist to the Pinochet regime in her own rights, was becoming an accomplished writer, and in the Chilean culture, writers, along with poets, enjoyed special recognition. Pablo Neruda, a world-famous Chilean poet and a Communist leader, had been a paradoxical example of culture values; he had been hated by the political right, and at the same time, he had been loved and venerated by them.

Maria, in the same respect, was hated by the leftists but also had a special place in their sense of values — she was a writer after all, and writers were a special sort of people.

Back in 1975, Colonel Manuel Contreras was next to Pinochet, the most feared and hated man in Chile. He had strengthened his position when the assistant deputy director had urged the State Department to invite Contreras to Washington, D.C., to meet the high officials of the State Department and members of President Ford's cabinet.

I could not help from grinning at the very thought of it. Contreras had achieved a greater status than Pinochet, whose request to visit Washington had been declined by the State Department. Contreras had not requested to visit Washington but had been invited by the State Department.

When Contreras had visited Washington, he was on a special mission: The military secret services of the countries of the Southern Cone (mainly Chile, Argentina, Paraguay, and Uruguay) were converging to form an alliance to eliminate Marxism and communism by all means necessary. Contreras had then convinced key people in Congress and within the State Department that an alliance of the countries of the Southern Cone against Marxism was essential to the interest of the United States and a recognizable deterrent to the expansion of the Soviet Union in the Americas.

On one occasion, Spencer and I attended a meeting with Contreras and other members of DINA. Contreras was very candid in expressing that Operation Condor would not acknowledge its existence to the American people, but it had the full support of President Ford, CIA Director George Bush, and Kissinger. Operation Condor was to be financed by the Americans, and the countries involved were to communicate with each other via telex through the Panama Canal Zone.

On this cold morning of July, as I reflected on these past events, I shivered with the intense coldness. I did not like being so cold, but at the same time it was a welcomed protective blanket. It seemed to slow down my thought processing. The thoughts were concise, to the point, and clearing my frame of mind.

My eyes focused on the water falling on the concrete floor. It froze at the touch of the concrete. I could not help but wonder about the differences one may find in similar settings at different places in the world. In Nam, the rain came with hot suffocating temperatures, and at times one could not tell the difference between being soaked by the rain or by your own sweat.

Here in Santiago at the foot of the Andes Mountains, the rain could be as cold as the Andes itself. Except for the people, the situations in Nam and Chile were just about the same — rain, wetness, uniforms, instruments of death everywhere, including oneself, and the awareness that somewhere in the shadows the enemy lurked ready to strike at any time. The difference was the temperature. In Chile the Andes made the difference — cold, indifferent, and always majestic. Towering above the city, the Andes stood impassive, naked to that intense blue. Its whiteness spoke of pureness, which made it distant, far away from us, not to be disturbed. Its majestic forms reaching the skies would not be bothered by the likes of us — pitiful, insignificant creatures full of a sick wanting and carrying this sickness to our own graves with a degree of proud accomplishment as if we were the blossom of greatness.

Now I was just like the rest of them, justifying revenge as if it were a sort of accomplishment in bringing justice to my pain. The wrongness of a few seemed to have given me a sort of achievement in cutting other lives short. Inside of me I knew that this was no achievement at all. What was driving me was a sense of warped justice, to eliminate those who had caused the death of Anne.

If once I had distaste for the Marxists and Communists, now I had a consuming hatred toward them. I was another Spencer. I was part of his world, constantly living at the edge of uncertainty, of madness. Every day was the same — always seeking a just answer to a question that seemed unanswerable, not realizing that I already knew the answer. The truth was there, but I had chosen to be blinded by my feeling of revenge. People die every day. Death was part of life. Anne's death should not have been any different. Death was expected to come upon us any time, unexpectedly.

In these stormy dark times, I also had moments of spiritual awareness that come to most men. In these moments of reflection, I wondered about myself. Really I had no excuse. I was fully aware of my wrongness, and yet I had this madness justifying my actions even though I knew that Anne would have not approved at all.

At times during and after the war, I had been touched by this sickness, a distorted wanting to get even. Even for what? I had asked myself that question, but it had also brought on self-examination, which had eased my troubled mind. I usually came out of such thoughts bordering on irrationality, but as for now? Hell, I could care less. Those bastards had to die, especially those who were in charge. There had to be some kind of retribution for Anne's and my baby girl's deaths.

But there was also Fuentes, who had died a horrible death at Villa Grimaldi at the hands of Michael and the biochemist Eugenio Berrios. Fuentes' voice was also calling for justice in a world filled with silence. Spencer had voiced his displeasure to Contreras when he learned that Fuentes had been covered with sores caused by a malignant virus that Dr. Berrios had been using to get information from him, but Spencer's protest was never acknowledged. And most recently was the untimely deaths of those two young Jehovah's Witnesses, which many times had turned my dreams into nightmares. I sensed their deaths had bothered Spencer for he was still waiting from Argentina for some sort of answer from Martinez.

It was at this time that I sensed that Spencer was not an ordinary operative, and I ventured to think that he now occupied the place of James. Contreras started giving Spencer several of DINA's missions, which prompted Spencer to rely only on a handful of agents, most of them Chileans and some Americans whom until then I had never met even though they had been in Chile longer than I had. Lately I had also been seeing the rise of Spencer within DINA's structure, especially in Operation Condor, where now he seemed to lead and control all affairs.

I was also impressed with the degree of loyalty that the Chileans themselves had toward Spencer. This was noticeable in a meeting we had recently when a colonel attached to Condor made the comment that if Contreras did not like the way Condor was conducting its business, Condor should flush Contreras down the toilet. Those listening broke in laughter to the comment that could have meant death for the colonel, but Spencer remained silent. Instead he grinned and continued unperturbed with the business of the day. There was no doubt in my mind that he was fully in charge of Condor. The following day, the colonel who had made the derogatory comment about Contreras was found dead, and no one wondered why.

Absorbed in my thoughts, I did not immediately notice the young face of a soldier offering me a cup of coffee. It seemed that he had been there longer than I had been there, longer than I would have liked him to have been.

Since Anne's death, I had noticed changes in my personality. One of these was that I did not care for anyone to just look at me without a word being spoken, especially when I was not aware. I became annoyed by the sight of the soldier, but seeing his smile, I smiled back and told myself several times to let it go, that it was not that important.

As I was about to take a sip of coffee, I noticed Spencer and an officer, probably a general, coming toward me. Spencer introduced him as General

Larios, a close friend of Contreras. I had seen him on several occasions, but I had never formally been introduced to him. I had heard that he enjoyed torturing prisoners and that he had introduced the "tunnel" at the stadium. In the tunnel, prisoners were seemingly given the opportunity to live, but none survived the ordeal. At the exit of the tunnel, Larios would be there to put a bullet in their heads. The prisoners had to run between two columns of soldiers with branding rifles. They would beat them up as they ran between them, presumably to safety; but in all cases, they were shot at the end of the ordeal. Two years earlier God had been kind to me for I had somehow been spared from going through the tunnel.

The thought of God intervening on my behalf now added uncertainty to my thinking for I had never thought of Him as being real, and lately this awareness was there too often to be ignored, and it was bothering me.

Both men were in good spirits and invited me to join them in an office in of the barracks. There were some other officers and two civilians I recognized as undercover agents. One of them was a sort of likable fellow called Clavel, who had joined some of us when we raided a compound in Concepcion and had been with us at the raid in Buenos Aires. Spencer had also told me that Clavel was with Michael when Prats had been killed.

Spencer passed me some papers that had a list of names of the Chilean resistance who had been recently eliminated in Argentina, Paraguay, and Uruguay — a total of 325 names. The names of those who had escaped from Chile to those countries and were still alive were under a column listed as pending. The list had been sent by SIDE, and it was addressed to Contreras and signed by General Otto Paladino.

The other list was from DINA, and it was being sent to SIDE with the names of the Argentineans who had been executed in Chile. The list came from different military enclaves — mostly from the Santiago zone — and it was signed by Contreras.

Recently Operation Condor had killed a prized item in Buenos Aires: Juan Jose Torres, the former president of Bolivia. Torres, after being ousted from power by a military coup, had been exiled to Argentina, where he had formed a leftist resistance group. DINA and SIDE would not tolerate the intrusion, and Condor ordered the liquidation of the former president.

I knew that Spencer had been part of the group that had executed Torres. When returning from Buenos Aires, Spencer had given me a simple statement to send to Panama via telex: "Minus El Cholo" — a derogatory Chilean term for a Bolivian.

As in the past, I knew we were not working entirely for the CIA. The death of Torres was not entirely backed by the CIA; it was not the policy of the United States to directly seek or order the assassination of any foreign leader. However if necessity demanded some assassinations, the United States would indirectly approved it. Panama seemed to be the only proper place to send classified information. Where was the information channeled to? I could only guess, and I would not ask Spencer. The assassination of Jose Torres seemingly was strictly a Condor operation.

Spencer told me that Enriquez, another leader of MIR, had been confirmed to have been executed in Argentina. MIR was no longer considered a threat to the internal security of Chile, but there were still some subversive cells operating in Europe and Mexico that required attention.

At the end of the meeting, Spencer took me aside and gave me a leather binder, which he told me to take with me. I opened the binder and glanced at the information inside. Seeing the startled look on my face, Spencer grinned at me and said, "It is signed by Contreras with the approval of His Excellency." He then proceeded to tell me that we were to meet with Contreras soon to go over the details of the planning.

Larios came to join us to let us know that Michael had flown to Miami to seek some help from the Cubans on neutralizing the Cuban influence in Buenos Aires. He made the comment that Castro needed to be taught a lesson and take his boys home. Condor was not going to allow Castro to set foot in the countries of the Southern Cone.

"We'll use the bastard this time," Spencer commented, and Larios laughed. I knew Spencer was referring to Michael.

Soon the meeting ended, and Larios invited Spencer and me over for a drink at the Carreras Hotel, where I was staying. I offered Spencer to stay at my place overnight because it was getting too late to go to Valparaiso, but Spencer had other plans and declined my offer. I was to meet him at Valparaiso the coming weekend.

On the way to the hotel, I kept to myself most of the time, and I commented only once in a while on some of the things that they were talking about — the first page of the papers in the binder kept flashing in my mind with intensity and clarity. The assignment was about Orlando Letelier, the former Chilean defense minister, a man that not only the Chilean government wanted dead but had been marked by Spencer as an unwanted liability.

Letelier was now on the agenda of Operation Condor. The implications that a Letelier assassination would bring were enormous, and I doubted it had the stamp of approval of the State Department. Our American image at home and abroad was tainted already, and it had suffered enough bad publicity. To kill Letelier was insane, but the coup of 1973 had also been an act of madness, and it had the approval of the American government.

I realized the assassination of Letelier in Washington, D.C, would have further ramifications and would cut deep into the American national sense of patriotism. It would undoubtedly bring the wrath of the people upon those who had dared the violation of their country. The idea of an assassination in the United States capital ordered by a foreign power was beyond reason. The American people would not accept the violation of their land, and the American government as a whole would reject a terrorist attack within its borders. It would not stand the violation of its sovereignty. Operation Letelier was a daring mission that, without a doubt in my mind, would bring deadly consequences upon those who would dare participate, including myself for I was part of Condor.

Putting aside my thoughts on this grave matter, I read the memo. Letelier was to be assassinated at his residence in Washington, D.C., at the very steps of the White House. It would be the first time in the history of the United States that a foreign power would dare to intrude on its sovereignty. Condor had decided to penetrate the skies of the American eagle in search of its prey, and it was not going to be stopped in its deadly flight.

However, the assassination of Letelier could be stopped if the world press got hold of valid information to that effect. The Chilean government that was desperately seeking world recognition of its legitimacy and was fully examining all avenues toward appeasement would have to reconsider its intentions and halt the assassination of Letelier. The State Department would not approve of the violation of the United States' sovereignty, no matter how detestable Letelier was to its diplomatic menu.

I was now in possession of vital, valid information that could stop the assassination of Letelier, and it had to be soon — before Condor would extend its wings. If I were to be found out, it would mean my death. But this time my death would be just retribution for the many lives so senselessly lost in an act of revenge that should have never been. Anne and my Ruth would have never wanted it. I had to stop the assassination of Letelier.

Part IX

August was passing — fast, furious, and as other months, bloody. September was pressing hard on the same path. Anticipating the death of Letelier, I could feel September's suffocating, heavy breathing, just like in 1973. The Chilean September of 1973, though smaller in its number of victims, had been as bloody as September of 1792, when thousands of royalists were killed in Paris during the French Revolution. I could not help from fearing September — it was a bloody month. President Salvador Allende had been killed on September 11, 1973. Was it not in September of 1974 when General Prats had been assassinated by DINA? I was not sure; it could have been. Now Letelier was on September's agenda.

I did not consider Letelier an item needed on the menu of Condor, but others thought it was essential for the good of Chile. Pinochet wanted him dead, and so Contreras and Spencer saw it as part of the equation of differences, and Letelier, in his ledger, made the difference.

Operation Condor was ravaging its prey. Just recently at the start of August, Condor had given Castro a bloody nose, and there was nothing Castro could do. A CIA operative told me that Michael and his Cuban buddies had done away with some of Castro's diplomats in Buenos Aires. Later I was to learn that actually Spencer had done the job.

A CIA agent codenamed Rusty who had been helping us became another casualty. He had been removed from Operation Condor and handed over by DINA to the CIA station. He was now considered missing because the station did not acknowledge Rusty on its roster. Rusty was in his early forties and was a well-seasoned operative. I sort of liked him, but in the business in which we were involved, friendship did not matter. Had DINA or the CIA done away with him? No one would ever know except the killer.

Spencer briefed me on the Rusty situation. Rusty was a mole planted by the CIA inside Operation Condor, implying that the agency did not fully trust Spencer and me. It was unofficially the general understanding within the agency and DINA that those inside Operation Condor were not to report to the CIA station in Santiago. Rusty had broken this understanding, and DINA had not taken kindly to this breach of trust. Operation Condor had no dealings with the American Embassy or those who would inform the American State Department of Condor's activity. Spencer had made that clear to all of us CIA operatives within DINA.

According to Spencer, at the beginning of August, Rusty had informed the CIA's local station about the Letelier operation. Consequently, the CIA station had informed the State Department, and now Kissinger was fully aware of the plot to kill Letelier. It was a political comedy with an impending tragic end of which the State Department, the CIA, and Ambassador Popper had already been aware. Kissinger had been informed several months prior to August that Condor was planning to strike outside the Southern Cone countries. Spencer put it very candidly by saying it was a world of pretenses. The problem was that the CIA had sent a cable, and now there was a paper trail that could in time be damaging to the State Department, the CIA, and DINA. In all probabilities, DINA had done away with Rusty, leaving the CIA holding the bag.

"Leave it to the CIA, and they'll screw up everything," Spencer commented. "As we see, no movement from the State Department, the CIA, or from Popper. DINA sees no reason not to go ahead with the operation. We must act quickly, however, before someone changes his mind."

Spencer also pointed out that it was possible that the State Department and the CIA thought that the enormity of the plot would dissuade Pinochet and Contreras from executing the plan, hoping that at the last minute there would be a change of mind that would end Operation Letelier. Kissinger and the CIA could also interfere once the killers left the country and bring the whole operation to a halt. The United States government would not allow an attack on D.C. Therefore, it was imperative that Condor would have no delays in its flight to the north.

The month of September had now been awakened with Operation Condor on the move. The killing of Letelier was several weeks into its process, and neither the State Department nor the CIA had made any move to approach DINA or Pinochet. The field for Condor to land was spacious and open; its destination was Washington, D.C.

At Spencer's insinuation, Contreras sent two of DINA's agents to Asuncion to get Paraguayan passports to travel to the States. Michael had already been dispatched to New York to pave the path for the rest of the assassins.

Spencer thought that the departure from Santiago of two DINA agents to the States could raise some suspicion at the American Embassy that could alert the State Department. The avenue for the assassins was to be through Paraguay, being that the Stroessner's government was a close ally of Pinochet. Spencer thought that the CIA would close in on Santiago but not Asuncion because Santiago was the obvious point of departure for Operation Condor.

The intensity and stress of the operation were taking a toll on me to the point that at times I wanted no part of it, and yet I was still in the midst of it. Staying inside the operation was necessary for I needed to know as much as I could so I could have concrete evidence to bring Operation Condor in Washington, D.C., to a halt. It was ironic to me that those in power in Washington who had helped to create Operation Condor remained aloof while their underlings were trying to prevent Condor from flying outside of the Southern Cone's perimeter. Unless a direct order came from Kissinger, the CIA in Chile was to be rendered incapable to stop Operation Condor.

I could not help but wonder about the mental states of Kissinger and Bush, who I felt were fully aware of what was transpiring. It was all right for them to eliminate human beings inside Chile, but it was against their policy to kill them outside its borders. Now Letelier was in the picture, and seemingly they were indecisive on what to do with him. In my mind from what I could gather, they were fully aware that Condor was on the move to kill Letelier.

Since the beginning of the plan to kill Letelier, I noticed that Spencer was keeping more to himself. He had personally approached Contreras on taking over the plot to kill Letelier, and as days passed by, I noticed the changes in his personality. Instead of his normal, easygoing personality, he was now somewhat distant. It was as if he wanted to separate himself from the rest of us. At the same time, he would ask me to stick around in case he needed me. He made it obvious that he did need me.

There was no doubt in my mind that the death of the general and his wife, Sofia, had left an unfinished issue inside Spencer's mind. The death of Anne had probably added more weight to his determination to kill Letelier — and to some degree the killing of the two Argentinian kids added weight as well. Although he had killed the girl in cold blood, the aftermath of the incident in which he found them not to be subversives had bothered him. If the girl had been a leftist, he could justify it in his warped sense of justice, but because she was not a Communist, it had bothered him for he could not justify it to himself. In the case of the Prats, he felt guilty because he could have prevented Sofia's death by killing Don Carlos himself.

Reflecting on these events, I could not come to terms with the common denominator that was driving Spencer on killing Letelier because all these past deaths were of our own doing. The Communists were not involved. All I could see was that he was using them as more wood to increase the fire that had been set to eliminate the Marxists at any cost.

I knew Spencer considered Letelier to be someone who could make the difference in Chile's future, and for that reason alone he had to be eliminated. However, Spencer's total dedication to the project seemed to trespass Letelier's importance in the operation. I sensed that something greater was lurking in the background of the operation, maybe more sinister than carrying out Letelier's death itself.

Once I asked him why we were spending so much time on the planning of the operation because we well knew that a dependable agent could do the job by just going to Washington and place a bullet in Letelier's head. It could be a simple job, and it would leave no traces of any kind. He looked at me in a thoughtful way and just said, "Precisely my friend. You are absolutely right." He then continued with his work.

He feverishly considered each point in the planning as to give the assassins ample room to succeed. He disliked Michael and the Cubans, who were in the front of the assignment, and he could have easily channeled the operation to failure. But at the same time, he was clearing the path for them to execute the assignment with a high degree of success. It was evident to me that he wanted them to succeed in something that I, now more than ever, wanted to be stopped. But how could I stop the assassination?

At this point, the urge to stop the Letelier assassination and get out of the organization was gaining momentum in my mind. The constant faces of my Anne, Julia, Mario, the kids, Frank, and most recently the deaths of the two Argentinian youths were pressing hard, leaving me no alternative but to consider a definite way out, and it had to be done soon. Knowing that I was part of the plot to kill Letelier was eroding my sanity. Retribution for my Anne's death had been completely wrong, and now it called for an offering of a different value, which could end my life. As I thought about it, I found it ironic. Placing my life as an atonement to my sin had come at a time when I also wanted to live and go back home. The house in Idyllwild was still there, and her parents were in need of my help.

I was weighed down by my conscience and the thought of what Anne would have said if she had been alive. My reluctance to inflict pain on others and refusing to be part of any more killing and my deep desire to take to the altar of Anne's and my baby girl's remembrances a different kind of offering led me to tell Spencer that the time had come for me to leave the agency. I was to resign from the CIA as soon as Letelier's deal was over.

He listened attentively to what I had to say. At times he moved his head downward in an agreeing manner, but he did not respond. Instead he asked me to help him with some of the details of the operation not yet finished. As I knew him well, his lack of response did not bother me. Instead I chose to leave the subject alone, knowing that in due time he would give me his advice.

Toward the end of August, Spencer stayed at my place for several days planning every aspect of the operation. The geography of the location of Letelier's home on Sheridan Drive in Washington, D.C., was important. The weather on this particular day was also important because the killers had to walk to the residence. Letelier usually would leave for work between 8:00 A.M. and 9:00 A.M.

There had to be more corroboration about who could be with him. Until now we knew that his children went to school earlier so there was no need for him to drop them at school. It was extremely important to avoid a situation like the one with General Prats and his wife, Sofia, and that fact came straight from Pinochet himself. Also it was imperative that Michael would plant the bomb underneath the car himself, for this was strictly a Condor 1 operation, and DINA wanted the credit.

Since the moment that I learned Michael and his Cuban buddies had been chosen to carry out Operation Letelier and not us, I was very relieved. The idea of committing to an assassination inside the United States border was foreign to my thinking, something that Spencer and I had discussed several times.

The breaking of the United States sovereignty was an issue for both of us; it did imply treason. At length we had engaged in conversations regarding the recent role of the CIA in the Watergate affair that had brought down top officials of the agency — not necessarily for the crime itself but because Congress prohibited the agency from operating inside the United States. Spencer seemed to have agreed on the principles involved, but he was determined to get Letelier or accomplish his real reason to carry the operation to its finish; there was no stopping his determination.

Spencer and I were not to execute the operation. That part of the operation was left to Michael, the Cubans, and two of DINA's agents. Though we were not direct participants in the act of the crime itself, we were just as guilty for being a part of it. At the final phase of the operation's planning, Spencer made it clear to me that except for himself and me, those Americans who were part of Operation Letelier were not to be told about the final details of the mission.

Knowing of my earlier reluctance to be participant of the operation, he did not get me involved directly with DINA's operational staff but kept me informed of what was transpiring at DINA's headquarters. Once in a while he would go over the details of the planning with me. He wondered aloud if President Ford would hear the bomb being detonated. Knowing the location of Sheridan Drive, I ventured to guess that the White House was within range of a loud sound coming from the distance that I had estimated to be around ten miles.

"If I am right and the wind is blowing in the right direction, the president and Kissinger are going to have a tough time digesting their breakfasts on that day," I said.

He grinned, and his steel-bluish eyes gleamed. "It serves them right, and don't forget our boss, but more so the whole damned government," he said, placing the documents in his brief case as he got ready to leave.

Just before reaching for the door, he turned and looked at me. I was still sitting across the desk, playing with a pencil in my fingers, and at that moment before he had said a word, I knew that he had planned the whole operation not just to eliminate Letelier but to get back at our own government for something which was not yet clear to me.

"Yes John, you have guessed correctly. Don't you know that I always could read your mind? Am I wrong in saying that you have some suspicion that it was not just Letelier's death in this ordeal?" he asked as he placed the briefcase down and sat on the chair across the desk. I looked down at the desk without a response and waited for him to continue.

"Yeah, you know me too well. It is not just Letelier but Washington," I said, breaking the silence. "You know well that this hit on Letelier is also a hit on the seat of our government. In the history of our nation, no one has dared commit an act of terrorism of this nature. Have you thought of the implication? Why this sudden change in your loyalty to the country we swore an oath to defend?"

"This is true, my dear friend. We went over this question more than once. I remember you many times cursing the government," he responded and paused for a moment. "The question we ask ourselves is: What happens when the government no longer represents its people? Do you really think that for the sake of security and comfort the American people in general would give their blessing to the senseless spilling of foreign blood? Or is it that American blood is better than the rest of the people on earth?"

I looked at him questioningly. For seconds I found myself questioning his loyalty to the sovereignty of the United States of America. But the questioning did not go any further. This was Spencer, an American, a marine whom I had seen so many times risking his life as he ventured into enemy fire to recover a fellow fallen American soldier. He typified the John Waynes, the Audie Murphys, the Davy Crocketts, and the George Pattons, the essence of the American soldiers of Iwo Jima, Guadalcanal, and the Ardennes. Name it, and he would have been there doing his share. He was a true American.

"You asked me about the implications of this job. I have also asked myself the same questions," he said, looking straight into my eyes. "At first we are going to feel the whole weight of the American wrath. The CIA will be told to eliminate us, and DINA will have to come up with an answer. I told you earlier John; this will be the first reaction of the American people and, of course, the government. But in time, the people will put it aside, and generations years from now will forget what happened in D.C. on September 26, 1976. Do you know why? It's because the people do not trust our government; they never did."

We looked at each other for a while in complete silence as if we were contemplating a passing moment that would not be easily erased from our memories. "Not just our people, most people in the world distrust their own government," I said. "There will never be a perfect government. Our imperfection as human beings will not allow it."

"There is one option left, my friend," he said. Seeing my expression of puzzlement, he added, "The messianic kingdom of Jesus Christ."

"The…the what?" I responded with some surprise in the tone of my voice for I had never expected that sort of statement from him. But I recalled his knowledge of the Bible. Anne had talked to me about that kingdom, which at that time had seemed more fictional than reality. I also had in mind that those two youngsters preached the messianic kingdom, but at this moment I chose to show my ignorance on the matter.

"The messianic kingdom — Jesus was the Messiah or the Liberator prophesied by the prophets of the Jews. He was to be the One who would liberate them from the Roman yoke. But in reality the Messiah came not to just liberate them alone but the whole of mankind from sin," he responded.

I kept my eyes on him, trying to figure him out. At times he could be a very complex individual. I knew he was not a religious man, but he did have knowledge of the Bible.

"What does Jesus have to do with our government or any government?" I asked.

I felt his eyes on me as if he was studying me, probing into my mind. "Sometimes I don't really know what to think of you, my friend. You are a well-educated man. The obvious, however, which does not escape the ordinary man does seem to escape your attention," he said as if he was gently scolding me. "Perhaps it's the lack of religion in your life. Maybe you if you had listened to your wife you would probably understand."

His words found a sensitive part in me. I looked at him resentfully, and as I met his eyes, I found my own conscience staring at me. He knew me too well. "I never took you as a religious man, my friend," I responded. "Anyway what is this messianic kingdom that you are referring to?"

My own response cut me deeper for I was denying something that, more than once, Anne had told me about. She had told me at length about God's kingdom on the earth. I had been too involved in my personal quest for retribution that I had seemingly forgotten what was important to her, and now in defending myself I was denying that kingdom.

Also there were those two youngsters who for some reason or another had hung on to their Bibles to the very end. I knew that this denial came from my rejection of a loving God who I believed could have prevented the killing of Anne and Ruth. God had not protected them, nor the Argentinian teenagers. When I returned to the States for Anne's service though, Carl and Mary Morris had taken time to comfort me and had presented me with a God that had nothing to do with Anne's death. At the time, it did little for me, and I rejected the idea of a loving God. Now I was still in denial of the Bible itself, though something very deep inside of me was telling me that it was the truth.

"According to the Bible, Jesus Christ will return to the world of mankind and will rule the earth for one thousand years. This period is known as the messianic kingdom of Jesus Christ. His kingdom will destroy all earthly governments," he said. Showing no emotion at all — more like stating a fact — he added, "That's what those two Jehovah's Witness kids were preaching the day they were killed."

"You don't really believe that. Jesus Christ could have established His kingdom when he was here on earth, not after being dead for two thousand years," I responded. Again my own response reflected denial, and it hurt because Anne had looked forward to this promise, and it was real to her and also was very real to those young Witnesses whose death weighed heavily on me.

"That is where you are wrong, John," he responded. "Jesus Christ for some people is very much alive. Some are convinced that He will come and establish a government of his own, a theocratic government."

"I don't see how people can think that way. Jesus is dead. And that is that… dead," I responded on the border of conviction for inside I was not so sure. Anne thought it that way too, and I wanted to be under that sort of government. We humans already had through the centuries tried out all types of governments, and we had failed miserably.

He did not answer and drew a faint smile, sort of a grin. At that moment, he could be measuring me as a fool or as a well-educated bastard. I was not sure. But I was sure that any measurements of his were accurate. I was a fool, a fool for bringing my Anne to this forsaken cruel land. A fool for denying what had been dear to her. A fool for not being part of that hope of hers.

Still with that faint smile, Spencer leaned toward me as if he was to share a secret. It was his usual gesture, a way to change the direction of the conversation. "We both have, in some ways, reservations about this deal. That is why I told Contreras that Michael was the man to carry out the elimination of Letelier, though he is a screw up. Michael dwells in recognition, and his specialty is blowing things up. As far as I am concerned, he pledged his allegiance to Chile. He is not an American, period. Contreras did not want him on this operation, but I convinced him that since it was a DINA operation that it was proper for Michael to execute the operation. After all, he is on DINA's payroll."

"I appreciate that you kept me out of the execution of the planning. But now tell me, after this is all over, not just the Letelier thing but the assignment in Chile, what then? What are you going to do? I am leaving, but what about you? Does anything come to mind?" I asked.

He did not respond and grinned. After a brief moment of silence, he thoughtfully said, "I don't really know. Maybe if the agency gives me an assignment to my liking I could give it a try. Would I go back to the States? No! Right now, with the Soviets in the Middle East, I could be of help to my Arab friends. I have some close ties with the Saudis and the Yemenis. I don't really know. Time will tell." He paused for several seconds and added, " Now before

I leave, I want to let you know that I have been thinking about your decision to leave the agency. Be extremely careful. I do not want you to become another Rusty. I will help you. You can be sure that I will help you. When you leave, never look back. Always remember that anyone of us could kill you."

We held our eyes level with each other for some time. He was right. I thought about the incident at the park. I always thought that it had been done by a subversive, but it could have been ordered by our own people. I had heard it before, and now it was right in front of me. At this time, those who had left the organization had been targeted for elimination.

"If the order came to you, would you…?" I asked him.

"The order did once come to me…but I failed," he responded and waited for my reaction. My reaction was one of denial. The incident at the park where I had been shot had occurred while Spencer was out of the country, prior to General Prats' death. It could not have been him because I knew that he was out of the country. James had confirmed it. Or…was he?

Seeing my puzzled expression, he asked me to calm down and listen. He proceeded to tell me that when he was told to eliminate Prats and he had sent me to Percil to find an excuse to avoid the assignment, that he had never left Chile. Instead he had gone south to the resort town of Villarrica where he had spent time fishing. Actually Percil had received my message on the swallow trying to fly north, but it never happened. Sir Percil and James had accentuated the lie by giving me the impression that Spencer had left the country.

It was at this time of deception that Spencer had received the order to kill me, and just like any other businessman, he had proceeded with the program. As Spencer put it, it was a necessity to seal his loyalty to the agency. Perhaps someone above wanted to put Spencer's loyalty to the test. Again he had misguided me into believing he had left the country. I was not upset; on the contrary, I was somewhat taken by the intrigue and suspense of the ordeal.

I managed a smile; his revelation made me feel good. To miss at that distance on purpose, it could have come only from him. No other agent could have missed, except for him. He was an extraordinary marksman.

"How did you explain your failure?" I asked.

"I was kidded about it. But that evening there was another agent with me who swore I had killed you. He was the one who drove the car where you laid down. I knew that you were alive, but he did not. He swore he saw you dead. And it was accepted as a lucky break."

"Why was I targeted?" I asked.

"You knew too much, and you were too loud. It didn't sit well with some of our people," he responded

"Were you told to do it again?" I asked.

"No. Someone changed his mind. Lucky break for me," he said.

"I asked you before: What about now? What may happen to me?"

"It is not a question of maybe. What will happen to you is for sure. Most likely they won't ask me this time. It could be anyone. So do not trust anyone. When you leave, just leave. Don't put your resignation in as other fools have done and end up somewhere in a ditch. I will help you back to the States or Europe. I will furnish you with another identity. There are thousands of our fallen buddies willing to give another marine a helping hand," he said in a reassuring way. "I will give you a complete rundown on the new identity that you will be taking. Once you have made it your own, destroy it. Just give me a few days."

His word gave me a new insight into a possible better outcome for my future. He was right, and that was something that I had in the back of my mind. Joining the CIA had been easy, but leaving it had turned into a dilemma, especially for operatives like me who were always at the edges of clandestine field work. I thanked him. I held his hand. I knew that this would probably be the last time we would really be this close.

I realized at this moment that this was the opportune time to ask the question about Pudahuel. Looking at him, I asked, "Spencer, was Pudahuel a MIR operation, a DINA, or a CIA operation? I need to know this. I must know this. All I know now is that the target was James, and Anne was a victim of circumstances. I need to know the truth."

"It was a combined CIA and DINA operation. James was a liability, and he had to be eliminated. The chief station here at Santiago was kept out," he said. He turned the chair slightly and fixed his eyes on the empty wall. Suddenly he seemed to withdraw into himself. He buried his head into his hands and muttered something, and for the longest moment, he just stared at the floor. I could tell he was very perturbed. When he finally gained some composure, he managed to say that he was deeply sorry for what had happened to Anne.

When he looked at me, his eyes were on the verge of tears, and I felt pity for him. I knew he had loved her very much. In this intense moment, I felt that he was vindicated as far as I was concerned. There was now no doubt in my mind that he had been part of the Pudahuel attack. Silence, as in the past, was now speaking, and that silence was more explanatory than any words could be.

He extended his hand and grabbed my arm and told me what had occurred. He himself was a CIA man, but he was also part of a team of special forces operating inside the CIA. They had received orders from their headquarters at Panama. I had been right all along; the CIA was a very complex world of cells within cells. At times these cells worked together, ready to eliminate each other for the interest of their own group. He would not give me any specifics, but I felt that it was probably army or Marine Corps special forces and yet still CIA.

The orders to eliminate James had come directly from Washington to them — not from the CIA headquarters itself, though it was some sort of a mutual understanding between them that James had to be eliminated. James, who had recently brought to Washington damaging evidence of American involvement in the torture and killing of Chilean subversives, had become a liability to the whole American secret spectrum and had to be killed. This was a stunning revelation. No one inside the secret service was to be spared by elements of the American high military command who would consider them to be a liability to the nation, and the CIA was no exception.

The plan was to execute the operation as a MIR hit due to the fact that several weeks earlier, MIR elements had attacked a military compound and taken some rocket launchers, which were recovered shortly after. The launcher was useful because the CIA used this as a disguise to put the blame on MIR. Unknown to Spencer, who had directed the operation, Anne was a passenger on the plane that was bringing James to Santiago. James was aware of Anne's presence on the flight and had probably offered a ride to our place. This was evident because the car had been blown up at the gates of Pudahuel.

"You know well that if I had only known that she was in the car, I would have aborted the whole thing. I had no way of knowing that she was in the car. We knew that there would be the driver and one of James' people, and all of them were expendable." He stopped talking as tears ran shamelessly down his cheeks, and it did move me for I had never seen him in tears. "If I had only known, John," he continued. "There have been so many times that I have asked the same question, over and over. I know well that to you — and it is true — at times I can be a calculating cold killer, and I cannot deny that, but Anne?...Never Anne! I loved her as much as I love you. I looked at her as a younger sister, and I always made sure that she knew how much I cared about her...and then when I learned that she was carrying a child...I just cannot tell you how sorry I am, " he said frantically in a despairing way.

"I know you too well, Spencer," I said, lowering my eyes. His burst of emotion had touched me for I knew well that he was not the emotional type. "There is no need for more recrimination. It happened, and maybe that is why I can no longer stay here. Maybe what happened to Anne is just retribution for all the damage I have done in this country. Not just the killing I have done working for the CIA, but before in the diplomatic field. It was us, the ones who created this mess in Chile, and I am guilty in the spilling of so much blood, so much suffering."

For several moments, we kept silent and looked at each other, trying to find something that could hold us to a place of understanding. I knew now that Spencer was the Gringo whom Fuentes had spoken about and perhaps the Gringo who agreed with the killing of Charles, but at this time I felt there was no need to ask any more questions.

"You asked me earlier, why I am turning against our government, why I am so determined to hit the heart of the government in Washington. You just said it, retribution…just retribution," he said, gaining some ease of composure.

After a brief pause, he continued. "I tried for years to justify our presence on foreign soil and the motives for American intervention on the politics of other countries. Even when I saw with my own eyes the callousness…the lack of concern for human lives…the abandonment of our soldiers by our government.…I always figured that it was just part of the puzzle, that somewhere there was the positive that would justify these negatives. I accepted my role as a necessary tool to achieve something greater for the national interest. At the same time, I was fully aware that I was not fighting for freedom and country — those things are not valid excuses when we are killing people in their own country. There were many occasions when I listened to you talking about things that I did not agree to it, but in those instances I could not afford to agree with you. It was sort of a disguise that was, at least for me, necessary. I had to keep on pretending. Giving you the impression that the full-blooded all-American boy was still there, always ready to follow his government's call, no matter what."

He paused for a while as he looked at me, seemingly waiting for a response, but I chose to wait. "The States have the best armed forces in the world," he said. "But we have the worst kind of people in Washington directing the affairs of the country. From the president down to the smallest politician, there is nothing but lies, greed, and corruption of all sorts. Look at our agency. It is the most cold-blooded, corrupted entity in the entire earth, worse than the KGB. You were right; we are nothing more than a bunch of killers turned loose by our government to achieve self-gratification for large corporations." He stopped talking, and I could tell that this change of thoughts had been a result of his own convictions as a soldier, of integrity, of dedication to the good of the States, an integrity that he himself had proved in the battlefield.

"But then…" he said, "when you are there, and you see the waste of young American lives for the sake of raw material that benefits the very rich and the politicians who represent the large corporations…then you begin to wonder. Remember after we left Nam? What President Nixon did at the end of the war? He could have gained peace with Hanoi, but no, he let it go for two years so Hughes could sell his precious helicopters to the army. In doing so, he prolonged the war and another few thousand of our boys were killed. And what about the Tet Offensive in 1968? By then you had already left. Our own general betrayed us by not telling us that we were surrounded by a large force of Viet Regulars. We knew by just seeing the thousands of gooks killed that something was brewing, and the CIA sent several agents to Washington to give the information in person to President Johnson, but they were killed by our own people before they reached the president.

"Yeah. You told me that," I responded.

"The Viets could have easily overwhelmed us if it was not for our own guts and resolve not to give in. Some units were overrun, but at the end we defeated them. But there was something I never told you. It was at Dai Do, a village near the demilitarized zone, that did it for me. We were ambushed, and in no time I lost several dozens of my men. Though I had lost many of my men in others battles, Dai Do did it for me. My guess is that everyone has his limitation, and I had reached mine. No sooner afterward, I asked the agency to end my tour; by then I had been in Nam eight years, and I was taken out. The CIA itself at this time had concluded that it was not worth it for its operatives to stay there, and I came home. Home?… There was no home for the soldiers that were returning. I was lucky for I became a civilian immediately, and I returned to the States via Mexico. A year later I was sent here." He stopped talking and became thoughtful. He looked at me and drew a faint smile. "Letelier is only a sand pebble on the shoes of a giant. It will bother him for a while, but soon afterward these sand pebbles will be shaken off and roll on the sand dunes of time and remain forever silent. But to me John, what matters is that it did bother him for a few moments."

I could tell he had reached a point in his life that demanded some sort of answer that he could not find — except retribution to justify his own participation in the affairs of the government. He now saw the government as an evil entity, and not just the United States government but all the governments of the world. He reminded me that Condor was not born from the needs of the Chilean people but from the dictatorship of Pinochet and United States foreign policy.

Spencer felt he had become part of the program to undermine their destruction. He said Condor was a bird of prey and needed to be fed, this time by the same system that had created it. Condor was to attack the very seat of the American government, right in the heart of Washington, D.C.

After Spencer left, I was left with the uncertainty of what was transpiring. Nothing was certain except the killing of Letelier on September 26, exactly two weeks away. The State Department and the CIA were now fully aware that something was going to occur and had made no attempt to stop the operation, unless something in their validation of the situation was definite.

Although I had agreed with Spencer on most of his assertions of our government, I was not totally convinced that killing Letelier in Washington was the right thing to do. Now that I knew that the CIA and DINA had been directly responsible for killing Anne, I felt that a different kind of retribution was more in line with the killing of my wife. Avenging Anne was to deny Condor its prey. Spencer would definitely be upset, but he had also been part of it. Denying them their prey was good enough for me. I had to act now; there was no time left.

There was nothing I could do against the CIA — only an act of God would bring this monster down. This thought had a profound impact on me. Somewhere in my heart, I felt the need to seek the God that according to Anne was always close by. All I had to do was to find him. Maybe the death of those two youngsters had helped in seeking a God that promised another kind of government. Maybe Jesus Christ had the right agenda for humanity. Now the most important thing for me to do was to stop the killing of another human being. Letelier was not to die for the wants of Condor. If the State Department needed something definite to act and order the halting of Operation Letelier by Condor, then I would have to provide them with something definite. That definite act was something that I already knew, the exact date of the assassination. This would give the agency time to stop Operation Condor inside Condor's borders, unless the agency really wanted him dead.

Though convinced that nothing would at this time change my mind on sending a direct message to Washington, I still refrained from doing it, and days kept passing away without me acting on my conviction. But then something happened that broke down my hesitation.

One night after putting away some of Spencer's work and going through the routines of securing my room from the unexpected that could happen to any of us dwelling in the clandestine world, I found the bag containing the belongings of the boy killed in the raid in Argentina. It was in the far corner of the closet where I kept my clothing. I remembered that after returning to my place from the raid in Argentina, and not wanting to know more about him or maybe in an effort to detach myself from the reality of those moments, I threw it in the closet. I did not want to deal with his death and the death of the girl.

Several hours later lying in bed, I opened the bag and brought the boy's Bible out and read his name that he had written on the first page. His name was Fabian Morales. Paging through the Bible, I read all the scriptures that he had underlined. What got my attention was one particular verse that was tainted with his blood. It was Daniel 2:44 which read, "And in the days of those kings the God of Heaven will set up a kingdom that will never be brought to ruin. And the kingdom itself will not be passed on to any other people. I will crush and put an end to all these kingdoms and it itself will stand to times indefinite." This was exactly what Spencer had said and what my Anne was expecting — a government under the rulership of Jehovah the Almighty God and of his Son Jesus Christ.

Hours afterward I was still awake. The clock was going on 2:00 A.M. I wondered about those youngsters' parents. Were they still waiting for them though many months had already passed? Did they know that they were dead? Would I ever have the answer to why they were there? Jehovah's Witnesses had no politics, so they were no leftists or subversives. I had no idea at that moment that the answer would be waiting a few hours ahead. Sleep soon came and so too the awakening when Spencer came shortly after 8:00 A.M.

I had a hard time waking up and keeping awake afterward. Finally after drinking the coffee that Spencer had prepared, I was ready to take in the day's agenda. This morning he was easygoing, jovial, and seemingly happy and even spoke with feeling about Michael whom he disliked.

"I just hope he blows up with Letelier," he said in a jovial way. It was a heartfelt, expressed feeling for I knew he wished in the sense that the world would be better off without the likes of Michael.

He sat on a chair by the table and asked me to listen to a letter that Martinez had sent from Buenos Aires in which he wrote that Fabian and Aurora Fernandez were brother and sister and that they were young pioneers for the Jehovah's Witnesses. On the date of the raid, they were visiting a secretary who had shown a desire to know about what the Bible teaches, and it was known by their parents and other members of their congregation that they had visited the factory on several occasions prior to the raid to distribute their brochures. Since it was found by SIDE that they were definitely not subversives their bodies had been returned to their family, and reparations to the family had been made.

"I know that to you I am a cold, heartless killer, and to some extent you are quite right — that is the nature of our business — but you have to believe me that I felt bad about those two kids. If I had not killed the girl, the Argentinians thinking of her as an Uruguayan, they would had no pity on her, wounded as she was and young as she was. She would have been a fair prize, and she would have been raped, tortured, and killed. I had to kill her for I would not allow that to happen to her," he said, not showing any emotion at all. Then he added, as if their deaths were just a part of life, "You know I am glad that they were not Communists, and thinking about what they preach..."

Before he could finish, I said, "What are you thinking, Spencer? You talk as if the only thing that matters is that they weren't Communists. Can you see that they were young lives, human lives as well?"

He looked at me with reproach and said, "I told you more than once that you can never be like us, and I know that it was a mistake to bring you in. You do have a hard time dealing with the unexpected, and it should not be. Life is a journey filled with the unexpected; otherwise it would not be living. Think about how those two kids died preaching the theocratic government, and here both of us are also fighting against these governments. Who knows, maybe in sort of a way we are paving the way for God's government."

I looked at him in disbelief and replied, "I know that I am bad, but you are evil and profane. I think that you are out of your mind. God does not work his purpose by destroying people but by loving them."

He did not respond. Instead he drew a grin on his face and placed some paperwork on the table and went to work as if nothing had occurred. I kept my eyes on him for several moments — an aura of coolness and calmness seemed to engulf him. I went to my desk and went through some of my work, pretending normality while inside I was fighting for survival in the middle of a storm. After a while, I told him that I needed to go out for a walk. He nodded approvingly, and I left, telling myself that I had to do it soon. Operation Letelier had to be stopped....It had to be now.

Several days later, through a contact at the embassy, I managed to send a direct cable to Ryan, a deputy to the assistant secretary to Kissinger. The cable provided him with the exact date and hour of Letelier's hit — the specific thing they needed to stop Condor from landing at D.C. on September 26. The State Department now had six days to stop Condor.

In the early hours of the day after I had sent the cable, Spencer unexpectedly woke me up. It had to be extremely important for him to come to my room, which still was in darkness, to wake me up. He told me not to turn on the light and to keep quiet and get dressed.

Immediately sensing the urgency of the moment, I proceeded to get dressed. In the back of my mind, I knew that it had to do with the wire that I had sent to the State Department. Something had gone wrong. Had my cable been intercepted? He did not tell me anything nor did I ask questions.

Using a small flashlight, Spencer got a hold of Anne's picture that I kept on my dresser and pulled the picture from the frame. He put the picture inside an envelope he had with him. I could see that there were more papers inside the envelope. Spencer then told me to remain put and stepped outside the apartment. Moments later he returned with Clavel. Spencer told him to stay until morning and to get rid of or destroy anything pertinent to me and that if anyone from the agency or DINA came to tell them that he had been sent by Spencer to take me into custody.

Outside the apartment, he asked for my wallet and gave me another wallet, which contained my new identity and a large amount of money. Carefully we avoided the security of the building and walked several blocks before reaching a black sedan parked between several cars in the parking lot of a night club.

Spencer approached the car, and he talked to the men inside. I could tell there was a driver and someone else in the back seat. After a while, he came to me and told me that we had to wait for a few minutes as one of the agents inside the car was using the car phone to get clearance for our departure. It was probable that we could run into the Carabineros' checkpoints on our way to Valparaiso, which was to be my exit out of Chile, and clearance was imperative.

I could see Spencer's expression by the light coming off the nearby lamp post. It was relaxed, at ease. He placed his hand on my arm and smiled.

"Stupid thing that you did, my friend, but sort of expected from you. Otherwise you would not be the John I know. I kind of think that it was what Anne would have expected," he said.

I could sense by the tone of his voice that he was not upset, which gave me a great deal of relief. "I thought that my contact was reliable and that this time my message would not be intercepted," I said.

"Your contact was reliable, and that is the problem. It went through," he replied. "After receiving your cable, the State Department placed our friend Letelier on its priority list, and at this very moment, they are contacting Ambassador Popper to tell Pinochet to stop the operation. They are placing field agents on alert." He paused for a second and added, "I got a call from the locals to bring you in. I was told that you have been assigned to another task. But knowing them, they want you dead."

"But I thought that the agency was not involved in this operation," I said.

"My naïve friend, you still don't get it. Everybody wants Letelier dead," he replied. "The important thing now is to get you through this alive, or you'll join the fallen ones."

"And become another star in the CIA wall of fame," I said jokingly. Just a few days earlier when we were talking about Rusty, Spencer had mentioned the upcoming placing of a star for Rusty at the CIA Memorial Wall at Virginia. The star was in remembrance of CIA agents who had been killed in the field.

Spencer was not laughing and did not respond to my remark. He proceeded to tell me that the agency had also contacted DINA with the order to bring me in. Contreras took it as interference in Operation Condor and told Spencer that if the CIA wanted me that they would have to come after me. DINA would not kill me. I had served them well. Spencer felt that Contreras was not a man to be told what to do, not by the CIA or even by Pinochet. Manuel Contreras was known to be tough with his men, but he always protected them, and I was one of his men.

DINA was giving Spencer plenty of time to get me out of the country and had provided some needed help to secure my safety. However, if we were to fall into the hands of the CIA agents, DINA would not interfere. Another American operative who was with Condor and had worked closely with Spencer for some time was also to help Spencer in taking me out of the country. This agent, whom I knew as Bronco, was part of the special units that were working inside the CIA in Chile. Having Bronco on my side gave me a high degree of trust and confidence. I would come out of Chile alive after all.

Knowing the importance of my cable to the State Department, I was intrigued by Colonel Manuel Contreras' reaction, and I asked Spencer about it.

"On the contrary, the colonel has known for a while that Washington does not want Condor to operate outside the countries of the Southern Cone, much less killing nationals or foreign dignitaries in the United State. That is politics, but the reality is different. Washington does want Letelier dead but chooses to remain behind the curtain while the show goes on the stage. The colonel took your action as a calculated effort to show them good faith from their operatives inside Condor. He admires your courage. You have shown a lot of guts by going outside Condor and out of the local CIA to reach Washington. Contreras is pleased that you gave them the date of the planned attack, and he knows that Washington will be upset when it finds out that it was the wrong date. But by then Letelier will be dead. Like the colonel said, 'Everybody makes mistakes,'" Spencer replied.

"Really?!" I exclaimed, sort of puzzled for I had given the State Department the exact date on which Letelier was to be killed: September 26. I was sure I had given the State Department the right date. However, I chose not to correct Spencer on the date I had given. At this point, my life was at stake, and I was grateful that the colonel sought my safety. The logical answer from Contreras should have been to kill me on the spot for he had to disassociate himself from the operation immediately by acting as if the operation had never taken place.

I looked straight at him, for still it did not seem right. "What's the difference between Rusty and I? The colonel had him killed for the same reason."

"Rusty was planted by the CIA; you were not. Also you and I are his people, and he knows that we are loyal to him, not to Pinochet. By now you know that inside DINA we have operatives who have been planted by Pinochet to keep an eye on the colonel and that does not sit right with the colonel. Pinochet and the CIA want you dead, but the colonel does not. I know Don Manuel Contreras — he is a man that keeps his word, and the word is that are you are to leave for the States alive."

And yet earlier I distinctly had heard what Spencer had told Clavel back at the apartment: to tell the CIA or DINA's people nothing about my whereabouts. Had he some doubts about the colonel? I was intrigued, for at this moment Spencer was protecting me with those loyal to him, and Clavel was very loyal to Spencer. Spencer was putting himself on the line, risking his life for me. Clavel and those who were helping him were also risking their lives.

However, no one seemed to be nervous or worried. They all acted as if Spencer was their boss and no one else, and all of them did work for Operation Condor. Was Condor preying on the CIA and DINA? Was Condor becoming a separate entity itself?

Part X

The soothing calmness of dawn was now engulfing the city at its usual pace, slow moving and inexorable, unchanging in its course to finality. Soon shadows and darkness would succumb to light and color. And the habitat of men would also follow the steps of dawn. The houses of forbidden pleasure, as well as lesser places of fleshy desires, would close their doors. Prostitutes, pimps, thieves, and drug addicts would return to their place to rest their empty lives and carcasses. Somewhere else the uninterrupted breathing of industry would release their prey and grab incoming new ones. Crying infants would seek a fulfilling life and the giving of their mother's breast, the crying of human illnesses and diseases would echo in hospitals, and silence would come to those who could not make it to dawn.

Dawn had again given me a sense of reassurance that life was there waiting, that a new day could always be better than the one we had left behind. Dawn was a prelude to moving forward —it kept us going. There was always a full day ahead. It was sort of strange to feel this way. For over a year, after Anne's and my child's deaths, my life seemed to end with the passing of each day. I seldom had wanted to live another day. Now as sanity had returned to me and had rescued me from the dark nightmare of the clandestine life, I was again feeling the gentle fresh breeze of Anne's life within me.

As the car passed the streets and avenues, I was somewhat glad and slightly struck by the resilience of people to survive. Years earlier, gloom, terror, silence, and despair had made these streets and avenues deserted. Now people seemed free as they hurried down sidewalks and across intersections. Merchants were bringing their produce for display to the street's market places while others were opening doors and placing advertisements on sidewalks.

Now and then people would shout excitement and obscenity into an air that was already getting intoxicated by the fumes and smoke of hundreds of vehicle exhausts and riveting engines that coughed incessantly. They had no limits as electric buses, cars, trucks of all sizes, cabs, minibuses, motorcycles, and bikes furiously raced forward. It was a world on the move as I was.

My world was moving fast, too fast. A few weeks ago I had some sense of security when my resolve to leave the agency had not totally surfaced. Though I had Spencer at my side, this was not the type of job where I could leave in a tranquil setting as most jobs were. I felt as though I was caught in a web, and my instinct for survival was throwing all sort of doubts in all directions. Spencer was my friend, but he was also a CIA agent and a DINA agent working for Operation Condor. Spencer himself had taught me that friendship in an operative existence was a liability. Now I was a liability to anyone connected with Operation Condor, and Spencer was a part of that operation — not only part, but he had run most of the affairs of Condor, and in some instances he had worked independent from DINA. Now the oddity was that being myself a liability to Operation Condor, I was now also being protected by it, which was puzzling.

I looked at Spencer, who sat in the front seat next to the driver. He seemed calm, unperturbed. For seconds I caught his eye as he turned his head slightly toward me. It seemed that he had read my thoughts and glanced as if to tell me to stop wondering. But his look had not reassured me at all. Questions and doubts were being raised in my mind. I could not help from wondering about Bronco, the other American, who was going to help Spencer get me out of the country. Spencer had not mentioned anything about Bronco's whereabouts, and I had not raised the question. Instead another DINA agent had replaced him, and Spencer had introduced him as Favio.

He was about fifty years of age with a light complexion and receding hair and had been recently assigned to Operation Condor. Favio was the smallest agent I had ever encountered, around 5 feet 4 inches tall with some encouragement. Because of his small stature, I assumed he had come from the civilian side of law enforcement; my assumption was short lived when Spencer told me he was a Chilean Navy officer, an expert in electronics and surveillance. Since the very first time I had met him, I was apprehensive about him but not alarmed. Doubting was part of our persona. One could not fully trust anyone in the clandestine world. In some cases there were degrees of trust; in his case, my trust in him was totally absent.

I knew the driver well. His name was Julio Cervantes. He was younger than I, in his early thirties, and he was definitely Spanish. Cervantes was a literary name, the author of one of the most famous stories ever told: Don Quijote de la Mancha. Julio had told me once that he came from the Castilians. I grinned at the thought. Most Spaniards that I knew would say that they were descendants of the Castilians. As far as I could tell, it gave them a sort of respectability among the Spanish world, where literature was always at the very top of their values. Don Quijote de la Mancha had been written by Cervantes, a Castilian born in the region of Castilla and De La Mancha in Spain. Looking at Julio, his ancestors had probably come from the region of Castillia, but his features were more Moorish, being that the Moors had once ruled Spain for several centuries.

My thoughts were brought to a halt as the Carabineros checkpoint came into view as we approached the main route to Valparaiso. Julio muttered something, and Spencer reached for his ID that would identify him as a DINA agent.

I glanced at Favio, who quickly removed his gun and placed it on the seat close to him. "You never know about these cops. Some of them are with us, and others are not," he said suspiciously as he flapped part of his overcoat to cover what was definitely a .357 Magnum.

I sort of chuckled as I wondered why little guys always carry big guns; I could not help from associating it with their height. It probably elevated their sense of security. Most of us want an edge over our adversary in a confrontation. A .357 Magnum at close range was in fact a huge edge. Favio looked at me inquisitively. "Don't you carry anything bigger?" I asked. He cussed me out sensing my sarcasm.

The officer in charge approached the car while his subordinate held his rifle ready and kept a prudent distance. Julio said something about the dark glasses that the officer wore, and Spencer grinned.

"Stupid fool, the sun is not even in sight," Favio said, still showing unfriendliness. "Unless he is trying to conceal himself."

"Not much concealing could be done with a nose like that," Julio remarked as he lowered the window.

The officer leaned in and looked at us. For an instant, I thought I had caught his attention, but I was not sure. Julio gave him Spencer's papers and after looking at them, he politely told Spencer everything was in order. He glanced at the rest of us and wished us well.

"What do you think?" Spencer asked Julio.

"I think it's all right. Otherwise he would have asked more questions. What do you think Favio?" Julio asked as he drove the car away from the checkpoint.

"It seems all right. I just don't like the bastards. They are more inclined toward Pinochet than Contreras. I never liked the paramilitary anyway. They are nothing more than civilians playing soldiers," responded Favio.

"He is just doing his job," responded Spencer. "Whether he likes it or not."

Then there was silence. It seemed as if each of us was guessing what the other was thinking. It was too disquieting for my sake. I wondered if DINA had taken Bronco to replace him for Favio, one of his own, for a different purpose than what Spencer had in mind. If there was anything different to occur than what I had been told, it had to happen before Valparaiso.

Soon we came upon Curacavi, a small town situated in magnificent greenery and forestry. Several years earlier, Anne and I had stayed here overnight. As we passed by Curacavi, I remembered Anne telling me that it reminded her of Bishop, a small town in the States situated at the foot of the sequoia where she said we could spend time fishing along the many streams. Now thinking about it, I could not help from having a depressing feeling. I could see her smiling face telling me all the things we could do. I could not tell if she even really liked fishing. Each time we went fishing, she was always preoccupied with finding a place for lunch and the gathering of wild flowers that she collected and kept between the pages of whatever books she was reading.

She was a reader. I wondered what had happened to that old Bible she carried around. Most of those flowers found a place in that bible before she placed them in her collection. I wondered how two people can live together and certain things pass by them unnoticed. Anne and I were married for nearly seven years, and we were ready to start a family. Surely seven years was enough time to have known everything about ourselves. In all probabilities, she knew more about me than I knew about her. Thinking about her, I could not help from smiling. She was something. Unknown to me, she had already started our family. I just was not there to see it. For a moment I thought of her being pregnant. She had carried our child for four months, and she had never mentioned it in our conversations. It did not bother me. I knew my Anne. She just wanted to surprise me, and it would have been a surprise.

For instance, that Bible she always carried was important to her but not to me. That old book really meant something to her. Even though I had found her reading it many times and sometimes she had spoken to me about it, I just listened and did not pay enough attention to it. I recall once she had become a little angry, saying that I did not care enough. It wasn't long before she was herself again. She was a forgiving person, maybe too forgiving. Now I wished I had paid attention. Now I could listen to her forever.

I knew she was not afraid of dying. Since her death, her belief about what happens after death was now a comforting thought to me. She thought of death as a long sleep and that someday she would wake up to life again. She deeply believed in the resurrection of the dead that was going to occur in the messianic kingdom of Jesus Christ. Once she had told me that we should never be afraid of being separated forever because we all were to be resurrected and that we were going to live forever. Thinking about that forever, it could be around the corner waiting for me now. Maybe that is why I was not too concerned about my life….Maybe in that forever I would run into her again.

Absorbed in thought, I did not realize that we had already passed Curacavi. It was the slowdown of the vehicle that brought me back to the present. Julio said something about getting a flat and slowed the car down to a stop.

Spencer went outside to investigate, and Favio followed him. Julio turned to me and told me to remain in my seat, which I found odd, and immediately I knew that something was in the making. I saw Favio standing behind Spencer, who seemed to be examining the front left tire. Then I saw Spencer say something to Favio, who then leaned down to check whatever Spencer was pointing at. Instantly I heard the shot, and Julio lost no time in leaving the car to join Spencer, who was dragging Favio's body. I heard the trunk being opened and, moments later, the trunk being shut.

I tried to remain calm and act as if nothing out of the ordinary had occurred, but sudden death had always been, at least for me, too brutal, too callous. I recalled the girl that Spencer had shot in Argentina and the boy that the other agent had killed on that occasion. The mind is never rigid, at least for me. It has the flexibility to adjust. In Chile it was constantly adjusting to the realities of my world. Next to me a few moments earlier had sat a human being filled with warm blood and thoughts of his own, and now he was a corpse.

Spencer and Julio returned without saying a word and sat down as we continued the trip. I looked where Favio had been and saw his gun still lying on the seat. I reached for it and placed it by my feet.

When we came to an area filled with tall trees where bushes blinded the sides of the forest, Spencer told Julio to turn, and he drove the car right through the bushes and stopped. We were surrounded by all sorts of vegetation, a most beautiful place for those who love life, and a convenient place for those who would deny it.

I stayed seated in the back seat as I watched them take Favio's lifeless body into the woods. If this was the moment to escape, I would have had a fair chance, but I kept faith that Spencer and Julio were on my side and that getting rid of Favio was something needed to accomplish my escape. I remembered well that Spencer had told me that Contreras had agreed to help me out unless Pinochet had something else in mind. Maybe he had planted Favio in our group to abort my escape.

I looked at the gun at my feet. I found that I had no intention to use it. Favio's death had intensified my belief that Spencer was really trying to protect me from falling into the hands of the CIA. Earlier he had told me that DINA had secured my exit through one of the freighters anchored at Valparaiso's harbor.

About ten minutes later, they both returned. Spencer was upset. He told me he had really needed Favio for Operation Condor due to his expertise in surveillance and that he did not want to kill him but loyalty to Condor was of greater importance considering the nature of the business in which we were involved He proceeded to tell me that Favio had been planted inside Condor without the knowledge of Don Manuel Contreras. He told me that before leaving Santiago he had sent a message to Contreras asking him the reason behind Favio replacing Bronco.

At the Carabineros checkpoint we had passed earlier, he had received the answer. The officer had planted a note on his paper, an order coming directly from General Contreras to get rid of Favio. Favio was working directly for Pinochet and had been ordered to deliver me to the CIA agents waiting at Valparaiso.

"Valparaiso is my playground, my friend," said Spencer to ease my apprehension. "I know them. Just take it easy. Everything will be alright."
I did not respond. I nodded at him to show a degree of composure, though at the moment it dawned on me that I was perhaps walking right into the lion's mouth. Valparaiso was his theater of operation just like Spencer had said. Now it seemed as though the lion's mouth was open, waiting for his prey. The deliverer was dead now though. This reasoning reassured me that Spencer was not going to deliver me to the CIA; otherwise he would not have killed Favio. I reached for him and patted him on the back. It was the perfect display. Being in his home territory, he could call the shots more so now. Julio seemed to be pleased. He glanced at me showing his approval. Yet I still could not shake

feelings of apprehension. My guess is that no one can when one's own death is breathing heavily on one's neck.

Something in the distance called for our attention. It seemed that there was an accident as emergency lights flashed ahead. As we came closer, we saw several people frantically moving around. Two cars seemed to have collided, and the paramedics with two men were trying to get someone out of one of the vehicles.

Julio stopped, and Spencer got out of the car. Julio followed him as they went to assist. At that moment, I realized that there were no police cars present. Carabineros were always at an accident before the paramedics, especially on road accidents. I reached for the gun at my feet to make a break, but the door swung open, and I found myself staring at a gun.

"Let it go John. We are friends," said a well-dressed man in English, aiming a gun at me. "Follow me and don't do anything stupid," he added with an accent that was not American but still English. He was about my age — late thirties — and tall and blond with reddish skin.

The flashing lights of the paramedic van stopped, and I could see that Spencer and Julio were being taken separately to the cars that had seemingly collided. I noticed that Julio was handcuffed. Spencer however was not, and he seemed to be arguing now with his two captors. As the cars moved onto the road, I knew it was a set up. We had fallen into it just like amateurs. I laughed knowing the state of mind Spencer was in. In a very complex world, he had fallen into its simplicity. It was clear to me that the CIA had anticipated Spencer's move by placing agents from other areas that jumped us before we reached Valparaiso, where Spencer had many friends.

My captor did not produce any handcuffs and asked me to follow him, which gave me a feeling of relief. It seemed that the agency had proved Spencer wrong after all. Otherwise I would have been killed by now. It was a most welcomed relief, but I was not totally free. Leaving the agency would not be an easy road to follow. I could still end up dead. Maybe the agency wanted to offer me some sort of formal training. I had never been trained by them....Maybe the Agency would offer me an alternative....Maybe I was more important as a diplomat....All of these "maybes" kept racing through my mind.

Inside the car, I sat in the back seat next to my captor. I was greeted by two agents seated in the front. They were waiting for the other car, which was carrying Spencer, to move first. The van had already left, and the other car with Julio inside had also left. My captor and I had never seen each other before, and the other two seated in front were also strangers. This sort of bothered me. I knew most of the agency's men in the Santiago and Valparaiso areas. These men were either new to the area or were new arrivals, perhaps, which was not unusual. Agents were constantly on the move.

"Sorry gent," said the agent seated next to me. He gave me back the .357 Magnum and added, "Don't you carry anything bigger?"

I smiled, recalling what I had said to Favio earlier. "It belonged to someone else. Powerful gun, though it doesn't really give you an edge," I said and placed the gun on the seat between him and me. "Keep it as a souvenir. It is too large to carry around."

He thanked me and put the gun under his overcoat. The expression that he had used was not American but British, and it had caught my attention. Nothing unusual — the agency had thousands of agents from all nationalities, but these three agents had something else in common. They had a sort of refinedness that made them different from the lot of us. I couldn't pinpoint exactly what it was, but it was there.

The other car began to move, but instead of moving ahead, it moved toward us. The man in the front passenger's seat lowered his window and signaled at our driver to wait. The car slowed down to a stop several feet ahead of our car.

"What now?" our driver asked. Before anyone could add a word, the doors of the other car opened, and Spencer and another agent left the car and moved in our direction. Spencer moved close to us and stopped. The other man walked up to our vehicle. He took a look at us and told me to leave the car. Spencer wanted to talk to me.

I left the car and went over to Spencer. Spencer was not as upset as I thought he would be. Instead he smiled and asked me how I was. Then he asked me to take a walk with him while the others waited.

For a few moments, we just walked in silent. I felt that he knew what was occurring, but I also knew that he would fill me in partly but not tell me everything. Seconds of silence at times somehow feel like long moments of wondering. Was he considering a break? This could be an opportunity, but when I told him that now was a good opportunity to make a break, he told me that there was no need. He opened his coat to show a part of the handle of his gun. He had not been disarmed. This was leaving a trail of questions that I chose not to follow. I waited for him to fill me in on what was happening.

We stopped near a massively tall tree. I looked at it, powerful branches filled with leaves of a soft light green color. "Is this an oak?" I asked to break the silence. Spencer was taking his time.

"What do I know about trees?" he muttered. He looked straight at me, his penetrating eyes looked into mine, and he said, "Well my friend, we have come to the end of our path though one never knows what is ahead. Maybe we will cross paths again. While it lasted, there was no other man who I could say was truly my friend. You are my friend." He lowered his eyes. Then he looked away as if he was trying to gain his composure or maybe trying to get to a point of reference somewhere in his mind. Maybe he had accepted the agency's decision to take me back with them. I felt for him; he was not the emotional type.

"You saved my life once or twice, and I saved yours a couple of times. What is important is that we both survived. I just wanted to let you know that I was doing the best I could to get you out of this country alive," he said "We were both a part of a special event in each of our lives. Nam was our world at that time, and we accepted that as such…but here? …This is not your world. You do not belong here. Your world is the world of Anne's. Go to it and do your best. I told you once that you could never be like the rest of us. It was my mistake to bring you into the CIA. I knew then that you could never kill in cold blood, but I brought you in anyway."

I looked at him and saw him as I had so many other times when we had shared such personal feelings. "I will always remember you," I said and added with sarcasm, "It seems that the agency has proved both of us wrong and why not? After all, I gave them enough time to save Letelier. I do deserve some form of gratitude besides a bullet."

He smiled and shook my hand, and abruptly he embraced me. "You are a good man, John. A damn good friend. Take care of yourself."

I grabbed his arm and asked with concern, "What about you and Julio?"

"They will let Julio go, and I will be back at DINA's headquarters. Condor must keep on flying," he responded.

"Why was Julio handcuffed and not you"

"He is a Chilean, and I am an American. I am still a CIA operative," he responded with a smile. "Courtesy of the U.S. government."

I welcomed his sarcasm. "I only know your mother through letters, but perhaps someday I will stop by Boston and pay her a visit. I will tell her that she has a fine son. That is if the agency lets me go."

"You do that John. She is one of the finest ladies in Boston," he responded. He held me by the arms and looked straight into my eyes. "Remember when we were discussing the War in the Pacific and what it meant for the marines to climb Mount Suribachi?"

I assented; I could still recall that discussion. It occurred in Vietnam when we were climbing a forsaken mountain that had no military value at all, and both sides lost so many young men. At that moment, Spencer had told me about the difference between Nam and the Pacific war. He told me about Iwo Jima, where one of his uncles had fought. It seemed odd that he was bringing this up at this moment, but his knowledge of Navy warfare always made me an avid listener.

"The important thing for the marines was to place their flag on top of Mount Suribachi as a statement for all combatants at Iwo Jima. It turned the tide of the battle into an American victory. I want you to think about this point. Our government is my Suribachi. I have climbed to its very top. Now Condor has landed on top of Washington, D.C. Condor is making a statement for the world to see," he said. "Condor's landing on D.C. is so insignificant that Americans, in two or three years from now, won't even remember what happened in Washington. You see, Letelier is not the point. The point is Washington. Only those of us who dare to climb the mountain will gain a victory of sorts. In consideration of all things, I have made my statement. It's the same as our soldiers' statement at Suribachi. Someone somewhere, another American perhaps, will see this government as I see it. That is what really matters."

I felt his penetrating eyes probing into my mine; it was important for him to know my thoughts. "I am really sorry that you did all that work for nothing," I said with a mixed feeling of regret. "I knew how important it was for you to let the world know what Washington really is. I may say that I agree with you to a great length, but I am one of those who don't dare to make such a strong statement because killing Letelier was a strong statement. It is not now, but it could have been." I nearly swallowed the last words. My saliva had dried up in my throat, but I managed to add, "I am sorry that I screwed up this operation. I know that DINA probably is getting its people out of the country by now. For Michael there won't be problem. He knows the country well."

Spencer grinned and did not seem sore at all as I had thought. "Don't be sorry. It had to end this way. As I told you before, I would have been disappointed if you had done nothing," he said. "This way we have shown our true selves, and believe me John, that is important. As for Letelier, he will be remembered for a while, but soon when this is all over, he will be forgotten by most people, except by those who got to know him."

I looked at him, and he lowered his eyes to the ground evasively, with his hand still having a strong grip on my arm. It seemed odd. He was talking as if Operation Condor was still an occurrence to happen, though by now the State Department was probably placing a high security alert to protect Letelier. The CIA had a week to put its people in place. I felt Spencer was in a state of denial knowing well that all doors were being closed to Condor at this point in time. The United States' long arms of justice soon would grab Michael and his group; it was only a matter of time. On the day the assassination was to take place, most likely all the would-be assassins would be under arrest. Then the State Department would sweep the whole mess under the rug, and Washington and Chile would continue its affair as if nothing of great importance had happened.

He raised his eyes and looked directly into my eyes and smiled, and I was glad for we were departing as good friends. He let my arms go free, and with a grin, he turned around and walked toward the waiting car. For a fast passing instant, I thought that I had seen the glare of moisture in his eyes.

I stood, sort of motionless, looking at him as he entered the car. As the car drove away, I felt a profound sadness, an awareness that let me know perhaps this was the last time I was going to see Spencer. I fought back tears. Besides Anne, he had been the closest friend I ever had. Strange thing, Anne had been a loving, caring person and Spencer was a cold killer who would not blink an eye when ending a human being's life. Between these two extremes I had lived, seldom giving this paradox a thought. Though at times the things I had seen Spencer do had bothered me, I had always managed to excuse his behavior, perhaps due to my love for him as a friend.

It also seemed odd that Anne and Spencer, being at the opposite ends of moral values, had brought me the hope offered by the messianic kingdom of Jesus Christ and everlasting life in a paradise on earth. Anne had lived her life with that kingdom in view, and Spencer had thought of it as an end to human rulership. Maybe that hope was only for the dreamers, and yet it was still the only hope left for me. Now both were gone, and my path was clear. Anne's world was waiting for me. Perhaps that messianic kingdom would someday arrive. Perhaps in time I would see my Anne again and so too my baby girl. But now I still had to face the agency. This was a sobering thought. I was now more than ever determined to leave this way of life. The CIA response could easily end my life, but at this point it was worth the gamble.

My thoughts came to a sudden halt when we arrived at Valparaiso. I became aware that our car was moving toward the opposite direction of the agency's headquarters located in the Harbor district. We were now moving inland. I glanced at the agent sitting next to me expecting a reaction, a change of expression, but there was none. He was impassive, seemingly enjoying the scenery. The others seemed unperturbed in the front seat, continuing their conversation about a soccer game. I found it unusual for most Americans would speak of baseball, football or basketball, but seldom would one make a conversation about soccer. These agents were not Americans, even though they worked for the company.

"Where are you taking me?" I asked the agent sitting next to me.

"You are in good hands, my friend. Your people won't be able to touch you. Just be patient," he replied with a touch of politeness in his voice and mannerism. He glanced at me and returned to his calm, don't-bother-me sort of attitude.

Guessing at this moment was unavoidable; he had referred to "your people." Who was he referring to — DINA or the agency? Or were these agents part of the special forces operating inside the CIA? It had to be. No wonder they had let Spencer go. Julio's fate at this moment could also be questionable; he could be dead by now. The question now was, "Why me?" Maybe someone wanted to expedite the process to stop the killing of Letelier….Maybe the agency wanted Letelier dead after all and these agents were trying to spare Letelier's life. Perhaps they wanted more precise information in the planning of Letelier's death, something that I could definitely provide. There was also a gap. Spencer was a part of their contingency also, and he should have cooperated, unless Spencer had refused as a matter of loyalty to Operation Condor. That also left other questions that had no answer at this very moment. Perhaps there had been a compromise between them — I was a willing informant, and I could help them as much as Spencer without compromising Spencer's relationship with Operation Condor and DINA. In retrospect I could see now why Spencer had not made any attempt to escape when the opportunities were there.

As we moved inland, I was informed by the agent seated next to the driver that they were taking me to the city of Quillota. At the upcoming Pan American Highway junction, I was to be transferred to another car. My final destination was to be the port of Coquimbo. While he was still talking to me, there was a short burst of beeps repeatedly coming from under the coat of the agent next to me. I looked curiously at him. I had heard before that some agents had recently been given a sort of wireless phone that could be carried with them. Spencer had recently told me that some phones were in the process of being available to the operatives in the field.

The agent listened attentively to the device and muttered an answer. He looked at me and then at the others who, by now, were silent, waiting to hear what he had to say.

"Well, my friend," he said to me, "now your people will waste no time in trying to get rid of you, but don't worry." Then he looked at the others. I noticed that the driver slowed the car down somewhat and glanced continuously at us without taking his eyes fully away from the road.

"I have been informed by the office that Condor struck Washington, D.C., an hour ago. Orlando Letelier and his assistant were killed in a car bombing at 8:30 A.M. Washington's time," the agent said in a voice that seemed to regret announcing the news about Letelier's killing.

"It is not possible," I uttered as I looked at them.

"Don't take the news so bad gent. Our friend is truly a master of deception. He let us think that it was to happen next week," the same agent said.

I leaned my head on the hard glass of the window and looked outside. All this time since Operation Condor had placed Letelier on its agenda, Spencer had dealt a double hand to me. I had proved him right, for at the very end when I thought I had deceived him by turning over the operation to the State Department, he had already played his last deceptive card: He said Letelier was to be killed on September 26 but instead had been killed on the 21st, something that Spencer had planned all along.

Since the beginning of Operation Letelier, an aura of irony had framed the entire operation. The White House, the State Department, the CIA and DINA wanted Letelier dead, but none of them except for DINA were willing to place the chips on the table, and none would turn over the cards to play their hand. The Americans, now on the verge of a devastating international fiasco, had pulled out as at Bay of Pigs and wanted to stop Condor at any price, by all means necessary. Condor had already landed on American soil, giving the State Department no time to stop the operation.

Spencer was a good player, a true player. He had told me in his own words the final phase of the game, and I was too naïve to even consider defeat. He had already climbed Mount Suribachi, and Letelier was now a statement to the world. Condor had descended on Washington and had taken his prey to the very doors of the White House.

As for me, the objective now was clear. I would take my fight to the college campuses and small communities in the States; to the factories, to the small shopkeepers, to the field workers, to those who made their living on sweat and tiresome tasks, to those whose hardships and stamina of spirit would endure the long hours at minimum wages that extracted from them their maximum efforts. Perhaps I could help in small ways those who were being treated unfairly by the justice system and be that friendly cop at the corner who understood the hardships of the poor and the pain of those who came from broken homes and the plight of the thousands of homeless Vietnam veterans that roamed aimlessly the roads and highways of America and lived in makeshift shelters under the bridges of superhighways for just the privilege of staying alive.

Conclusion

It was now dawn, and I had not slept since the prior day's dawning. I was now at the Port of Coquimbo waiting for the boat that was to take me to the freighter Coppernico, a Greek ship flying Panama's flag. I looked at the ship, a large stationary object on the calm waters of the bay, and it filled me with a feeling of relief. Finally the road to total freedom was there waiting for me. It was so close that I could just extend my hand and touch it.

The morning was cold but pleasant as the gentle marine breeze touched my face. I looked at Sir Percil. He was standing beside me, and his pleasant smile reaffirmed my sense of security.

Leaning on the steel railing, I observed the dying lights of an awakening city across the bay located on the northern shore of Coquimbo Bay. I asked Sir Percil for the name of the city.

"That is the city of La Serena," Sir Percil said, looking toward it. "La Serena seems to sleep unperturbed by time — very rich in its culture and sort of affluent in the makeup of its inhabitants, but too serious. It lacks that peculiar vibrant Chilean flavor. To make matters worse, it lacks the protection and richness of a harbor. On the other hand, the Port of Coquimbo is rich in history. Its inhabitants are sort of commoners but a resilient, vivacious lot."

He turned toward me and said, "As you know, this is Independence Week and not too far from here is a place called La Pampilla. Right now it is filled with thousands of people still celebrating Las Fiestas Patria. Lots of cuecas and cumbias, not to mention lots of concha and toros and pisco. Too bad we cannot make it there. This celebration played right into taking you to the freighter without awakening the suspicion of the locals. Really we are not too concerned about the military here, DINA or the CIA."

"Yeah, that is what the driver who brought me here told me. It seems that you British have a history of your own in these parts," I said.

"Quite right, we even have a cemetery of our own that dates back to the 1600s. You know, Sir Francis Drake plundered La Serena and Coquimbo around the year 1578 if I am not mistaken; it was a week after he sacked Valparaiso. Rumors are that Davis and Sharp also left their impressions here."

"Really?!"

"Absolutely," he said. "Then in the 1800s, English settlers came to Chile, particularly in the south but some settled in these parts. We are part of the Chilean culture. We have the respect and friendship of the Chilean Navy."

I could tell he was enjoying our conversation. I was sort of reluctant to change the subject, but necessity does call for harshness. I thanked him for coming from Santiago to see me; it was a privilege for me to be acknowledged by Sir Percil. His diplomatic status always preceded him, giving him an aura of respectability. Now its presence in this clandestine work added, on my part, a touch of admiration. Seldom had I been aware of a diplomat of his caliber being seen with the likes of us. Diplomats had their own security, but these men accompanying him were definitely British agents, most likely MI6 operatives.

Hansen, one of the men who had brought me to Coquimbo, had already told me that Sir Percil had served for years with the British secret service when MI6 was known as MI5 during the Second World War and well into the '50s. Hansen had already prepared me for my meeting with Sir Percil but volunteered no information on what had caused this special treatment of an American. All he knew was that I was not to be taken by the CIA or DINA. He also could not tell me why I had been abducted from Spencer, who was to help me out of Chile. All he knew was that Sir Percil was in charge, and there was some sort of agreement between the CIA and the British. But he also knew that there were some unfriendly elements inside the CIA who wanted me dead.

As I listened to Sir Percil's brief comments about the history of the British presence in Chile, I could not help from admiring him. He had a different sort of imposing figure. Whether I was to look at him as a diplomat, a Navy man, or as a retired agent, he was the true picture of a gentleman, a British gentleman.

Sir Percil's brief comments about the history of the British presence in Chile were well known, especially by the coastal people. The British Navy and the Chilean Navy had a comradery of their own. At Chile's southern section, the British segment of the population was considerable. The British tone permeated throughout Chile's history pages. Lord Cochrane was the father of the

Chilean Navy, and many others had joined the Chileans in their war of independence from Spain. Englishmen became heroes, which resulted in some of Chile's ports being named after them.

After a while, I finally changed the course of our conversation and gently placed my hand on his arm. "Now Sir Percil, why did you interfere on my behalf? The CIA will be displeased."

He smiled, seemingly enjoying my last words. "What the CIA does not know will not hurt them, will it? Besides, our cousins are not really that bad. But the KGB? That is a different story." He stopped briefly and thoughtfully looked at the calm water of the bay. "This bay has the calmest, most peaceful waters of any bay I have seen. Do you know what Coquimbo means?" he asked, without taking his eyes off the water. He continued without waiting for the answer that I did not have. "The natives of this region named it Coquimbo because of the calm, tranquil waters of the bay. Coquimbo means "place of calm water." I do not know exactly if the word comes from the Quechas or the Moluches. In ancient times, they were the ones who inhabited these parts. I could be wrong, which will motivate me to do some studying on the subject."

He had managed to elude my wondering thoughts by the soft tone of his voice and the soft expression of his face. The thickness of his gray brows made his eyes shine with lives of their own, vibrant and yet peaceful. His thick gray moustache, well-trimmed and elegant, went well with his lips, which seemed to be always on the verge of a smile. He portrayed the typical grandfather that every boy wishes to have. The furrows on his face, just appearing, introduced old age with graceful kindness. I guessed that he was in his early seventies. His appearance in general was pleasant to the eye and portrayed wisdom in its entirety — the things that we want to know, the experience and knowledge that most of us eagerly seek.

Then unexpectedly, he looked at me. I felt the intensity and strength of his eyes. He fully smiled this time, and it felt good. "Why you?" he asked. "Since I met you, my young friend, I felt your honesty, and it was apparent to me that you really were the friend that Spencer never had. I remember the time when you came to me for answers that I could not provide. At that time, some young Americans had been killed by the military, and it had a profound impact on you. After you left, I asked myself: Why would a man who had gone through the carnage and atrocities of Vietnam be affected so much by the death of two men? In proportion to the killings in Vietnam, it seems as if it would be of no consequence at all."

I looked at the silent figure of the freighter smoothly moving with the slight, gentle movement of the sea. There she was waiting — waiting to take me away from this madness. Sir Percil was right. Why had a man like me, seasoned on a war of attrition that Vietnam came to be, taken it upon himself to save two men when he did not know them? I had asked myself the same question when I tried to save Frank and Charles, and I did not have the answers then nor now. It just had to be done; it was the right thing to do at that time.

Aware of my silence, he paused for a moment before he continued. "Then afterward I found out that your parents had been killed in an automobile accident when you were fourteen. You had no family. The court placed you into different homes, and as soon as you turned eighteen, you joined the marines."

Still with my eyes on the freighter, I fought tears, and for a long moment, I just looked at the water. This old gentleman was taking me apart. This part of my life had remained closed since the day of my parents' deaths in 1957. Only once or twice had I talked with Spencer about it, and only once had I really opened that chapter of my life to Anne. She kindly closed it as to not ever reopen the wounds again. Strangely I did not question or wonder about how Sir Percil had obtained information so personal to me, and it did not bother me. Instead I listened to each word he was saying.

"You see, you are a special person to me and particularly to Spencer. In some ways, both of you lived a sort of parallel life. As I will not see you again, I thought it proper to fill in some of the gaps of your ordeal," he said and held my hand as tears trickled down my face. I was not bothered by the tears as I listened to him. "You see, Spencer lost his father at the Suez Canal in 1956.... As you know, his father was an American operative."

He lowered his eyes and left my hands free. He rested his hands on the railing. Now he looked down at the splashing water below and kept silent. I noticed an expression of sadness in his face. He took his left hand to his mouth and coughed several times. "Seems that I am catching a cold," he said and turned toward me, a smile appearing at the corners of his mouth. "I rarely become emotional, and this is one of those rare occasions. Seems to me that at times people like me should be excused for these rarities. Don't you think so?"

By now I had regained my composure as I assented in silence. I wondered where this conversation was going; he seemed to know Spencer quite well.

"I had no idea that you and Spencer had this kind of friendship. How long have you known Spencer?" I asked, thinking that he had not known Spencer as long as I had. I should have guessed it. Spencer had been in Chile since 1970, but I had known him since 1963 in Vietnam.

"Known him?" he asked himself, and for several moments, which seemed to last forever, he just looked at me. "Spencer is my grandson....Stella is my daughter.... I know him quite well. Otherwise I would not be here."

I was dumfounded. I had never suspected that there was any connection in the sense of family ties. Who would have guessed? Now as I heard him telling me about Spencer, things started to make sense. What had drawn Spencer to Vietnam was his hate toward the Communists, who he felt was responsible for his father's death. According to Sir Percil, during the skirmish between the Egyptians and British, Spencer's father had probably been killed by the KGB. I was wrong about Spencer's real motive for going to Vietnam. His dislike for the Soviets had been overshadowed by what had occurred afterward. Now I could understand why his hatred toward the Marxists was imbedded so deep inside him — not only he had lost his young girlfriend in Vietnam, but he had also lost his father to them.

Sir Percil continued, "After William died, my daughter decided to take Spencer to America so that Spencer would have an American education. Spencer at sixteen had already graduated from Cairo University. He had a masters in linguistics."

"Sixteen? Did I hear you right? A masters at sixteen?" I interrupted.

Sir Percil seemed pleased. "Hard to believe, but you see, Spencer was one of those gifted children. His gift was his ability to learn any language that he chose to learn. Not just learn, but master any language. At age fourteen, he spoke twelve languages. The first time I heard him speaking a language besides English was when he was about ten years old. It was amazing. The family had been in Amman, Jordan, for not even two months when we heard him speaking with some children in Arabic. It was then that my daughter shared Spencer's gift with me. At that time, Spencer had already learned French."

"Amazing. No wonder it's so easy for him to assimilate the local accents. Sometime he speaks as a Chilean, other times as an Argentinian, and he also speaks Portuguese effortlessly," I said. I recalled the many times I had heard him changing the sound of his voice into the different accents of the Spanish spoken in the countries of the Southern Cone. In Nam, he spoke not only Vietnamese but also many of the dialects of the tribes.

"Yes, he is an extremely intelligent man," he responded. He kept silent for a while and then wondered aloud about the whereabouts of the boat that was to pick me up. I looked at my watch; the needles were marking 5:30 A.M. I looked toward the two waiting cars. Several agents stood outside the vehicle looking at us. Further down the pier, two agents were exchanging smoke and speaking with three Chilean Naval officers. I wondered about my exit; it seemed that I was not leaving unnoticed. Sir Percil, perhaps seeing the concern on my face, assured me that all they knew was that I was a British subject travelling under their protection. I could now sense the kind of unspoken camaraderie existing between the Chilean maritime and the British.

"To tell you the truth, at times I did think that Spencer's dislike for the Communists was beyond reason. Now that you've told me that his father was killed by the Soviets, I can understand the sort of hate which grew in Nam. A young girl whom he took a liking to was tortured and killed by those gooks," I said, turning my attention to him.

"Perhaps — and the death of his father could also have been part of it. But what really turned him against the Communists was what happened to a young Cuban girl refugee whom he met at the University of Miami," he said.

My attention grew tenfold as my eager heart fully grabbed each word that was coming out of his mouth. Finally I had come to the point where I could truly understand Spencer.

Sir Percil continued, "My daughter told me that when Spencer turned seventeen, he was courting this Cuban girl. She was the first girl in his life. He loved her deeply. Her name was Margarita. Margarita had come to the United States several years prior to Castro's taking over the government of Cuba. At that time, she was attending the University of Miami, the same university that Spencer was attending. According to my daughter, their meeting each other was what some would call love at first sight." He stopped briefly as he recalled events in Spencer's life that were totally new to me. Never once had Spencer mentioned the Cuban girl to me.

According to Sir Percil, Margarita was staying with her aunt while attending school and went periodically to Cuba to visit her parents. Her father was an officer in the Cuban Army. Then in 1959 when Castro's forces overthrew the Cuban government of the dictator Batista, it forced the rich and upper class of Cuba to flee to the United States. Among them were the families of the officers of the Cuban Army. Margarita's family was allowed to leave Cuba but not her father, who was a colonel in Batista's Army.

As Sir Percil spoke, I felt a tightening in my throat, which seemed unusual for I was not doing the talking. I kept my eyes on his face, absorbing each word that came from his mouth. Now he slightly coughed as he sought for a breath of air to continue his narration. "Shortly after Castro overthrew Batista, Castro (who was no different than Batista) ordered the execution of over one thousand people who were once Batista's supporters. Among them was Margarita's father," he said. Again he paused, but this time it was in an effort to remember for he became thoughtful.

It was as if he was seeing in present time with his own eyes an event that had occurred nearly two decades ago. "It was a ghastly thing to see," he continued. "You see, Fidel Castro ordered the executions on national television for the entire world to see. It was madness! If Castro wanted the world to take his side, it definitely was not the thing to do. My daughter told me that Spencer was with her family when her father was executed. I was in London when I watched her father being killed. Being an officer of His Majesty who had fought in a world war, I was revolted at what I saw. It was unimaginable what that poor girl and her mother went through when they saw his death. In time that event affected Margarita so badly that she lost her mind. Several months later, her insanity drove her to commit suicide…and my grandson stayed with her until the day she died."

For several moments, Sir Percil kept silent as his eyes sought relief on the calm water of the bay. Again he looked at me, and I swallowed my salty saliva as my throat felt very dry.

He coughed several times in an effort to clear his throat and continued. "Then afterward, Spencer disappeared. My daughter looked for him everywhere. I contacted some of my people located in the Florida area, but we did not hear from him until July of 1963 when he was on his way to Vietnam. My grandson suddenly came into my life as a fully matured man; he had just turned twenty. He was by now a CIA operative and was going to Vietnam as an adviser to the South Vietnamese Army. He did not mind telling me that he was a CIA agent; he knew that his mother and I were British operatives and that his father was a CIA operative. You know, he is an expert weapons man. He learned that trade from us when he was just a lad. I learned from him that after Margarita's death, when he was eighteen, he joined some Cuban exiles that were returning to Cuba to overthrow Castro. He was at the Bay of Pigs, and you well know what happened at Bay of Pigs. I just do not know how he survived. He was the only American survivor who made it to Guantanamo, where he stayed for over a year in special training."

I finally understood Spencer's hatred. His hatred did not just brew from the Cuban Marxist government killing the love of his young life, but it had been further fermented from what had occurred at Bay of Pigs, where the American government bluntly betrayed the invading forces that it had sent to liberate Cuba from the Communist menace. Their hatred had taken roots in his young life, roots that grew deeper into his soul and spirit as he drank the bitter water of Vietnam, another American betrayal of its soldiers. Now I understood his hatred toward the Marxists and Communists as well as his hatred toward the American government. All these years he had been a man on a mission of restitution, a quest for retribution. It did not matter the place or the time. As a marine, I felt the depth of his disappointment toward our government. All of us in the marines who were aware of what had occurred at Bay of Pigs in Cuba were ashamed and embarrassed. It had that sort of feeling we felt when we left Vietnam; we felt not just betrayed by our government but also by our own people.

It was a historical fact that after the Cuban exiles expeditionary force known as Brigade 2506 had disembarked at the shores of Bay of Pigs in Cuba in April 1961, they were betrayed by the president of the United States, who had approved the planning and execution of the landing and had offered support to the invasion.

When Brigade 2506, a force of more than 1,300 Cuban exiles and their American advisers, landed at the beaches of Bay of Pigs, President Kennedy halted American support. He withdrew the marines who were waiting at landing crafts at sea to join the invasion. The carriers never launched one plane to help those who were already fighting Castro's forces. Hundreds of the invaders were killed or taken prisoner, including American advisers. There was no report of any American being taken prisoner; the assumption was that they all had been killed, except Spencer, who escaped to the American base at Guantanamo Bay. If one bothers to look into the geography and the distance between Bay of Pigs and Guantanamo Bay, he would truly wonder about the type of man who would survive that kind of ordeal.

Sir Percil looked down the pier and said, "Here comes our man. Be on your way. God be with you."

I shook his hand and said, "What about now? Wouldn't he resent you interfering? After all what he wanted was to take me out of Chile himself."

"John, my dear boy, he asked me to interfere. He had no way out. You see, he could not allow you to fall into the hands of the CIA or DINA, and he could not allow you to leave this country alive. You know too much about Operation Condor. This way the CIA will think that DINA took care of you, and DINA will point the finger at the CIA. By allowing me to take over, he would not have to pull the trigger. In his mind, it is acceptable that I, as a third party, would make the final decision on whether you live or die. Why? Besides his mother, I am the only family that he has left after all."

"What will happen to him?" I asked as I started descending the stairs.

"Nothing can happen to him. He is Condor....He has no bosses. Contreras does not run the show, neither Pinochet....You know," he said smiling. "And what about you, my young friend....What will you be doing?"

"I, Sir Percil? Perhaps I will be teaching and seeking," I responded as I stopped momentarily descending the stairs.

"Teaching? Teaching what, my friend?"

"What I learned here, Sir Percil," I replied as I kept going down.

"And seeking what, my friend?"

Again I stopped and looked toward the sea at the freighter being gently moved by the water, but in my mind I was not seeing the ship or the ocean. I was seeing the unfolding scenes of my dream; I was seeing my Anne and that little girl extending her tiny hands at me.

"The kingdom, Sir Percil. Seeking the kingdom!" It seemed that the breeze had swallowed my voice. I looked down at the wooden steps as I continued descending and raising my voice, I said aloud, "Seeking the kingdom — God's Kingdom!"

At the bottom of the stairs, I looked back to where he had been standing, but he was gone. It felt good to know that my friend had someone who really cared about him. In his final gesture, it showed he still wanted me to live. He knew that his grandfather would allow me to live. He knew that the British had nothing at stake with Operation Condor or the killing of Letelier.

As I came to the boat, a large, muscular, older man jumped off. He rushed by me and told me to find a place on the boat and wait for him. He had to say hello to his friend, who I assumed by his shouting was Sir Percil. "Mister Jim! Mister Jim!"

I jumped onto the boat and sat at one end. Placed beside me was the briefcase that contained my British ID and my documentation as a representative of Her Majesty. My destination was now the Port of San Pedro in the United States. This is where I would assume a new identity. However, my identity was not going to be what Spencer had given me — that I had already decided.

I looked at my watch; it was now 5:55 A.M. I looked at the sky. It was somber and cloudy, but it would bring no rain. Like in most ports along the

Pacific and coastal Chile, the sun would probably break through in another two hours. The old sailor came back, and I liked him instantly. When people say that a particular person has a smile from molar to molar, this was the man they were describing. He introduced himself as Pedro James and in no time was telling me stories of his life. He told me that he was of English stock; his family had been in these parts since the 1700s. I became aware that he had Chileanized his English; it was colorful.

I asked about how long he had known Sir Percil, and I immediately became sort of fascinated. His answer had the tone of a story at the edges of fiction.

"Sir Percil is Her Majesty's given name, but in these parts and most places in southern Chile, he is well known as Jim William. He is a direct descendent of John William, who founded Port William," he said with pride.

He continued on, telling me the history of the Williams. "You know, during the Second War, Mr. William and my father went to England to defend our homeland. Several of the young ones, who were all brothers and cousins, also joined them. Most of us came back, but my father and two of my uncles did not make it. Mr. William returned, but he kept going back to England, where he had a daughter and a grandson. I believe that his wife died in England when she was very young. To tell the truth, I do not know too much about that side of his life. All I know now is that he does represent Her Majesty even though he is a Chilean citizen. He was born here."

I looked at the menacing sky as the ocean breeze started gaining strength. It felt warm. The water started getting agitated. "Rain is coming," I commented.

"Nah!" he replied. "Just the usual spell of morning. Not as long as his majesty makes his rounds," he said, pointing at the sky.

I followed his pointing, and I saw nothing but grayness above. He looked at me and again pointed at the sky. "There, sir. You see that black dot moving at the very top of that whitish formation of clouds?" After a while, I was able to see the black speck now changing direction toward the east. I wondered aloud about what it was. I didn't know what it could be. It was not a plane.

"That is his majesty, the condor, the envy of most monarchs, including Her Majesty the Queen of England," he said as his muscular arms arched as he buried the oars into the moving water.

"It's here — in these parts of the country? We are too far north," I said with my eyes fixed on the black speck now disappearing into the vastness above.

"Wherever the Andes are, he is there. The condor rules unopposed over the Andes," he said approvingly.

I looked at the harbor now diminishing in the distance. It seemed empty, deserted. As we moved closer to the freighter, I felt a sudden sadness. It was as if the sea was detaching me from what had been my world for nearly six years. My eyes reached for the sky again, desperately searching for the condor. I wanted so badly to see him…but he was no longer there. I closed my eyes and smiled. Condor would always be with me. After all, I had flown on the wings of Condor.